MUSIC IN
THE HILLS

Books by D. E. Stevenson

Music in the Hills
Vittoria Cottage
The House of the Deer
Gerald and Elizabeth
The Young Clementina
Crooked Adam
Sarah's Cottage
Sarah Morris Remembers
The House on the Cliff
The Marriage of Katherine
Katherine Wentworth
The Blue Sapphire
Fletchers End
Bel Lamington
The Musgraves
Still Glides the Stream
Anna and Her Daughters
The Tall Stranger
Summerhills
Amberwell
Blow the Wind Southerly
Five Windows
Mrs. Tim Flies Home
Shoulder the Sky
Young Mrs. Savage
Kate Hardy

Mrs. Tim Gets a Job
The Four Graces
Listening Valley
The Two Mrs. Abbotts
Celia's House
Spring Magic
Mrs. Tim Carries On
Rochester's Wife
Alister & Co.
The English Air
The Green Money
A World in Spell
The Story of
    Rosabelle Shaw
The Baker's Daughter
Smouldering Fire

Omnibus Volumes

Miss Buncle *containing*
    Miss Buncle's Book *and*
    Miss Buncle Married
Mrs. Tim of the Regiment
    and Golden Days

MUSIC IN THE HILLS

D.E. STEVENSON

HOLT, RINEHART AND WINSTON
NEW YORK · CHICAGO · SAN FRANCISCO

Library of Congress Catalog Card Number: 76 -160440
First published September 1950
New edition 1972

SBN: 03-080287-3
Printed in the United States of America

Foreword

PREFACES are seldom necessary but, in the case of *Music in the Hills*, there are a few explanations to be made about the location of the story, the characters and their conversation.

Mureth and Drumburly and the river that links them are not one farm or town or river in the Scottish Borders but a composite picture, an artistically true one, I hope, which will appeal to those who know the country and will serve as an introduction to those unacquainted with its beauties.

The characters in the story are imaginary, not drawn from real life. It is necessary to emphasise this because the Scottish Border Country is a small world, somewhat isolated on account of its hilly nature, and, as is natural in a small world, many of its inhabitants know one another—or at least know of one another—but I can only assure them in all sincerity that if they think they recognise a character in this story as the portrait of a real person they are mistaken.

It has been difficult to choose names with a local flavour without using names belonging to individuals. I have tried to accomplish this well-nigh impossible feat. If I have failed I apologise here and now.

In depicting the speech of the district I have ignored dialectic spelling and relied upon Lowland Scots idiom and turn of phrase to convey the desired effect. Dialect is tiresome to read and I see no great advantage in writing it. Those who know the Scottish Borders need no guide to the local dialect, and those who have not heard it for themselves could never appreciate the sound of it from the written word.

Here and there, in this novel, there may be a Scots expression unfamiliar to one who happens to have been born in some other part of the world, but in every case the context makes the meaning clear. For instance when Daniel has sprained his ankle and announces that he hirpled down to the road-end it is obvious to the intelligent reader that his gait was unsound.

As regards the pronunciation of the place names, Drumburly should be *Drum burly* with equal emphasis on the two first syllables. Mureth should be *Mure* eth, the first syllable accented and to rhyme with endure.

Lastly, although this novel is in reality a sequel to *Vittoria Cottage*, it is complete in itself and can be read quite separately and without any reference to its predecessor. I hope to write more about James.

D. E. STEVENSON

Part 1

1

*S*PRING HAD come to the valley. The house of Mureth lay
sleeping in its sheltered nook like an old grey tabby. There were
trees round the house, fine old beeches and a few gnarled oaks,
their branches tipped with buds, so that from afar they seemed to
be shrouded in a pale-green mist. The little burn, leaping down
the hillside, dawdled through the garden and then quickened its
pace and threw itself with glad abandon into the river below; it
was like a child at play who suddenly catches sight of his mother
and runs to her arms. Such a happy laughing child was Mureth
Burn, and useful too, for the old house was supplied with its
clear water and lighted by its power and the garden was made
fruitful and pleasant by its wanderings. Birds came to bathe and
to drink, alighting upon a convenient stone and preening their
feathers; they came at all times of the year for even in the winter
when the ground was hard as iron Mureth Burn still ran. Jock
Johnstone who had lived at Mureth all his life could not remember
a winter when the burn was completely frozen. The spring was
slightly warm where it bubbled out of the hillside high above
the house and it had no time to freeze before it reached the river.

Jock Johnstone had been born in Mureth House, so had his
father and his grandfather. It was a pity he had no children to
carry on the tradition, to run about the old place and waken it to
life with noise and laughter, but in other ways he was fortunate
and knew it. For one thing he had Mamie, and no man had a wife

3

that suited him better, for another he had health and strength (his fifty years sat very lightly upon him), and for a third he had one of the most prosperous farms in the county: hills and moors for his sheep, lush meadows by the river for his cows, a fine steading with barns and byres and, last but not least, half a dozen neat cottages for his men.

Jock Johnstone was fortunate but his circumstances were not entirely due to luck for although he had inherited good property he had improved it by his own efforts. He had drained the low-lying holms and built fine new byres and he had renovated the old tumble-down cottages and brought them up to date. This last had seemed an extravagance at the time for he could have used the money to improve his herd, but Mamie had insisted that the cottages must be improved; water must be laid on, windows must be enlarged, baths and sinks and stoves must be installed. Jock had spent a small fortune on the cottages and had received little thanks for it (and a good deal of chaff from his friends) but now he was reaping the benefit of the outlay; now, when good farm-hands were as valuable as diamonds—and much scarcer—there was never any difficulty in getting the pick of them for Mureth Farm. Every shepherd's wife in the county had a covetous eye upon the comfortable, well-found Mureth Cottages.

Recently Jock Johnstone had had to advertise for a new shepherd and had had a sheaf of letters in reply. He had shown them to Mamie. "That's your doing," he had said. "Duncan of Crossraggle has been trying to get a shepherd for weeks." "Mind you choose a nice one," Mamie told him with a smile.

Jock had chosen his man and, on this particular spring morning, the shepherd was moving in—and Mamie Johnstone walked up to the little cottage on the hill to welcome the newcomer.

Well Cottage was the nicest cottage on the farm, Mamie thought, for it stood by itself in a dimple of green grass near the spring. There was a little garden surrounded by a wire fence to keep out the rabbits, and a wood of conifers sheltered it from the east. Mamie arrived in time to see the furniture being carried in; everything looked clean and good, it was thoroughly sound, old-fashioned, cottage furniture. Mamie was pleased, for the cottages were her pride and joy and she was aware that people who owned good stuff were usually good stuff themselves.

A small, thin, wiry-looking man was directing operations, he was wearing a very neat brown suit and shining brown shoes. Mamie Johnstone herself was anything but neat for she had been working in the garden and was suitably attired for the job. A butcher's apron, striped blue-and-white, covered her old tweed skirt and blue pullover; red, knitted socks and hob-nailed shoes, caked with mud, completed her costume. Her light-brown hair had become loosened from the coil at the back of her neck and was blowing about in the breeze, her cheeks were rosy and her deep-blue eyes were sparkling.

Mamie did not go forward at once for she was a shy person and she was afraid of appearing inquisitive or interfering. Of course she must see these people sometime and make friends with them but perhaps it would be better to wait until they had settled in. Perhaps it would be better to come back in the afternoon and have a chat with the shepherd's wife.

She hesitated and at that moment the small brown man looked up. He waved to the men to continue their task and came over to speak to her. In spite of Mrs Johnstone's curious attire there was something about her which proclaimed her identity.

"It's a fine morning," he said as he approached. "I'm lucky

to have it fine for moving. I'm Daniel Reid. You'll be Mrs Johnstone, I'm thinking."

He was a very curious-looking man with a brown weather-
beaten face and a large nose and bushy eyebrows—rather an
ugly man, but in spite of his ugliness Mamie liked him. She shook
hands with him and welcomed him to Mureth.

"I hope you'll be happy here," she said gravely. "I came up
to see if there was anything you wanted. Mr Johnstone had to
go to Dumfries."

"There's nothing, thank you. It's a fine wee house. I'll get
settled in half no time."

"Perhaps Mrs Reid . . ." began Mamie, looking round somewhat vaguely.

"Mrs Reid?"

"I mean your wife."

He chuckled. "There's no Mrs Reid."

"But who looks after you?"

"I look after myself," said Daniel Reid firmly.

Mamie was surprised. She was pretty certain that Jock would
not have engaged the man if he had known there was no wife,
for Jock always said that men settled down better and worked
better if they were well looked after at home. And the cottage
was so nice! What a pity to have no woman living in it, to keep
it properly, to clean and scrub and take a pride in it!

"I'll keep it spick and span as a new pin," said Daniel smiling
at her. "There's no woman on earth so pernickety as me."

"But I never said—"

"You'll see," Daniel told her. "If there's another cottage on
the place as neat as mine I'll eat my boots."

They both laughed. Mamie decided that this was a very unusual sort of shepherd. What was his history? Did Jock know what a very extraordinary man he had chosen? Would Jock like him? Jock was a dear, of course, but he liked people to be ordinary —as opposed to extraordinary.

"But I hope you won't be lonely, living here all by yourself," Mamie said doubtfully.

"I'll not be lonely," Daniel assured her. He looked round as he spoke, looked at the greeny-fawn, rolling hills and the blue sky with its high, white clouds, looked down towards the shining river winding its way between the fertile meadows. "No, I'll not be lonely," he repeated softly.

It was Mamie's turn to read his thoughts. "Yes, it is beautiful," she agreed.

"And homelike," nodded Daniel. "I've been all over the world and now I've come back to Mureth."

"Come back?"

"I was born here in the wee cottage in the steading. My father was Mr Johnstone's cow-man. That was old Mr Johnstone, of course. I often thought I'd like to come back and now I've come."

Mamie was too surprised to speak . . . and yet why should she be surprised? It was quite natural, really.

"Maybe I should have mentioned it to Mr Johnstone," continued Daniel in doubtful tones. "I thought of mentioning it in my letter, and then I thought— Och well, I thought I'd as lief be taken, or not taken, on my own merits. That's the truth."

Mamie nodded.

"I thought I'd leave it," he said. "I thought maybe I'd just tell him one day when we were on the hill, but you'll tell him. It's better that way. Maybe he'll remember me; there were three of us and I was the middle one. I was rising twelve when Father

died and we went to Edinburgh to live with our grandmother
. . . but you'll not be interested in all this, Mrs Johnstone."

"Of course I'm interested! Mr Johnstone will be interested
too—and pleased. I wonder if he'll remember you. How old was
he when you left Mureth?"

"The same age as myself," replied Daniel with a twinkle.
"Many's the time I've worn his breeks—aye, and his shoes, too,
when he'd done with them. He was always bigger than me."

Mamie smiled. It was funny to think of this tiny man wearing Jock's outgrown garments. Jock was so tall and broad-
shouldered, a giant of a man.

"I've seen you, too," Daniel continued. "Many's the time I've
seen you at the kirk with your father and mother—Mr and Mrs
Armstrong. There were three of you—three wee girls—and you
were the youngest."

"There were four of us—four girls—but Harriet was much
younger. How funny to think you should remember us!"

They were silent for a few moments. Mamie was looking
back and remembering those far-off days when she and Jean and
Caroline used to drive in to Drumburly Kirk with their father
and mother every Sunday morning. Mr Armstrong was one of the
first in the county to give up his horses and replace them with
a motor car, an Argyle, with brass fittings which glittered and
gleamed in the sunshine. Mamie had never liked that motor car;
it was high off the road and swayed about a good deal and made
her feel slightly seasick, and the wild rush through the air frightened her. The others liked it, of course. They enjoyed the stir it
made. Goodness, how long ago it seemed!

"What happened to your brothers?" asked Mamie at last.

"Alexander lives in Edinburgh," replied Daniel. "He's married and has two children. He was always the clever one and he's worked hard and done well for himself. He's respectable," declared Daniel with a grin. "He's a wee bit ashamed of me, to tell the truth. You see I've been a rolling stone all my life. I've rolled all over the world. I've seen things and done things and enjoyed myself fine—but I'm not exactly a success by Alexander's standard."

Mamie nodded. She had wondered why Daniel Reid was "different" and now she knew. He had travelled widely and had made the most of his experiences. It was curious that in spite of his long sojourn in foreign parts he still retained his Lowland Scottish accent. Of course he spoke much less broadly than the ordinary, stay-at-home country folk (whose speech was so broad as to be almost unintelligible even to Mamie, who had lived amongst them all her life) but he phrased his sentences in the Lowland Scots manner and his speech was enlivened by the good old Scots expressions, for which there is no satisfactory translation in the English language.

"And what happened to your other brother?" Mamie asked.

"He was apprenticed to a butcher in Edinburgh," replied Daniel. "It was a good opening, but he didn't make the best of it. I couldn't just say what he's doing now. We've lost sight of Jed."

"Jed?"

"Jedediah, his name is," said Daniel smiling. "Mother was a great one for the Bible; but Jed was easier when you were in a hurry. That was the way it got shortened down."

It was time for Mamie to go home and let Daniel Reid get on with his work so she said good-bye and told him to come to

the house for his tea. Lizzie would give him tea in the kitchen
—it would save him the trouble of making it for himself—and
Jock could see him afterwards and have a talk with him.

Daniel accepted the invitation gratefully. "That would be
fine, if it wouldn't be a bother," he said. "Lizzie will be the cook,
I suppose."

"Yes, she's been with us for years," Mamie told him. "She
was evacuated from Glasgow at the beginning of the war and
she's been here ever since. She has two children, they go to school
at Drumburly, but they'll be back at tea-time. Don't be late," she
added as she turned away.

"I'll be there on the dot," said Daniel. "And thank you kindly,
Mrs Johnstone."

It really was a lovely day. The sun was warm and golden;
the larks were singing; the buds upon the hedges were bursting
open and showing little frills of pale-green lace. There was a
curious sort of excitement in the air, thought Mamie as she went
down the hill, it was akin to the feeling in a theatre before the
curtain goes up . . . and of course that was just what it was!
Winter was over and the curtain was rising for summer and all
the pleasant things which summer brings; summer on the farm,
long light evenings, warmth, fruitfulness.

Mamie thought of all this, not clearly but vaguely. She was
full of the joy of spring. Daniel Reid was part of her happiness.
Mamie liked him. She hoped sincerely that he was good at sheep.
If he were not good at his job Jock would not keep him and that
would be a pity for Daniel Reid was the right kind of person
to live at Mureth. Mureth was so isolated that it mattered a lot
what sort of people lived here. It was not like a town where you
could pick and choose amongst your neighbours and have your

own friends. Every one of the twenty-odd people who lived at Mureth contributed to the atmosphere of the place. It was not so bad in summer when people could go into Drumburly and meet outside friends or see a picture, but in winter when Mureth was more or less cut off from the rest of the world it was sometimes rather difficult. People got on each other's nerves, they formed little cliques. One day they were close friends and the next— for no sensible reason—they were deadly enemies. (Mamie often thought that Mureth, in winter, was like a desert island with a company of wrecked mariners thrown together upon it.) Jock did not notice the undercurrents of feeling in the place, or if he noticed them he passed them off with a laugh. What did it matter if Mrs Dunne and Mrs Bell were not on speaking terms? If a man were good at his job and a woman kept her house clean Jock asked no more . . . but Mamie asked a good deal more. Mamie would have weeded out the malcontents, she would have made Mureth a Utopia if she could have had her way. People who grumbled and quarrelled and were uncharitable to one another were unfit to live upon Mureth soil.

Mamie was completely happy at Mureth. She was devoted to Jock and had plenty to do; she was fond of housekeeping and gardening and she was very musical. Few days passed without Mamie having spent at least an hour at her piano practising and studying classical composers. She liked listening to music, as well, and usually managed to arrange her day so that she had time to listen if there happened to be a good concert on the radio. What more could any woman want?

2

$\mathcal{A}$s MAMIE went down the hill she saw Lizzie coming up to meet her, Lizzie in a print dress with the sun shining upon her sleek brown head. Something unusual had happened—that was obvious—for it was now nearly twelve o'clock and by rights Lizzie should be in the kitchen . . . and Lizzie was a creature of fixed habits nor did she have any love for walking on the hills. On any ordinary day Mamie would have jumped to the conclusion that something dreadful had occurred, but today was no ordinary day. It was the sort of day when pleasant things happen, when everything goes well and all the little details of everyday life take on a sort of brightness; and take on this brightness as a personal blessing, as if Heaven had sent them all—the sunshine, the lark's song, the bursting buds—as a sort of birthday present to gladden one's heart.

"It's her leddyship!" shouted Lizzie, waving violently. "She's wanting the master but she says you'll do!"

"I'm coming," cried Mamie, waving back.

Here was a surprise—in fact quite an event—for, although there were several houses scattered up and down the valley, people were too busy nowadays to drop in for a friendly chat and Lady Steele was one of the busiest people in the county. She took an active part in social life, she was president of half-a-dozen different committees, and every charitable institution had her

12

name on its list as one of its most energetic patrons. Lady Steele was small and thin with fluffy grey hair and bright brown eyes (rather like a cairn terrier, Mamie sometimes thought) and her bark was so fierce that few people waited to see what her bite was like; the whole county was terrified of her.

Oddly enough Mamie was the exception to the rule; she was not frightened of Lady Steele, in fact she was rather sorry for her. Lady Steele was always so busy over other people's affairs that she had no time to look after her own. Mamie would have hated to sit on committees every day, to rush madly all over the country addressing Youth Clubs and opening Bazaars. Mamie would have hated to be out every night of the week and not have any proper home-life at all. She never could quite make out whether Lady Steele liked her good works or whether she was activated by a strong sense of duty. Perhaps it was both, thought Mamie, for of course Lady Steele held the opinion that she was indispensable. If *she* were not there everything would fall to pieces. Bazaars would remain shut, Youth Clubs would wither and die, Blanket Funds would fail and Women's Rural Institutes would be forced to close down for want of patronage.

Mamie hastened down the path and found her visitor sitting in a small pony-cart which was drawn up at the front door.

"No petrol," cried Lady Steele, waving. "Besides, Toby wanted exercising; he gets skittish if he doesn't have a run now and then."

"Goodness!" exclaimed Mamie breathlessly. "Didn't Lizzie ask you to go in?"

"If I'd wanted to go in I'd have gone in. It's very pleasant sitting here in the sun."

"She should have asked you."

"She never thought of it. Why should she? But all the same you're very lucky to have her."

"Of course I am!" said Mamie hastily. "Lizzie is a dear. I don't know what I should do without her."

"Do you ever think of the first time you saw her?" asked Lady Steele.

They looked at one another, remembering that nightmare evening in the little schoolhouse. The German bombers had raided Glasgow docks and the plans which had been made for just such an eventuality had suddenly been put into effect. A message was received saying that a bus-load of mothers and children were being evacuated from the devastated area and would arrive in Drumburly some time in the afternoon. The schoolhouse was made ready to receive them, bedding and food were collected, and a committee of ladies prepared to welcome them and to distribute them to various houses in the neighbourhood. What a nightmare it was! What a heart-rending affair! How vividly it brought home the horrors of war to the quiet peaceful valley! One bus-load was expected but three bus-loads arrived —mothers and children, weary, miserable, frightened and incredibly dirty had staggered into the schoolhouse and subsided onto the nearest seat—and the most miserable of the whole contingent was Lizzie Smith. Small, pallid, dirty, her face swollen and blotched with tears, one tiny child clinging to her hand and another imminent, she was scarcely a guest that anybody would choose to welcome.

"You'll take her, won't you, Mrs Johnstone?" said Mrs Duncan of Crossraggle in honeyed accents, and of course Mrs Johnstone had taken her. She had bundled the little family into her car and driven home. The other ladies had smiled at one another in relief.

"How long ago it seems!" said Mamie thoughtfully. "Poor Lizzie, she was very ill when the baby was born. She was so frightened and queer, we could do nothing with her—and then gradually she seemed to get used to us. Of course she hated Mureth at first; she found it too quiet and dreadfully dull. She was always going, but she never actually went."

"She has her children of course," Lady Steele pointed out.

"Yes," agreed Mamie, but she agreed in doubtful tones, for Lizzie's children were not much comfort to her. They were queer children (quite different from Lizzie in appearance and character) and Lizzie seemed to have very little in common with them. She treated them in a detached sort of way, as if they did not really belong to her, and they in their turn tolerated Lizzie and no more.

"She's a widow, I suppose," said Lady Steele.

"Yes," agreed Mamie. "Yes—a widow."

"You don't seem very sure."

"No," said Mamie vaguely. "Lizzie doesn't know—not really. He was a sailor in the Merchant Navy, you see. Jock tried to find out if he was dead or alive but they couldn't trace him. Smith is such a common name, isn't it?"

"But surely—I mean there are all sorts of ways—"

"Lizzie wasn't keen about it, so Jock gave it up."

"How extraordinary!"

Mamie was silent. She had a feeling that if you did not care for your husband you might be happier without him, but the feeling was too nebulous to put into words.

"Oh well," said Lady Steele regretfully (for there was noth-

ing she liked better than setting other people's affairs in order),
"oh well, if Lizzie doesn't *want* to find out . . . but I must say
I think it's very unsatisfactory."

"Yes, I suppose it is."

Having finished with Lizzie's affairs, her ladyship proceeded
to her own. "I wanted to see Jock," she said. "Lizzie says he's
gone to Dumfries for the day."

"Lizzie said I would do," said Mamie.

Lady Steele gave a little snort of amusement. In spite of the
fact that Mamie refused to take an active part in social affairs
she liked Mamie quite a lot. Mamie amused her. "You'll do if
you can give me a bag of meal for the hens," said her ladyship
frankly.

Mamie said she could. She was aware that Jock supplied an
occasional sack of meal to Drumburly Tower; she was aware, also,
that the transaction was illegal . . . but hens had to be fed.
They tied the pony to a ring on the wall which had been put
in for this purpose by Jock's great-grandfather, and walked round
to the steading together.

"I like Mureth," declared Lady Steele. "There's something
about Mureth . . ."

"It does things to people," Mamie agreed.

Lady Steele considered this. It sounded silly but was it
really silly? People said that Mamie Johnstone was a fool, and it
was true that sometimes she said things that sounded foolish . . .
but the things she *did* were wise. Look at Lizzie, for instance;
Lizzie had been scarcely human when she came to Mureth Farm
and now she was a useful, civilised member of society.

They had reached the door of the barn. "What does Mureth
do to people?" asked Lady Steele.

"It soothes them down—sort of," said Mamie vaguely. "I've seen it happen quite often. I'm too silly to explain, but I know there's something magic about Mureth."

"It's peaceful and quiet—" began Lady Steele.

"Lots of people don't like quietness. No, there's something magic about it. But of course it doesn't *always* work," admitted Mamie regretfully. "It didn't work with Leda. You met her, didn't you, Lady Steele? My niece, Leda Dering, who was staying with us."

"Yes, I met her," said her ladyship shortly.

"She isn't like her mother."

"No indeed. She isn't like any of you. She's exactly like her father. I never could bear the sight of Arnold Dering. Of all the selfish, disagreeable creatures on the face of this earth!" said her ladyship with spirit. "How Caroline ever managed to stand him! I was thankful, for Caroline's sake, when I heard the man was dead, and even more thankful when I heard Caroline had married again. She deserves a little happiness. But tell me more about Leda. Why didn't Mureth have the desired effect upon Leda?"

Mamie had disappeared into the shadows of the barn; her voice came out of the shadows, a disembodied voice, low and clear as a bell. "She was too wrapped up," the voice said. "Jock and I did our best to amuse her and interest her in things, but she was very unhappy. She was engaged to a man and then he married somebody else. Do you want a big sack, Lady Steele?"

"Two if you can spare them."

"Leda was all wrapped up," continued Mamie, appearing in the doorway with a large sack of meal and standing it up against the wall. "She was like a person with too many clothes on, you know. She couldn't feel the warmth of the sun."

The sun poured down into the yard. The clean grey cobbles and the old, red-stone buildings reflected the warmth and seemed to bask happily in the golden rays. Lady Steele felt them upon her back, warming, comforting, health-giving, so she understood.

"Mamie," she said. "I don't know why you pretend to be stupid."

"I don't pretend," replied Mamie. "I was always the stupid one of the family—no good at lessons or anything. Caroline and Jean were clever, and Harriet was the cleverest of all. If you have three clever sisters you know exactly where you are. I used to be rather unhappy about it, but not now. Jock likes me as I am."

Lady Steele had seated herself upon the edge of an old red-stone drinking-trough; she seemed in no hurry to go, and Mamie was never in a hurry. Mamie always had leisure for her friends. In most houses nowadays (thought Lady Steele) there was a feeling of unease. Time marched on and everybody ran madly to keep up with it; even pleasure was taken at a gallop. Yet what pleasure was there that could compare with this peace, this quiet sunlit moment? It is good for me to be here, thought Lady Steele. The thought surprised her; it would have surprised her friends even more, for humility was not one of her attributes.

Even Mamie was surprised to see Lady Steele sitting peacefully upon the edge of the drinking-trough, for her ladyship was usually in a tearing hurry . . . but Mamie said nothing. It was nice here in the sun. Two pigeons, perched upon the roof of the barn, cooed gently. Jock's riding horse moved in his loose-box. In the distance was the faint sound of sheep and lambs calling to one another upon the hill.

Presently Lizzie appeared. "Will Lady Steele be staying to her lunch?" enquired Lizzie.

"No," said Lady Steele rising. "No, I really must go. I've got a meeting this afternoon."

"It's pork," Lizzie informed her. "Spare ribs of pork and apple sauce."

"Don't tempt me, Lizzie," said her ladyship regretfully.

They walked round to get the pony-cart and to load on the sacks, and now that the spell was broken they began to chat again. Mamie enquired after Sir Andrew and the young Steeles—Ian and Eleanor—and learnt that Ian was now at Edinburgh University and Eleanor was doing lessons at home with a daily governess from Drumburly.

"She's fourteen now," said her mother. "Rather a troublesome age. So dreamy—always in the clouds. Andrew gets rather annoyed with her. Of course I haven't much time. We've got Holly staying with us just now. You remember my niece, Holly Douglas? It's a pity there aren't more young people about the district or we might have a party."

"James is coming to stay with us," said Mamie. "Poor James had a dreadful time in Malaya, in the jungle, chasing bandits. Caroline was very worried about him. Now he's home he wants to be a farmer so he's coming to Mureth to learn."

"I like James," declared Lady Steele. "I always liked James. He was a nice, fat little boy and Caroline spoilt him. How does he like his new stepfather?"

"He likes him," replied Mamie, but she said no more for as a matter of fact she had been wondering how James felt about his mother's marriage. His letters were cheerful, but you couldn't really tell from letters.

By this time the two sacks of hen-meal had been stowed into the pony-cart. Lady Steele got in and gathered up the reins.

"Good-bye, Mamie," she said. "You must bring James over to see us. It would amuse Holly."

*I*T WAS Jock Johnstone's habit on entering his house to stand in the hall and shout for Mamie. Whether he had been upon the hill, looking at his sheep, or over the river at Boscath Farm (which he ran in conjunction with Mureth) or whether he had been away all day at Lockerbie or Dumfries, Jock's first thought upon returning to his home was Mamie; his urgent need was to see her, to make sure she was there, to make certain that nothing untoward had happened to her in his absence and to tell her all his news. Today was no exception to the rule. He opened the front door and shouted for Mamie in a deep-chested bellow which resounded through the house . . . and Mamie came running down the stairs as if she were a girl of seventeen instead of an old, staid matron of nearly forty.

"Hullo!" said Jock. "I've had quite a good day. What sort of a day have you had?"

"A nice day," Mamie told him. "Lady Steele came over for some hen-meal and the new shepherd has arrived and I had a letter from Caroline."

"What are the Reids like?" Jock wanted to know.

"He's nice," said Mamie. "Oh Jock, I do hope you'll like him. He's not an ordinary shepherd."

"Not an ordinary shepherd!" echoed Jock in surprise. "I hope he's a competent man. He had a very good reference; so good that I took him without seeing him, which is a thing I've never

done before. He was head-shepherd at a big farm in the Pent-
lands and they offered him more pay to stay on but for some
reason he wanted to come here."

"Because he was born here," explained Mamie. "He was
actually born here, at Mureth . . ." and she went on to tell Jock
all about Daniel Reid.

"Well, I suppose it's all right," said Jock doubtfully.

"Of course it's all right," declared Mamie. "He knows Mureth.
You were saying the other day that it was always difficult for a
new shepherd because he didn't know the hills. Daniel Reid
played on the Mureth hills when he was a boy so he knows every
bit of them."

"You seem very taken with the man."

"I like him, Jock. He's ugly, but ugly in a nice way. He's the
sort of a person we want at Mureth."

"It seems to me that the man is not open," replied Jock. "He
might have told me who he was. Of course I remember the three
Reid boys perfectly well. One of them was a perfect devil—and
it may be this one for all I know. And why didn't the man tell
me he had no wife?"

"Did you ask him?" asked Mamie chuckling.

"You expect sheperds to have wives," replied Jock with a
smile.

Mamie could not deny this of course, for she had expected
the same thing herself. "But I *do* like him, Jock," she said. "He's
a real person. I think you'll like him too."

"I'll like him if he does his work well," said Jock.

Having finished with the subject of Daniel Reid, Mamie took
Jock upstairs to see the room which was being prepared for James.
She had decided not to give James the spare-room, for he was

to be here for an indefinite period, Mureth was to be his home.
She had chosen a room facing east because it had a lovely view
over the river and away to the hills on the other side. It was a
good-sized, square room with a stained, wooden floor and an
open fireplace with a basket-grate. On the floor were a couple
of brightly coloured rugs; curtains to match hung at the window;
the furniture was old-fashioned and slightly shabby but very comfortable; there was an arm-chair, a solid table and an oak bookcase. Mamie had tried to make it a sort of bed-sitting-room, for
James might like to sit here sometimes when he got bored with
his uncle and aunt.

"You've taken a lot of trouble over it," Jock said. "He ought
to be pleased, and I'm sure he *will* be pleased."

"Oh well," said Mamie in a deprecating way. "I thought perhaps he might be feeling a little unhappy. I mean about Caroline's
marriage."

"I don't see why? He'll be getting married himself one of
these days."

"There was something odd about Caroline's marriage."

"What was odd?"

"There's something odd about the whole thing," said Mamie.
"I thought from Caroline's letter that Mr Shepperton was going
to marry Harriet—she was staying at Vittoria Cottage at the time
—and then quite suddenly Harriet wrote and said Caroline and
Robert Shepperton were engaged . . . and now Harriet is going
off to America."

"Harriet has always wanted to go to America. It's the spiritual
home of successful actresses."

"I know, but—"

"I wouldn't worry," said Jock comfortably. "They know their

own business best—you can't do anything about it—and Harriet'll
have the time of her life in America; she'll marry a millionaire
most likely."

Mamie sighed. Jock was a dear but sometimes he didn't
understand things.

"Why are you worrying?" urged Jock.

"I don't know exactly," replied Mamie, smoothing the cover
on the bed as she spoke. "I suppose I'm worrying about Harriet.
Her letters are rather too gay, if you know what I mean, but as
you say she's sure to enjoy America. Is there anything else you
can suggest for James?"

"You've thought of everything," Jock told her. "He's coming
tomorrow, isn't he? I must remember to tell Willy Dunne to take
the car and meet him at Drumburly Station," and so saying Jock
took a large white handkerchief out of his pocket and solemnly
tied a knot in the corner of it.

Everything was just the same, thought James as he opened
the big front door and walked into Mureth House: the wide hall
with its faded blue carpet, the long dark-oak table with the huge
gong (which was used not only to herald meals but also to sum-
mon Aunt Mamie from the garden when somebody called or
wanted to speak to her on the telephone); the stairs swept up
with the same lovely curve. Everything was just exactly the same.
It was five years since James had been at Mureth and in those
five years he had been halfway round the world. He had sweated
in the steamy jungles of Malay; he had hunted bandits, had suffered and fought and watched men die. James thought he had
left childish things behind him, but now, here, at Mureth, the

childish things returned and rushed in upon him with a flood of memories. James felt like a small boy again.

Aunt Mamie was not a day older . . . in fact she seemed younger to James. He had thought her "quite old," his mother's contemporary, a grown-up person and therefore a different sort of being from himself. Now she seemed almost his own age. He had caught up on her as it were.

"Darling James!" cried Mamie, kissing him. "How big you are! I shouldn't have known you. Caroline said in her letter that you were simply enormous but I didn't believe it. I mean of course I believed it in a way, but not in my bones. I expected to see the same James."

"I am the same," he replied, smiling. "I'm the same inside," but it wasn't really true.

He followed her into the drawing-room where tea was laid on the same round table with the little lace mats. There were scones and honey and an enormous fruit-cake—the kind that Uncle Jock liked—there was the same willow-pattern china, and the same big silver tea-pot with its comfortable round belly, reflecting the room. The room was exactly as James remembered it, slightly shabby but extremely comfortable . . . the cretonne covers, the pictures of long-dead Johnstone ancestors on the walls. Aunt Mamie's piano stood in its old place beneath the round mirror in its gilt frame, and Uncle Jock's chair stood by the fire. James had always thought it a giant's chair, eminently suitable for the benevolent giant to whom it belonged. He was pleased to see that it did not seem to have shrunk.

"Sit there," said Mamie, pushing him into the chair. "Sit there and tell me everything. How did the wedding go off?"

"Oh yes—the wedding," said James. "It wasn't a big affair, you know. It went off all right." He hesitated and then went on in a determined sort of voice, "Mother looked lovely. Her dress was blue and she had a blue hat. I can't—I mean it's difficult to tell you much about it."

Mamie nodded. "But it's a good thing, you know."

"Of course," he agreed quickly. "And I like Robert awfully. It's just that it was such a—such a surprise. I suppose I was a fool not to see it coming, but—"

"But you thought he was going to marry Harriet."

James was amazed. How did she know? He had never told a soul. He had never intended to tell a soul.

"I suppose poor Harriet was in love with him, too," added Mamie.

"Oh!" exclaimed James. "Well, I must say—but—but—"

"Of course you feel it," continued Mamie. "It wouldn't be natural if you didn't feel it, but if he's nice—as you say—it's a very good thing for Caroline. Someday you'll get married yourself."

"No," said James quickly. "No, never. I mean you couldn't ask a girl to live miles away in the country—on a farm."

"A girl might like it," suggested Mamie.

"She wouldn't be happy," said James.

Mamie smiled. "I'm happy," she pointed out. "I'm as happy as the day is long. How do you know she wouldn't be happy, James? Have you asked her?"

James laughed in a slightly embarrassed manner. "You're a sort of witch, Aunt Mamie," he declared.

"It wasn't very difficult to guess."

"Her name is Rhoda," said James, who felt a sudden urge to tell Mamie everything. "Rhoda Ware. I wish you could see her, she's so beautiful, so lovely, so *alive*. I can't imagine anyone more beautiful. Her hair is absolutely pure gold—and she's gold all through. She's studying painting in London. I don't mean as a hobby but as a profession. She's really good, you know. I went to supper with her one night and she showed me some of her pictures. They were wonderful—quite breath-taking, really—and of course she wants to go on painting. You can understand it, can't you? If I were good at anything I should want to go on doing it all my life so I can't blame Rhoda. That's how it is, you see."

"Yes, I see," said Mamie.

"I shall never marry," continued James in a low voice. "I mean once you've seen somebody like Rhoda . . . well, nobody else is any good."

Mamie was silent. Several arguments came into her head but she realised that they were silly so she did not advance them. It was obvious that James had proposed to Rhoda and been refused. What an idiot the girl must be, thought Mamie. How blind! James was such a dear; he was so kind and considerate—as well as being extremely attractive; he would make an admirable husband. Mamie decided that if she had not been married to Jock and twenty years too old she would have married James herself. Poor James! He had lost his mother and his love at one blow. No wonder he looked thin and pale.

"Have another scone," said Mamie. "Take lots of butter with it—and honey. It's all home-grown, you know. Jock likes to be self-supporting. We can't *really* manage it, of course, because tea and coffee and sugar wouldn't grow here. Tobacco grows here beautifully—but I won't tell you about it because Jock will tell you himself."

She took out her work-basket and began to mend an enormous hole in one of Jock's enormous socks, and as she worked she continued to talk. Her talk was slightly incoherent, but James found it soothing. He ate large quantities of scones and butter and listened to her.

"I wish I could have gone to Caroline's wedding," said Mamie. "I remember her first wedding very well. I must have been about twelve." She counted on her fingers and said, "No, I was eleven. Jean and I were bridesmaids. We had white satin frocks and little pearl caps. Harriet was much too young to officiate. Poor Caroline didn't have a say in anything; Mother arranged it all, she even chose the bridegroom. Arnold gave Caroline the most beautiful presents. He was rich, but oh dear, he was *dull*. I know I shouldn't say that about your father, James, but he really *was*. I think that was the reason Jean and I chose our own way."

James laughed. He said, "Go on. I like to hear about far-off things. Tell me about you and Uncle Jock."

"I met Jock at the blacksmith's," continued Mamie smiling. "Of course I'd seen him before at shows and otter-hunting and things, so I knew who he was, but I had never spoken to him properly. He was getting a horse shod and I was getting a pair of fire-dogs. There they are," said Mamie, pointing to them. "I wouldn't part with them for anything."

"And I suppose that horse-shoe—the one over the mantel-piece in Uncle Jock's study—"

"Yes," said Mamie, blushing like a girl. "Yes, it is. You

wouldn't think Jock could be so silly, would you? We talked for quite a long time that day, because the blacksmith was busy, and after that we met several times by accident . . . and several times *not* by accident."

"Naughty!" exclaimed James.

"Yes, dreadfully naughty," agreed Mamie. "But we had to. I knew Mother wouldn't have let me if she knew. One afternoon we met at Drumburly at the Steele Arms and had tea together: it was a wet afternoon and Mrs. Simpson put on a fire in her own private parlour and gave us tea there, all by ourselves. It was so cosy and comfortable and we were very happy. Jock didn't propose *properly:* he just said, "Wouldn't it be grand if we could always be together like this?" and I said, "Yes." When he told Father he wanted to marry me there was a dreadful row and it all came out about our "secret meetings," as Father called them. I can't see that there was anything very wrong about arranging to meet Jock and having tea with him, but Father and Mother thought it was terrible of me, and they thought I ought to do better for myself—as if I could possibly have got anybody better than Jock! They made every sort of objection. They said I was too young (though I was older than Caroline was when she was married) and they said the County wouldn't call!" Mamie threw back her head and laughed. "Oh, James, how funny it sounds *now*."

"Did it sound funny *then*?" James wanted to know.

"Not really. It just sounded not a bit important."

"What happened?" asked James with interest.

"The next thing that happened was Elmer appeared on the scene. He was staying with the Steeles at Drumburly Tower and we met him at the Hunt Ball. He had come over from America on business, just for a month, and the moment he saw Jean he

decided that he would marry her and take her back with him. I
remember he said to me he had fallen for Jean in a big way. He
certainly was very much in love with her—and she with him.
Father and Mother didn't want them to get married but they had
no chance against Elmer. He just walked through them, kindly
but firmly. When Jock saw how it was done he took a firm line
and we were married on the same day. Sometimes, when I look
back, I feel rather sorry for Father and Mother," said Mamie
thoughtfully.

"They still had Harriet," James pointed out.

"Yes, and Harriet was the apple of their eyes. Harriet could do
no wrong, she was perfect. Then Harriet went to stay with a
friend in London and met somebody who was on the stage, and
the next thing they heard was that Harriet had decided to go on
the stage herself. They were terribly angry but nothing they could
say or do had the slightest effect . . . so, after a bit, they came
round and forgave her. I'm afraid they were lonely, poor dears.
It seemed rather bad luck to have had four daughters and not
to have one left at home . . . and none of their daughters was
much good to them. Caroline never could leave Arnold—he was
so awfully selfish—Jean was in America and Harriet was simply
wrapped up in her theatrical career."

"But you were here, quite near them!"

"Yes," agreed Mamie tepidly. "Yes, but they weren't—they
weren't very . . ." She paused. She was busy trying to find the
exact shade of brown for the sock she was darning.

"They weren't very—what?" asked James.

"Very proud of me," said Mamie. "There was nothing to be
proud of, was there? They had nothing in common with Jock. I
don't mean there was a feud but they just weren't interested in

Jock's kind of things . . . and of course I had no children."

James was silent for a moment and then he said lightly, "And last, but not least, you weren't on calling terms with the County."

"Oh, but I *was*," said Mamie, smiling. "That was the funny bit. I didn't care a hoot whether they called or not but they all *did*." She paused again and then added, "I seem to have been talking an awful lot. You've got a very talkative aunt, haven't you?"

"You don't *seem* like an aunt," said James. "If you don't mind I shall just call you Mamie."

"Of course," agreed Mamie.

"You seem just the same age as me."

"That's because I'm stupid," she told him gravely.

James laughed and laughed, and Mamie had to laugh too.

4

*J*AMES SLIPPED a torch into his pocket and let himself
out of the front door. Supper was over in Mureth House and
James had offered to go up to the shepherd's cottage with a message. He was glad to have a walk after his long day in the train,
and it was a beautiful evening, clear and bright with a red glow
in the west where the sun had disappeared. James had forgotten
how beautiful Mureth was—how peaceful. He had forgotten
quite a lot about Mureth but the actual lie of the land was familiar
to him; it had a homey sort of feeling.

Looking back at his talk with Aunt Mamie he felt surprised
that he had told her so much. She had not questioned him but
somehow it had all come out. The fact was one was apt to under-
rate Mamie's intelligence. You thought she was a bit vague and
then suddenly you found she understood too much—or at least
far more than you intended. But he was glad he had told her;
it was a relief to tell somebody and she was a good person to
confide in because she didn't make silly suggestions as to what
you should do or shouldn't do, she just listened. He felt less unhappy now that he had told somebody about it.

James went up through the orchard and began to climb the
stony track which led to the shepherd's cottage. The burn ran
down beside the track, leaping and swirling and chuckling mer-
rily. Mureth *was* lovely. He was going to like his time here. He
would work like a black and learn all he could and then he would

be able to stand on his own feet and rent a farm. It would be a good life, full of worth-while work. If only he could have Rhoda too! But Rhoda would never marry, she was absolutely wrapped up in her painting. Even if he decided to live in London she wouldn't marry him. She had said so. "There's no room for marriage in my life," she had said. It seemed a waste. She was such a marvellous person—so beautiful with her golden hair and her clear, frank, blue eyes. You felt, somehow, that Rhoda ought to have children, golden-haired children, beautiful and free and happy like herself . . . but it was no use thinking about Rhoda. Think of something else.

James paused on the wooden bridge which crossed the burn and leant on the railing. The burn leapt and prattled and raced away beneath his feet. Darkness was falling, but the water still seemed full of light—almost as if there were light in the water and not just the reflection of the sky. It will pass, thought James. People don't go on being unhappy forever. Soon I shall be able to see a gold head without feeling as if someone had stuck a dagger into my heart . . . soon I shall be able to think of Mother without feeling as if she were dead. Selfish hound, said James to himself. Mother will be happy with Robert. He's decent. I like him awfully. Why on earth do I feel as if I were an orphan child? He laughed, but without much merriment, and walked on.

The shepherd's cottage was in a little hollow and, as James approached, he saw a light in the square window—a red glow shining through red curtains. He went up to the door and knocked, and the door was opened almost immediately by a small man with a weatherbeaten face.

"I'm James Dering, Mr Johnstone's nephew," explained James.

"Mr Johnstone would like to see you tomorrow morning early."

"I'll be there," said Reid nodding. "Come in, Mr Dering."

James had intended to give the message and come away but he liked the look of the man so he accepted the invitation. The room was very cosy. An oil lamp stood upon the table and a peat fire glowed in the grate. There was brown linoleum on the floor and a multicoloured rag rug lay in front of the fire. There was a grandfather's clock in the corner and two large oak chairs with high backs and cushioned seats stood on either side of the fireplace.

James found himself sitting on one of the chairs. "You're very comfortable here," he said.

Daniel Reid nodded. "I've never been so comfortable in my life. I like comfort when I can get it. Maybe you'd take a cup of coffee, Mr Dering. I was just going to take a cup myself."

A brown jug stood in the grate. Daniel lifted it and produced two thick white cups from the cupboard.

"Look here," said James as he accepted the cup. "Look here, you didn't learn to make coffee like this in Scotland."

Daniel smiled. "It's not a Scottish drink," he agreed. "Folks here can't abide the stuff—it's tea all the time. Mind you I like tea, but I've learnt to like coffee too if it's well made; I like it in thick cups, the way they have it in France."

"You've been in France?" asked James.

Daniel Reid had been in a good many places and was quite willing to talk about his travels. He was ready to listen, too, and encouraged his guest to talk about Malaya. Some of the stories James told were pretty grim but he realised there was no need to spare Daniel the grisly details of the campaign against the Terrorists. Daniel could take it.

"Gosh!" said Daniel at last. "You've seen some queer sights, Mr James. You've been through some pretty nasty experiences."

"I don't talk about them to everybody," said James with a little smile. "As a matter of fact I don't think about them much. It's apt to give me nightmares."

"I know," agreed Daniel. He, too, had suffered from nightmares in his time.

James had had time to look round. There was a bookcase in the corner, a well-filled bookcase, and a violin lay upon the top of it.

"I play the fiddle a bit," said Daniel who had noticed his guest's interest. "It's good company when I'm alone."

"You've got some nice furniture."

"It's my mother's. Alexander wasn't wanting it so I bought it in. Alexander likes a suite—a whole room of furniture all the same that you buy in a store—but this seems more homelike to me. I remember Father and Mother sitting in these chairs, and Mother polishing the old clock and making the rug. There's not a thing in the house but puts me in mind of Mother."

"Isn't it rather sad?" asked James, who felt that to him it would be intolerable to have Caroline's desk and Caroline's chair and all her other little treasures but no Caroline.

Daniel looked thoughtful. "I know fine what you mean," he said. "But your Mother's a young woman and my Mother was old. It's a natural thing for old folks to die. She'd had a good life and she wouldn't have wanted to live and get so that she couldn't do things. It says in the Book, 'The days of our years are three-score and ten and if, by reason of strength, they be fourscore years; yet is their strength labour and sorrow, for it is soon cut off and we fly away.' That's very true, Mr James."

James nodded. "You think things are all arranged for the best."

"I wouldn't say that, exactly. Things are not arranged for us—not by my way of thinking."

"You mean we make our own lives, success or failure?"

"My brother, Alexander, thinks I'm a failure," said Daniel with a little smile. "He's a success, I'll admit that, but all the same I wouldn't exchange with him. There's two sides to life, work and play, and his are separate—office and home—but mine are mixed. I wanted to see the world and I've seen a good bit of it; I've seen more than most folk. I've enjoyed working my way along; it's what I like. I'm a shepherd by trade but I've never stuck up my nose at any sort of job: I've been a steward on a liner, I've served in a shop, I've worked on a railway, I've dug, and driven a car. I've fed my mind, travelling and seeing things, and all the time I've worked to feed my body."

James understood. He said, "You're a success because you've done what you meant to do. You're a success by your own standard and it's your own standard that matters."

"That's my feeling about it," admitted Daniel. "Of course I know other people think differently. Lots of folk think your life is arranged and sent to you by God—especially troubles. They're not so sure when it's good things that come, but troubles come to them done up in a paper parcel with their name on the label."

"My sister Leda is a bit like that," said James smiling.

"Lots of folk are. Do you know this, Mr James; when Alexander's wee girl died one of the Elders of the Kirk came round to visit Alexander, and he said, 'These things are sent to try our faith, Mr Reid.' That's what he said. Did you ever hear the like!

He believed God had sent suffering and death to that innocent bairn as a kind of experiment . . . to try out Alexander. That's not my idea of God. I'd think poorly of a human being who would do a thing like that."

"Yes," agreed James thoughtfully. "I've heard people say troubles are sent to try our faith—I suppose they're thinking of Job—but when you put it like that I see what an absurd idea it is."

They were silent for a few moments.

"Would you care to see over the house?" asked Daniel. "I've got settled now. It's an awful nice wee house."

James saw that Daniel was anxious to display his new abode and the arrangement of it, so he rose at once and said he would like to see it.

"I'll show you the kitchen first," said Daniel. "You can see all over and maybe you would tell Mrs Johnstone if you think I've got it nice. She was worried at me not having a wife to keep it clean."

The tiny kitchen was bright and shining; the row of aluminum pans glittered like silver on the shelf above the sink. Outside the back door was a shed with a motor-bicycle in it: rather an ancient bike but clean and serviceable.

"I'm putting up a shelf here for medicines," declared Daniel. "Sheep medicines and such-like. It's a handy wee place, this."

James agreed.

When he had admired all these arrangements sufficiently James was conducted up the steep, narrow stair to the bedrooms. In the larger room, which was quite a good size, there was a four-poster bed with a patchwork quilt of gay colours; there was a solid mahogany dressing-table with brushes and combs and

other toilet necessaries, and a photograph of an elderly woman
whose features resembled Daniel's.

"Your mother?" asked James.

"Aye, that's Mother. You're thinking I'm like her, Mr James.
And yet Mother was a good-looking woman when she was young!"
He chuckled delightedly.

It was difficult for James to comment upon this, for nobody
could have said with truth that Daniel Reid had any pretensions
to good looks. He was definitely ugly (with his wide mouth and
his big nose and his bushy, brown eyebrows) but his expression
was so benevolent and humorous that when you had spoken to
him for a few minutes you forgot his ugliness.

Fortunately Daniel did not expect any comment. "It's a pity,
mind you," he said thoughtfully. "Father was as nice-looking as
you please, but Alexander was the only one of us that took after
him."

Opposite the fireplace stood a huge mahogany chest of
drawers, as tall as its owner. The deep drawers were so beautifully fitted that they ran in and out as smoothly as if they had
been set on rollers.

"You don't get work like that in modern stuff," said Daniel
as he demonstrated this fact with pride.

The smaller bedroom was unfurnished except for an iron
bed and a mat on the floor, but it was as clean as the rest of the
house and nothing could have been cleaner.

James had almost come to the end of his adjectives of praise
and admiration; almost, but not quite. "Everything shipshape,"
said James as they came down the stairs.

"That's it," agreed Daniel. "If you have a place for everything (so that you can lay your hand on it in the dark) it saves

a deal of trouble, and that's one of the reasons I like to live by myself. Women are just a bother."

James laughed.

"I'm not against women, mind you," declared Daniel. "If I could have got the one I wanted I'd have taken her. But second-best was no good to me."

"I know what you mean," said James rather sadly.

Daniel glanced at him with interest but did not pursue the subject. He took a large china dog off the mantelpiece and offered his guest a fill of tobacco. It was strong rank stuff and James was thankful to be able to say he had not brought his pipe.

"But that's an awfully nice piece of china," said James, taking the dog in his hands and looking at it admiringly.

"It's old," Daniel told him. "I couldn't just say how old it is. You open it by giving its head a wee twist, see?"

James saw.

"Mother kept the housecleaning money in yon dog," continued Daniel with a smile. "I can see her now, taking it down off the chimney-piece to pay the butcher."

It was getting late and James took leave of his host and went home, but not before he had received and accepted an invitation to come again soon.

5

$\mathscr{J}$AMES WANTED to start work at once (he had come to Mureth to learn farming so the sooner he started the better) but his uncle and aunt had other views on the subject.

"You need a holiday," Mamie said. "Once you start work Jock will keep you at it."

"I'm a slave-driver," smiled Jock. "You'd better have your holiday before I get my clutches on you."

"But it's wasting time," objected James. "I've got to make the most of it while I'm here. It may take me months to learn—"

"Months!" exclaimed Jock. "It'll take you years to learn farming. I've been farming all my life and I'm still learning."

"Uncle Jock! But I can't—"

"Never mind him, James," said Mamie quickly. "He's teasing you. There's no need to worry. If you like farming you'll soon learn, but it's no good rushing at it." She looked at Jock as she spoke.

"That's it," said Jock, nodding. "You'll not go far wrong if you do what Mamie says. Take your gun and go up the hill— we could do with a few rabbits—or take a rod and get us a basket of fish. Look about and get the feel of the place and talk to the men; you'll not be wasting your time."

Mureth was a pleasant place in which to spend a holiday— not that this was a complete holiday of course. James looked upon it as a period of preparation for work and acted accordingly.

He took his gun and Uncle Jock's spaniel and walked over the hills. It was as good a way as any of getting into training. He went into the byre and watched the milking and talked to the men. *Look about and get the feel of the place.* Yes, it was good advice.

James liked kitchens. He soon formed a habit of dropping into the Mureth kitchen and chatting to Lizzie Smith. He knew Lizzie of course (she had been here for years) but he had not spoken to her much on his previous visits. When he had come to Mureth with his mother and sisters he was a visitor and no more, but now he was here by himself and for an indefinite period, so it was important to be on friendly terms with Lizzie. He had always got on well with his mother's cook, who rejoiced in the name of Comfort Podbury, and he had found it useful as well as pleasant to have a friend and ally in the kitchen. Lizzie and Comfort were as different as two women could be. Lizzie was small and thin, a wisp of a woman with a practical outlook upon life. Comfort was fat and simple and extremely romantic. Lizzie was humourless (occasionally she said things that amused James a good deal but she said them quite unconsciously). She rarely smiled; she had never been known to laugh. Comfort was garrulous, she loved fun and laughed immoderately at the smallest and most feeble jest. Still, in spite of all these differences there was *something* alike about them. They were sisters under their skin.

James had often teased Comfort and she had enjoyed it. "Oh, go on, Mr James, you *are* orful!" she had exclaimed. Lizzie was not averse to a little gentle badinage. "Och, away!" Lizzie would say. She would say it in a scornful manner, with a toss of her head; she would say it with impatience or with feigned impatience; she would say it incredulously; sometimes she would say it bridling —"Och, away!" On Lizzie's lips it was capable of conveying a dozen different moods and emotions. James was so intrigued with the expression that he practised it in front of the mirror, whilst shaving, and discovered that even he, born south of the Border and only half a Scot, could imbue the simple phrase with a variety of meanings.

He did not see much of Lizzie's children for they were at school all day and, if by any chance they happened to be in the kitchen when James looked in, Lizzie would drive them forth as if they had no business to be there . . . almost as if she were ashamed of them.

"How are they getting on at school?" asked James.

"Och, well enough."

"Duggie is thirteen, isn't he? I suppose his real name is Douglas."

"It's Duggie. Duggie Fairbanks Smith."

"Oh," said James. "Then Greta's name is Greta Garbo?"

"Uh-hu," agreed Lizzie. "Greta Garbo Smith, her name is." She said it defiantly as if she expected James to doubt her word or perhaps to object to her choice of names for her offspring.

There were three cottages by the steading and two on the hill (Daniel Reid's cottage and another, higher up, for the under shepherd). The three near the steading were slightly larger than the others and had the benefit of electric light from the house. Willy Dunne lived in one of them with his wife. The Bells lived next door: Willy Bell and his wife and baby and his wife's sister, Daisy, who helped in the dairy. Daisy was young and pretty and she was usually at loggerheads with Mrs Dunne who hated her like poison. The two Willys worked on the farm, of course, and as they shared the same Christian name everybody always called them Willybell and Willydunne—as if it were all one word. Even Mrs Bell had been heard to refer to her spouse as Willybell; but Mrs Dunne was the exception to the rule and called her Willy "Mr Dunne" in a respectful manner.

The third cottage was full to overflowing; it was tenanted by Joseph Couper, his wife, Jean, and their three children and old Mr Couper, Joseph's father. Old Mr Couper had been a ploughman at Mureth but was now too old for work; he sat in an arm-chair by the window and watched all that went on, or, if it was fine, his chair was moved into the porch and he sat there basking in the sun.

One morning James was going up to the hill for a couple of rabbits and stopped at the cottages to speak to Mr Couper.

"You don't remember me, Mr Couper," said James.

"Noo, let's see," said Mr Couper. He put on his glasses and looked at James.

"I'm James Dering," said James. "My mother is Mrs Johnstone's sister. We used to come to Mureth when we were children."

"Och, aye, ye're Jeames. I mind noo. Guid sakes, ye've grown! Ye were a wee laddie the last time ye were here. Ye must have been eating an awfu' lot o' parritch," declared Mr Couper gravely.

James realised this was a joke so he laughed.

"Oatmeal is guid for weans," continued Mr Couper. "It's guid for pigs, too." He paused and glanced at James's gun. "Ye'll be after rabbits, Jeames."

"Yes, my aunt wants some."

"I'll tell ye whaur ye'll get rabbits. Noo, listen, ye'll gang up the burrn tae the wee bridge and bear lift doon the track tae the sand-pit. There's aye plenty o' rabbits in the sand-pit. I've seen me getting hauf a dizzen in yon sand-pit. They're guid eating, mind you."

"I'll bring you a rabbit, Mr Couper."

"Aye, you bring us a rabbit. That'll be fine. I've no sae many teeth, Jeames, and I canna eat meat but I can eat rabbits. Ye'll get plenty in the sand-pit. I'm auld, ye ken. I'm ninety years auld," added Mr Couper proudly.

"Are you really?"

"I've seen Queen Victoria. There's no many folks can say that. There's naebody in Mureth but me that's seen Queen Victoria. You never seen her, Jeames."

"No, I'm not old enough."

"I've seen her," declared Mr Couper. "It was in Aberdeen. She was a wee leddy, mind you, and she was wearing a bunnet wi' strings tied beneath her chin but for all that she was a queen."

"She looked like a queen?" asked James with interest.

"She looked like a queen," nodded Mr Couper. "And there's nae ither body in Mureth that's seen her but me."

Mrs Couper came out of the cottage and greeted James. "It's nice you're back, Mr James," she said. "Maybe you'll be staying the summer here."

It was a question of course. James had been asked the same question several times—how long was he staying—and he found it difficult to answer. Fortunately he did not have to answer it.

"I was telling Jeames I'd seen Queen Victoria," announced Mr Couper. "I was telling Jeames—"

"Ye're an awful auld blether," said his daughter-in-law affectionately.

James found the sand-pit quite easily; he approached it with care, crawling up the side of the hill where the brambles grew thickest. He was not out for sport; he was pot-hunting, so he would shoot his rabbits sitting if he could. Mamie wanted two or more and he had promised one to old Mr Couper; perhaps he had been a bit rash.

When he reached the top of the slope he raised his head and looked over the edge of the sand-pit: there were three rabbits in view. One of them was lopping about near its hole, but the other two were sitting together on a sloping bank of sand. They were enjoying the sunshine. Poor brutes, they would not enjoy it long! James felt a trifle compunctious but he steeled his heart and took aim carefully. It was a very easy shot—nobody could have missed those unsuspecting rabbits—and James did not miss. He went down and collected the two limp bodies, they were both stone dead.

"That means rabbit-pie for dinner tomorrow, Mr James!" The speaker was Daniel Reid. He was standing on the edge of the sand-pit with his colly beside him.

"Hullo Daniel!" cried James. "I've got two, but I've got to get another."

"You'll need to wait a bit. They're all scared but they'll soon forget. They're foolish creatures."

James went back to his former position and Daniel sat down beside him. The colly lay at his feet panting. It was a bitch, black and white, with a sharp-pointed muzzle and pricked ears.

"We've been up the hill, Gyp and me," said Daniel. "There's a pool up there where the sheep come to drink; it's near the old quarry."

"You know Mureth well, of course."

Daniel nodded. "It's queer how well you remember places

you knew when you were a laddie. You go away across the world;
you see a thousand different places; you never think of the old
places for thirty years—it's getting on for forty years since I was
here, Mr James—but somewhere at the back of your head there's
a wee corner—"

"A corner full of Mureth," suggested James.

"That's it. I've taken Mureth out of the corner and dusted it."

There was a little silence. James put his hand on the colly's
silky coat. "What a nice creature!"

"Aye, she's grand. We understand each other, Gyp and me.
She's more sense than many a human being, yon beast."

"Daniel," said James, stroking the dog. "How long will it
take me to learn enough to be of use on a farm?"

"That depends," said Daniel cautiously. "Maybe you're thinking of renting a farm, Mr James."

"That's the idea."

"You'd need a grieve," Daniel told him.

James sighed. He said, "A good grieve would need a big
salary, wouldn't he? I don't think I could afford that. I suppose
it would be years before I could stand on my own feet?"

"It would take a while to learn," agreed Daniel.

"How long?"

Daniel could not answer that question. Nobody seemed able
to answer it, thought James, and yet it was quite a reasonable
question. In any other profession you knew exactly how long it
would take before you could stand on your own feet and begin
to earn money. James had money of his own, left to him by his
father, but not enough to support him for an indefinite period.
Perhaps he had made a mistake in deciding to be a farmer. Per-

haps he ought to give it up and try for a settled job, but he did not want to do that.

"I'd leave it," said Daniel. "Things'll work out all right. Mr Johnstone would never have asked you to come to Mureth without he had some plan for you."

"But Daniel—"

"Wheesht, there's your rabbit, Mr James!"

A rabbit had emerged from a hole at the other side of the sand-pit. It looked round timidly.

"Wait now," Daniel whispered. "Wait a wee. It's a long shot, Mr James. If you wound the brute it'll whisk down its hole and you'll not see it again."

James waited. The rabbit hesitated, but, seeing nothing to cause alarm, it lolloped down the bank to a patch of green grass and began to eat. James shot it successfully; he had his three rabbits now, and Daniel took out a knife and cleaned them for him.

6

DRUMBURLY WAS the nearest town to Mureth. It was
five miles by road, though a good deal less as the crow flies, for
the road followed the windings of the river. Mamie went to
Drumburly twice a week to do her shopping and, as she happened
to be going on the Thursday after James's arrival, she asked James
to go with her. It was a lovely drive, the road was hilly and winding, it twisted this way and that; then, climbing gradually to the
shoulder of a hill it suddenly revealed the little town below, close
beside the river, revealed it as a huddle of grey stone houses with
blue-grey slate roofs. The spire of Drumburly Kirk could be seen
in the midst of the houses, tall and slender.

There was one main street in Drumburly with some remarkably good shops. There was also the Kirk and the Town Hall, an
ancient building with a statue of Robert the Bruce over the wide
doorway. At the lower end of the street was the Steele Arms
Hotel presided over by the same Mrs Simpson who had befriended
Mamie and Jock. Mrs Simpson was old now but still active and
the Steele Arms was clean and comfortable. Leading from the
main street were narrow wynds where the people lived; they
lived very close to one another but the little houses were comfortable and cosy enough. The river flowed past the lower end
of the town confined by stone walls and spanned by a narrow
eighteenth-century bridge which was a favourite meeting place
for the Drumburly folk. On fine evenings, when their work was
done, the men congregated upon the bridge, smoking, talking,

leaning over the parapet and watching the clear water as it
swirled through the arches; or perhaps, resting their backs upon
the parapet, they lifted their eyes to the hills and to Drumburly
Tower which brooded over the little town as a hen broods over
her chickens.

Drumburly Tower belonged to the Steeles; it was a Border
Keep with thick square walls of solid stone, such as can be seen
all over the Border Country in varying conditions of repair. The
tower reared its proud head above a cluster of forest trees and
from the top of it there was a fine view up the river towards
Mureth and down the river to the low-lying plains and the distant Cumberland Hills. In the old days Drumburly Tower was
a place of refuge not only for the Steeles themselves but for all
their friends and dependents. In Border Raids it was possible to
see the approach of the enemy many miles away; then the cry
went up "The English! The English!" and Drumburly was warned.
Men seized their weapons, women caught up their children and
made with all speed for the safe refuge of the Tower.

But a square peel-tower with walls five feet thick is not a
comfortable residence so, when the Borders became peaceful and
law-abiding, the Steeles forsook their stronghold and built a house
near-by, a good-sized family mansion. Succeeding Steeles altered
and improved the place, threw out bow-windows and put in bathrooms and electric light. They built stables, planted trees and
walled in a piece of meadow-land to make a garden. The Tower
was kept in repair of course for it was an interesting historical
monument, a family relic and a landmark which could be seen
for miles.

James remembered the Tower and was interested to see it
again, standing upon its eminence above the town.

"It looks as if it owned the whole countryside," he declared.

"So it does, really," said Mamie. "It has stood there for so long that it has every right to be proud. There's a rhyme about it, you know:

> *While Drumburly Tower stands*
> *The Steeles will keep their fruitful lands."*

"I don't think much of the rhyme—as a rhyme," said James laughing, "but the sense of it is perfectly clear. No wonder the Steeles keep the old Tower in good repair."

They parked the car in the town and Mamie took a basket and went off to do her shopping. James had some things to do, too. He bought some shaving cream and chatted to the chemist and then he crossed the street and went into the stationer's for some writing paper. Lady Steele was there. She was leaning upon the counter arranging for cards to be printed for a Whist Drive which she was inaugurating for the Woman's Rural Institute.

"I must have them by Friday," she was saying. "And when I say Friday I don't mean the middle of next week."

James knew her at once. She looked a bit older than the last time he had seen her but she still looked like a cairn terrier (Mamie's description of her ladyship) and she had not lost her drive. Even if James had not recognised her he would have guessed who she was by the manner in which she was laying down the law and by the meek way Mr Wilson was accepting her instructions. Old customs die very slowly in the country districts of Southern Scotland and the Steeles had always been respected in Drumburly (respected and loved and feared) for they were a power in the land. Newcomers, however high their rank, would have to wait their turn if they wanted cards printed, but nobody expected Lady Steele to wait.

"Yes, your ladyship," said Mr Wilson. "I'll put them in hand immediately. I'm sorry about last time, it was a mistake, I was away with a cold and my assistant didn't understand. It won't happen again."

"You have too many colds, Wilson," said Lady Steele. "You should take cod-liver oil; a small capsule three times a day all through the winter. Sir Andrew used to have dreadful colds so I put him on cod-liver oil and now he scarcely ever has one at all. Now don't forget. Tell Mrs Wilson, she'll see you take it regularly."

"Yes, your ladyship."

"If you don't tell her I will," said Lady Steele firmly. She turned as she spoke and her eye fell upon James who was waiting to be served. "James!" she exclaimed. "It *is* James, isn't it? Mamie told me you were coming. Goodness, how you've grown!"

"Yes," said James uncomfortably. It really was the limit the way everybody he met commented upon his growth—as if he were twelve years old instead of nearly twenty-five.

"And you've got a moustache," said Lady Steele. "Goodness! I remember you when you were a little, fat boy. You used to come to our Christmas parties."

"Yes," agreed James. "They were very good parties."

"Where's Holly?" said Lady Steele, looking round the shop. "She was here a minute ago—my niece, Holly Douglas—you must meet her."

Miss Douglas, hearing her name, appeared from behind a large bookcase with two Penguins in her hand. She was a tall girl, slim and elegant, with dark hair and sparkling brown eyes.

"Oh, there you are!" exclaimed her aunt. "I couldn't think where you'd gone. This is James Dering."

Holly smiled at James. "I've heard about you," she said. "You were in Malaya, weren't you? My brother is out there now. I suppose it's rather horrible, isn't it?"

"It is, rather," said James vaguely. "Of course it depends where you are exactly. I mean . . ." he paused.

"You mean you couldn't possibly tell me about it here and now," nodded Holly. "Of course you couldn't, but I *would* like to know because John says absolutely nothing in his letters."

"James must come over and tell you all about it," said Lady Steele firmly. "Come to lunch tomorrow at one o'clock."

It was a royal command rather than an invitation. James did not want to go but how could he refuse? He murmured something about petrol.

"Petrol!" exclaimed her ladyship. "Of course you can't use petrol. You can walk or borrow a bicycle, I suppose."

James supposed he could.

Mamie was waiting for James at the car park and as they drove home together he told her what had happened. He was surprised to find that she was enthusiastic about his invitation to lunch at Drumburly Tower.

"You'll enjoy it," she declared. "It will be good for you to have a little change. Jock and I were afraid you might find it dull at Mureth but if you get to know people round about it will be much more cheerful and amusing for you."

"I don't think it will be very amusing. I'd much rather have a day's fishing."

But Mamie was not listening. "Holly Douglas," she was saying thoughtfully. "I haven't seen her for years. She's Lady Steele's brother's daughter—Lady Steele was a Douglas, of course. Holly was a very pretty little girl, she used to stay at the Tower quite a lot. Did she seem nice?"

"She seemed quite decent," said James tepidly.

"You won't see Ian," continued Mamie. "He only comes down from Edinburgh for occasional weekends, but you'll see Eleanor. She's about fourteen. She has lessons at home."

"Is that all the family?" James enquired.

"There's Sir Andrew," said Mamie.

They had arrived at Mureth by this time so James asked no more. He was not particularly interested in the Steele family.

$\mathcal{T}$HE FOLLOWING day James rode over to Drumburly Tower upon a bicycle borrowed from Willy Dunne. The bicycle was too small for him and the brakes were faulty so not only had he to walk up all the hills but down them as well. The weather was perfect for fishing, warm with a nice westerly breeze. James felt extremely cross.

As he approached his destination he began to envisage himself arriving and wished he had made further enquiries about the Steele family. He ought to know about them, of course, but he had forgotten. There was Sir Andrew and Lady Steele. He knew Lady Steele but he could not remember having seen Sir Andrew. Ian Steele was in Edinburgh and came down for weekends (surely he ought to remember Ian, but no, he had no recollection of young Steele). And Eleanor was a schoolgirl! Probably she was fat and spotty with spectacles, thought James, making the worst of a bad job. Then there was Holly Douglas who wanted to know "all about Malaya." If she bothers me too much I shall damn well tell her, thought James.

Having arrived at this desperate decision James found he had also arrived at the Tower. He dismounted and surveyed it thoughtfully. The Tower was about fifty yards from the house. It was massive and dignified; its square walls of brown and grey stone, pierced by narrow windows, rose from the ground as if they had grown from the soil. James had to tilt his head to see the top of the Tower, cutting a square section in the blue sky. The Tower looked permanent as a mountain crag, it had stood there for hundreds of years and looked good for hundreds more. The old Tower would still be standing, four-square to the winter storms, when the modern house had fallen into ruins.

James was still looking at it when Holly appeared from amongst the trees. She was wearing a green frock and a light straw hat with a green scarf twisted round it.

"Hullo!" she exclaimed. "I'm glad you're early. I hoped you would be."

"I wasn't sure how long it would take," explained James.

"You were looking at the Tower. It's a fine old place, isn't it? Have you ever been to the top? There's a marvellous view on a clear day—as the saying is."

She laughed and James laughed with her.

"I'd like to see it and this is a clear day," he told her. "But perhaps I'd better put the bike somewhere first."

They put the bicycle into the garage and went across to the Tower. The key of the door was hanging on a nail, Holly took it and opened the door and they went in. The ground floor was on a level with the ground, it was cold and dark for there were no windows. Holly explained that, long ago, when the Tower was in use the animals were kept here.

"Horses, I suppose," said James looking round.

His supposition was confirmed by the discovery of large iron rings let into the walls and of a stone drinking-trough in one corner. There was a low archway at one side of the chamber and from here a spiral stair of stone led upwards. The stairs were like those in a lighthouse but the steps were very worn and uneven. Every here and there a narrow aperture gave a glimpse of the outside world. James and Holly went up the stairs slowly, groping their way and talking in low voices; there was something a trifle eerie about the old place.

"I wonder if an enemy ever got inside," said James. "You could defend this stair pretty easily—very easily indeed if your enemy had nothing but a sword. The spiral is built so that the defender's sword-hand would have the advantage over his opponent's. The old chap who built this place knew what he was doing."

"Yes," agreed Holly. She was a little breathless and she was having trouble with the uneven steps. Her high heels were not intended for climbing.

On each floor there was one large chamber with rough stone walls pierced by arched windows, reinforced by iron bars. The windows gave very little light because the walls were at least five feet thick. The floors were of wood and had been mended recently. In some of the rooms packing-cases were stacked and broken furniture and other rubbish.

"I'd clear this out if the place belonged to me," said James.

Holly agreed. "It does seem rather a shame. The poor old Tower must hate being made into a sort of rubbish heap, but of course if you have a place like this it's almost bound to get cluttered up with things. Even cupboards get cluttered unless you're ruthless."

"Are you ruthless?" James asked.

"I have to be," she replied. "I haven't got a Tower to keep things in."

"It's no use keeping lumber. Look at that horse-collar for instance; who could ever have thought it could be used again? It's done. It's dead."

Holly looked at it. "You might start a bonfire with it," she suggested.

"Yes," agreed James quite seriously. "And that's the very best thing to do with lumber—not only old horse-collars but rubbish that clutters up one's mind."

"Old worn-out love affairs," said Holly in a low voice.

James glanced at her.

"It's true," she continued. "It's better to be ruthless."

There were five storeys, five large stone chambers with wooden floors. The top one was slightly more comfortable—or less austere—than the others for it boasted a fireplace. Perhaps this room had been used by the Steele family when the remainder of the Tower had been full of refugees from Drumburly Town.

"But I hope they didn't have to live here *long*," said James, looking round in disgust.

Holly laughed. "They lived here until the house was built. It was their home. I suppose it could be made more comfortable. You could put up curtains to keep out the draughts and have a rug on the floor. I don't know how they cooked, and of course they couldn't have a bath."

"I'd rather live in a tent any day," declared James.

At the very top of the Tower there was a stone gallery with a parapet, a marvellous look-out post. Holly and James leant upon the parapet and looked down. They looked down upon the tree-tops, upon the walled garden with its rows of vegetables. They looked down upon the little town and—miles away—to the plain and the winding river and the far-off English hills.

James had said that the old chap who built the Tower had known what he was doing. He had known how to build. Now James saw that the old chap had known how to choose his site.

The view in every direction was uninterrupted. One could see down the river and up the river, one could see across the river and far up the narrow valley on the other side. No other site could have equalled the site chosen by the old chap for his look-out Tower. If you took the trees away (and of course the trees were not there when the stronghold was in use) you had a very satisfactory field of fire, thought James. Modern weapons would soon put paid to the fortress but the fortress had not been designed to resist modern weapons.

"Worth it?" asked Holly after a little silence.

"Well worth it," replied James smiling at her. "The whole adventure is worth while.

"You know, I remember you," Holly told him. "You and your sisters came over to a Christmas party; it was ages ago, at the beginning of the war. You were staying at Mureth of course. You don't remember me, do you?"

"Did we—did we hide . . ." began James doubtfully.

Holly laughed. "You *do* remember! We were playing hide-and-seek. We hid in a big cupboard together. It was a gorgeous place, nobody found us, and then you made my flesh creep by pretending you couldn't open the door for us to get out."

"What a brute I was!"

"Yes, weren't you! But I enjoyed it, really. It was so deliciously terrifying."

James remembered now. He remembered the pretty girl with the dark curls. It had been fun teasing her. "Wait," said James. "Wait a minute. Your were wearing a red frock and you had a red ribbon in your hair."

"Oh James, how nice of you to remember. I can call you James, can't I? Because we're old friends."

"Definitely," agreed James. "I couldn't possibly call you Miss Douglas after hiding in a cupboard with you."

James was enjoying himself a good deal more than he had expected. It had been interesting to see the old Tower and to reconstruct its history . . . and Holly was fun. She was friendly and amusing and very pretty. Fortunately her hair was dark so James could look at her quite comfortably.

"We had better go down now," Holly said. "It must be nearly lunch-time and it's a frightful crime to be late for meals."

They talked as they went down. James told her something of his plans and his anxieties.

"But you haven't definitely decided to be a farmer, have you?" Holly asked.

"I have, really," said James. "I mean I want to be a farmer more than anything, but I'm beginning to see the snags. I never thought it would take so long to learn. I can't stay on at Mureth indefinitely."

"What will you do when you leave Mureth?"

"Goodness knows! I suppose I was a fool not to think it all out before."

"My plans are frightfully vague too," said Holly with a sigh. "I'm not properly trained for anything. I can type but that doesn't take you far. I shall have to get some sort of a job—in London of course."

"In London? You don't *like* London do you?"

"No, of course not. I'm really a country person."

She did not look like a country person. Even James, who knew very little about women's clothes, had a feeling that Holly's green frock was a town rather than a country garment and her shoes had been made to walk upon London pavements rather than in country lanes. He took her hand to help her down the uneven steps.

"I like the country best," he said. "That's why I'm going to be a farmer, but it isn't everybody's choice."

"Oh, I love the country," she declared. "It's so peaceful and beautiful, but I shall have to live in London because Mummy likes it. Mummy has a flat and I wouldn't be able to make enough money to be on my own."

"Nice for her," said James. "And for you, too, of course." He thought of his own mother as he spoke. If things had been different he and Caroline might have arranged to set up house together—and how pleasant that would have been!

Holly evidently did not share his views. "Such a bore," she said. "Older people are so narrow-minded, aren't they?"

8

IT WAS exactly one o'clock when James and Holly entered the drawing-room. Lady Steele shook hands with James and introduced him to the rest of the party which consisted of Sir Andrew, Miss McGill and Mr Fairburn. Sir Andrew was tall and thin and grey, Miss McGill was short and dark and Mr Fairburn was elderly with a great deal of very white hair and a red face.

"Lunch is ready," said Lady Steele. "We'll go straight in, shall we?" and she swept her guests into the dining-room and arranged them at the table.

James found himself sitting at Lady Steele's left hand with Miss McGill on his other side. There was a vacant seat between him and Miss McGill but no mention was made of it. Mr Fairburn sat opposite James with Holly Douglas upon his right, next to Sir Andrew. Holly looked across the table and smiled at James with lifted brows as much as to say she was sorry they were seated so far apart. James was sorry too, it would have been easier to talk to Holly than his hostess.

"Did you ride or walk?" asked her ladyship whose conversation was usually made up of question and answer.

"Both," replied James. "The bicycle has faulty brakes so—"

"Very unsafe," declared Lady Steele. "You should take it straight to the blacksmith and get them put right before an accident happens. Don't go to MacDonald. Aitken is much better."

Sir Andrew seemed to be on a diet for he refused soup, wav-

61

ing it away as if it were poison. He also refused casserôle of
pigeon.

"Bring me a poached egg," said Sir Andrew with the air of
a martyr.

"You can take pigeon, Andrew," said Lady Steele.

"Not in brown gravy," replied Sir Andrew firmly. "Brown
gravy is not what it used to be. It should be coloured with fried
onions, but nowadays they use stuff called browning which is
bought in a bottle at the grocer's and contains preservative."

James hid a smile. It looked as if Lady Steele did not have
things all her own way at home.

"Everybody uses browning," Holly said. "If you go to a
hotel—"

"I never go to a hotel," declared Sir Andrew.

"You live up the valley, don't you?" said Mr Fairburn to
James. "I wonder if you've met a friend of mine, he lives—"

"If you mean old Brown he's dead," said Sir Andrew, butting
into the conversation. "Quite time, too, if you ask me. He let the
place go to rack and ruin. It was a nice place in my father's time."

"Dear me!" exclaimed Mr Fairburn in regretful tones. "He
was an exceedingly good chess-player."

"Chess!" said Sir Andrew scornfully. "Chess doesn't take
you far. He had a bee in his bonnet about Highland cattle but
that didn't take him far either. Tassieknowe was sold to a London
man—a fellow called Heddle. There are all sorts of rumours about
him."

"I wonder, now," said Mr Fairburn thoughtfully. "That
wouldn't be the director of Amalgamated Quisters, would it? No,
it couldn't be. He's rolling in money, what would he want with
a sheep-farm?"

"This man's rolling in money," put in Lady Steele. "People say he's pulling down the old house and building a new one."

"Good heavens!" exclaimed Mr Fairburn. "Old Brown thought no end of the old house."

"It's a pity he didn't take better care of it," barked Sir Andrew. "Other people take care of their property. I spend hundreds on the Tower simply to keep it from falling down."

James glanced across at Holly, who was smiling. "There's a rhyme about the old Tower, isn't there, Uncle Andrew?" asked Holly.

Sir Andrew looked displeased. "Perfect nonsense," he declared. "Nobody believes these things nowadays. I keep the Tower wind-and-water-tight because it would be an eyesore if it crumbled to ruins and because it would take an army of workmen years to demolish it. The Tower is a white elephant," added its owner peevishly.

"A very beautiful and interesting white elephant, sir," said James.

Sir Andrew snorted. "Can't afford white elephants with income tax at its present penal level. We're all on the road to ruin; Heaven knows where it's going to end." He stuck a monocle in his left eye and looked across the table at Mr Fairburn. "How is your arthritis, Fairburn?" he enquired.

Mr Fairburn seemed reluctant to discuss his arthritis. "Much the same," he murmured.

"You should give up wine," Sir Andrew told him. "Wine and meat are absolute poison to anybody with arthritis."

"I don't get enough of either to harm a fly," said Mr Fairburn bitterly.

"Arthritis is a disease affecting the joints," continued Sir

Andrew. "Many people think it is a form of rheumatism but in reality it is quite a different complaint."

"There's a new cure for it," put in James. "In America they've discovered a new drug called Cortisone and—"

Sir Andrew did not listen. He merely raised his voice, which was extremely strident, and continued to describe the disease to Mr Fairburn and to describe it in detail, pointing out that the knuckles of Mr Fairburn's left hand were swollen and distorted and assuring him that very soon he would find the trouble spreading to other parts of his body.

It was during this dissertation, which the unfortunate Mr Fairburn bore with visible annoyance and impatience, that James felt a movement beside him and a small fair girl slipped unobtrusively into the vacant seat.

"Sorry," she murmured.

"Didn't you hear the gong, Eleanor?" asked Lady Steele.

"No, I was reading."

Sir Andrew had now finished telling Mr Fairburn all about arthritis; he turned his attention to his daughter. "You were reading," he said. "It may surprise you to know that other people besides yourself can read, but other people stop reading and come to table at the proper hour for meals. Other people brush their hair and wash their hands for meals. I am speaking of civilised people of course."

He paused but nobody spoke.

"If you spent your time more profitably I would find it easier to overlook your unpunctuality," continued Sir Andrew, changing his tone from sarcasm to complaint. "If you would read history or biography and endeavour to improve yourself instead of filling your head with romantic nonsense."

Eleanor did not reply. Her eyes were fixed upon the plate of pigeon and potatoes which had appeared before her and which she now began to eat with avidity.

Sir Andrew's eye fell upon James. "You were in Burma," he said. "Somebody told me you were in Burma."

"Malaya, sir," replied James. "But not during the Jap Invasion. I only got out there after—"

"Interesting place," declared Sir Andrew. "I was in Singapore for a week in 1925. The Malays are of Mongolic origin; some people are of the opinion that they are of Polynesian origin. The Malays are mild and patient, fond of fishing and of agriculture."

"The ones I met weren't like that," said James.

"Their language is soft and harmonious," continued Sir Andrew, taking no notice of the interruption. "They are very artistic and excel in working silver. A large part of the peninsula is covered with thick forest and there are a great many rivers, few of which are of use commercially."

"When I was there—" began James.

"It struck me as being remarkably civilised," continued Sir Andrew. "The development of the Federated States is one of the outstanding achievements of British rule. Roads, railways, hospitals and schools are all up-to-date and there are large and well-managed irrigation works to supply the flourishing rice-fields."

"Tell me about your mother, James," said Lady Steele. "I suppose she will live in London now."

"No," replied James. "They're going to stay on at Vittoria Cottage. Mother likes the country and so does Mr Shepperton."

"What does Mr Shepperton do?"

"Nothing—I mean he hasn't any business. He went through

a very bad time in the war, so he isn't fit to do much at present."

"Lucky fellow!" exclaimed Sir Andrew. "Hanging up his hat in Caroline's hall, eh?"

James did not reply; he was angry and embarrassed.

"Wish I had nothing to do," continued Sir Andrew. "I have far too much to do and the Government won't give me enough petrol to do it. Does your mother get enough petrol?"

"She hasn't a car," said James shortly.

"No car! How on earth does she get about without a car?"

"What are your sisters doing?" asked Lady Steele.

"Leda has got a job as assistant matron in a school. Bobbie will go on living with Mother, of course."

"Pretty girl, Leda," said Sir Andrew. "She came over one day when she was staying at Mureth; but she hasn't much life about her. I like a girl to be bright and cheerful. Leda'll never get a husband if she mopes about with a long face."

It was true, of course. James had thought the same thing himself, but it is a very different matter to think things about your sister and to hear her discussed unsympathetically by a total stranger. James was furious. He decided that Sir Andrew was intolerable. It was all James could do to prevent himself from telling Sir Andrew exactly what he thought of him.

"Don't listen," said a soft voice in his left ear.

James was so surprised that he looked round, but Eleanor was eating industriously (obviously trying to catch up with the rest of the party) her head was bent over her plate. All he could see was the side of her head, soft, straight hair—like floss silk—which had fallen forward and was hiding her face. Had she spoken or not? Could it have been his imagination?

Sir Andrew was talking about Ireland now. Miss McGill was

Irish so it should have interested her a lot to hear all about Ireland. Sir Andrew had spent some weeks fishing in Donegal so he was able to give her a full description of Ireland and the Irish people. Unfortunately Miss McGill was not as appreciative as she should have been, she tried several times to interrupt the flow of information which was being poured into her left ear, but Sir Andrew merely raised his voice and continued. His voice was so powerful that James felt quite safe to speak to Eleanor.

"Did you say, 'Don't listen'?" he enquired without looking round.

"It's the only way, sometimes," she replied. "And the louder it is the easier it is not to listen. Like the radio, you know. If you have it on too loud you can't hear a word; it's just a noise."

"What are you saying, Eleanor?" asked her mother.

"I was just saying you shouldn't have the radio on too loud if you want to hear it properly."

Sir Andrew had stopped talking for the moment so everybody heard Eleanor's reply and looked at her in surprise.

"Quite true, of course," said Sir Andrew sarcastically. "But hardly relevant to the subject under discussion. I wonder what Mr Dering thinks of such a very penetrating remark."

"I agree with Eleanor," said James gravely. "If you have it on too loud it's just a noise."

Eleanor spluttered. It was not a very ladylike performance because her mouth was full of food, but James was delighted with it for it showed she had a sense of humour and was not absolutely and completely brow-beaten. He wondered how she had managed to prevent herself from becoming brow-beaten. One week of Sir Andrew would have sapped all the spirit out of James.

"Have you finished your pudding, Eleanor?" asked Lady

Steele. "If so you can go back to the nursery. You don't like coffee, do you?"

"I think I'd like coffee today," said Eleanor. "I mean—"

"Not today, dear. We'll have coffee in the drawing-room," said Lady Steele. She smiled at James and added, "I know Holly wants to talk to you about Malaya."

The talk about Malaya was not as bad as James had expected; in fact it consisted of a few small details about the country which Sir Andrew had omitted to mention. Holly was not really very interested in Malaya and soon turned the conversation to more amusing topics.

James and Holly sat on the window-seat in the big drawing-room and chatted. Time flew quickly and, when Lady Steele approached and enquired whether Holly was coming with her to Dumfries, James looked at his watch and discovered it was three o'clock. He leapt to his feet and said he must go.

"Don't go," said Holly.

"If you're coming with me . . ." began Lady Steele.

"Of course I must go. I had no idea," declared James. "I mean it has been so—so interesting."

"You must come again," said Lady Steele.

Holly had to prepare herself for the expedition to Dumfries so James took leave then and there and went off to find his bicycle. It had been an odd sort of lunch-party. Parts of it James had enjoyed and parts of it had been almost unbearable. It was over now and he need not come again. He did not want to come again . . . at least . . . not really. Not to lunch, thought James.

The door of the garage was open and a small, slim figure in a white frock was seated upon the running-board of Sir Andrew's Daimler.

"Hullo, Eleanor!" exclaimed James in surprise.

"I was waiting for you," said Eleanor. "You've been an awful long time but I knew you couldn't go away without your bike."

"It isn't my bike," said James hastily. "I wouldn't own it for anything. It belongs to Willy Dunne. He's the chauffeur and mechanic at Mureth—drives the tractor and all that."

"He ought to take more care of his bike. It's frightful. There's a slow puncture in the front tyre, but I pumped it up and I think it will get you home all right."

"How kind of you, Eleanor!"

"I liked doing it," she said.

James hesitated with his hands on the handlebars of the bike. The little figure looked droopy and dejected. "What do you do all day long?" he asked.

"I do lessons in the morning with Miss Clarke. She comes from Drumburly."

"What else?" James wanted to know.

"Nothing much—except reading of course. I wish I were older," said Eleanor with a sigh. "If I were older perhaps I could go out with Mother sometimes—like Holly does."

"Of course you will," agreed James. He noticed a book lying on the running-board of the car. "What sort of books do you like?" he enquired.

Eleanor picked up the book and showed it to him. It was a copy of Shelley's poems.

"Doing your prep.?" asked James.

"Oh no!" exclaimed Eleanor in surprise. "Poetry isn't lessons."

"It was lessons when I was at school."

"Was it? I just do sums and French and things like that. Dull things," said Eleanor.

"You ought to go to school," declared James roundly. "You'd find lessons much more interesting and you'd have lots of friends."

She looked thoughtful. "But perhaps I wouldn't have so much time for reading. I shouldn't like that. I've just been reading a lovely, lovely poem," said Eleanor turning over the leaves of the book. "It's about a girl called Emilia—but sometimes he calls her Emily—and he wants her to fly away with him to a perfectly beautiful island where they can be happy together and not be bothered with other people."

James noticed that she handled the book as if she loved it, supporting the back of it with her hand. He noticed, too, that her hands were beautiful, very small and white and soft. As she leant over the book her silky hair fell forward, as it had done at lunch, hiding her face. It was not gold—like Rhoda's hair—it was so fair as to be almost silver, and perfectly straight.

"Read the poem," said James.

"Oh, it's long," she told him. "Pages and pages. I'll read tiny bits of it if you like—if you aren't in a hurry."

James was not in a hurry. He leant upon the handlebars and listened.

> "It is an isle 'twixt Heaven, Air, Earth and Sea,
> Cradled, and hung in clear tranquillity; . . .
> The winged storms, chanting their thunder psalm
> To other lands, leave azure chasms of calm
> Over this isle, or weep themselves in dew,
> From which its fields and woods ever renew
> Their green and golden immortality . . .
> And all the place is peopled with sweet airs;
> The light clear element which the isle wears

> *Is heavy with the scent of lemon flowers,*
> *Which floats like mist laden with unseen showers,*
> *And falls upon the eyelids like faint sleep;*
> *And from the moss, violets and jonquils peep . . .*
> *We two will rise and sit and walk together*
> *Under the roof of blue Ionian weather*
> *And wander in the meadows, or ascend*
> *The mossy mountains where the blue heavens bend*
> *With lightest winds to touch their paramour*
> *Or linger where the pebble-paven shore*
> *Under the quick faint kisses of the sea*
> *Trembles and sparkles as in ecstacy . . ."*

The light childish voice read on, for once Eleanor had started she found it difficult to stop. James did not want her to stop. It was extraordinarily intriguing to hear the poem of passionate love fall from the innocent lips of Eleanor. What did she know of "Sleep, the fresh dew of languid love, the rain Whose drops quench kisses till they burn again"? What did she know of "burning souls," of "one passion in twin hearts"? Obviously nothing. The words fell from her lips sweetly but coolly like dew.

"Thank you awfully," said James when she had finished.

"It *is* lovely, isn't it?" she said dreamily. "I wish I had been Emily. Do you think she was a real person?"

"Yes, I think so," said James. He tried to remember which of Shelley's friends the poem had been addressed to, but it was so long since he had been at school that he had forgotten . . . and anyhow it was better that Eleanor should not know too much about Shelley's affairs.

"Do you read other books besides poetry?" he asked.

"Oh yes. *Waverley* and *Redgauntlet* and lots of others. I love *The Lay of the Last Minstrel* because it's all about this part of the country—and *Marmion*. I *adore Marmion*, don't you?"

James made a sound of assent. He couldn't remember anything about *Marmion*, except a sort of little picture, faint and vague, of a knight escaping from a fortress and the portcullis falling behind him and shaving off the plume in his helmet.

"And *Ivanhoe*," continued Eleanor. "I was finishing *Ivanhoe* before lunch and I just *had* to finish it and see what happened. That's why I didn't hear the gong, you see."

"Yes," agreed James. He hesitated. He had a feeling that it was not very good for Eleanor to spend her whole life reading Shelley's poetry and the romances of Sir Walter Scott (not her whole life, thought James uncomfortably) yet apparently there was nothing else for her to do. "Haven't you any friends?" he asked. "Don't you go out to parties, sometimes?"

"There aren't any parties."

"We're going to have a party," James told her. "There's going to be a dance in the barn at Mureth. You must come."

"Oh James! Would you ask me? I'm not too young or anything?"

"Of course I shall ask you. I'm asking you now," declared James, smiling at her. "But you shall have a proper invitation as well. Good-bye, Eleanor."

"When will you come again?" asked Eleanor, anxiously.

James did not know when he would be coming again. He paused with his foot on the pedal. "I'll see you at the dance anyhow," he said. "Perhaps I'll see you before."

"Good-bye, James," said Eleanor in a sad little voice.

9

THE EVENINGS at Mureth were very peaceful. Jock and James would read and Mamie would sew. Sometimes Jock would say, "We might have some music, Mamie," and Mamie would smile and sit down at the piano. Sometimes Mamie played without being asked, or at least without being asked in words.

Quite often, James noticed, Jock and Mamie communicated their ideas to one another without words. They were so near each other, so perfect for one another, they were two halves of a complete whole. It was a good thing to see, but it made James's heart ache. How lovely it would be to have somebody like that, thought James; to have somebody who cared frightfully if you had a headache or happened to cut your finger, somebody who shared everything with you, who knew your faults and weaknesses and went on loving you more and more!

Mamie's music was unlike any music James had ever heard. She sat down and her fingers strayed over the keys of her piano as if she were thinking and her thoughts came out in melody. All sorts of songs and tunes were mingled in her playing and she went on from one to another without a pause. She was catholic in her choice, old songs and new songs, melodies from *Oklahoma,* from Gilbert and Sullivan's Operas or from Schubert; she would play "Old Man River" and "Love's Old Sweet Song" and from these she would stray into "Annie Laurie," "Hear My Song," "Violetta," "Linden Lea" or the "Green Hills of Somerset." You

73

recognised something and it was gone before you could put a
name to it. Sometimes Jock would sing the bits he knew in a
pleasant bass voice, sometimes he would ask for "Oft in the Stilly
Night" or "I Hear You Calling Me" or some other old favourite
but more often he was content to listen and dream.

One evening Mamie suggested a game of cribbage and Jock
agreed with alacrity. He fetched a green-baize board, two packs
of cards and a long strip of cherry-wood with holes in it and pegs.
Jock had made the marker himself and polished it.

"Cribbage?" said James as he watched the preparations. "I
thought cribbage was the sort of game played by maiden aunts;
old ladies with little shawls over their shoulders, with mittens
on their hands and footstools under their feet. There ought to
be a parrot in a cage and a pussy on the mat in front of the fire."

"Nonsense," said Jock smiling. "Cribbage is an excellent game.
The best game going for two people. Some people say piquet is
better but give me cribbage. We must teach you to play cribbage,
James. Then you can play it on winter evenings with your wife."

"I shan't have a wife—ever."

"Of course you'll have a wife. All farmers have wives," began Jock in a teasing voice . . . and then suddenly he stopped.
James felt certain Mamie had stopped him though he had seen
no look pass between them.

"Do you ever play chess, Uncle Jock?" asked James.

"I used to play," replied Jock. "There was an old chap at
Tassieknowe who was mad on chess, far too good for me, but
he hadn't many people to play with so we used to play together
sometimes."

"They were talking about him when I had lunch with the

Steeles," said James. "They said the place had been bought by a very rich man from London. Is that true?"

"It's true enough," nodded Jock. "There have been all sorts of queer rumours about the man but I was hearing the true story today, and as Tassieknowe is our nearest neighbour, no more than four miles up the valley from here, its fortunes concern us pretty closely." He went on to explain that Tassieknowe was a very old house, built upon the site of a Roman Fort. Old Mr Brown had been interested in archaeology and always said that the fort had been named after Tacitus, the great Roman General. Other experts disagreed with him about this and the subject was argued and discussed with a considerable amount of acrimony. When Mr Brown died Jock had decided to buy the farm; for the hirsel of Tassieknowe marched with Mureth and Jock wanted to expand in that direction. The hills of Tassieknowe were even higher than the Mureth hills and the two farms could be run together. He had expected to be able to buy the place cheaply on account of its dilapidated condition, but a London agent had appeared unexpectedly at the auction and had bought it for a client, a certain Mr Heddle. The sum paid for the place—which was little more than a ruin—was quite preposterous and out of all proportion to its value. It was said afterwards that the agent had been instructed to buy Tassieknowe regardless of cost.

The whole thing had been a nine days' wonder in the district: who and what was Mr Heddle? Why should a London businessman want a tumble-down farm-house in a remote Scottish valley? All sorts of rumours were afloat: Mr Heddle was putting in a grieve to run the farm and intended to use it for weekends and holidays; Mr Heddle was giving up business and was coming

to live at Tassieknowe and farm it himself; he was married and
his wife was delicate; he was a bachelor and would live alone;
he was old and wanted a quiet life; he was young and sociable
and would fill the house with his London friends. As regards the
house itself some people declared that Mr Heddle intended to
pull it down and rebuild it, others said he was going to excavate
the ruins of the Roman fort.

The rumours had died down and gradually, from all these
contradictory reports, the truth had emerged. Mr Heddle was the
director of a big combine and an extremely wealthy man, he was
neither very young nor very old—probably about forty-five,
said those who had seen him—he was a widower and his sister
was coming to live with him at Tassieknowe. There was no question of pulling down the old house but the renovations he was
making were extremely thorough and, instead of employing local
labour, an army of workers had been imported from Liverpool
to carry out the repairs and alterations. Nobody knew how Mr
Heddle had obtained permission for this and there was a certain
amount of bitterness engendered in the district by the fact that
he was able to do so. Many landowners up and down the valley
had been struggling for years to obtain licences to rebuild barns
and byres, to put bathrooms into their cottages and to make other
convenient alterations to their property but had found their way
strewn with obstacles and their projects hampered with yards of
red tape. Some of them, by dint of dogged perseverance, had
managed to achieve the most urgent of repairs but apparently
this Mr Heddle—whoever he was—had achieved miracles.

"It seems very odd," said James, who had listened to the
account with interest.

"It *is* very odd," agreed Jock. "I'm sorry about it, really, for

I'd rather have had a more comfortable sort of neighbour. Mr Heddle is not likely to take much interest in his farm, but we'll just need to make the best of it and be as neighbourly as we can."

"I suppose I'll have to call," said Mamie doubtfully. "I always feel so silly calling on strange people—I always have the feeling they don't want me—and I shall feel even worse with the Heddles because I shan't know what to talk to them about."

"Och, wait and see," said Jock. "They may be quite ordinary sort of folk like ourselves. I wouldn't worry, Mamie."

Jock took up the cards as he spoke and the game of cribbage, which had been delayed by the discussion, proceeded peacefully.

James watched them for a bit but he felt restless. He decided to walk up to Well Cottage and see Daniel Reid. He had been to see Daniel once or twice since their first meeting for he had a feeling that Jock and Mamie liked to be alone sometimes in the evenings. They were very kind to him and never made him feel unwanted, but all the same . . . He took Daniel books to read and he made Daniel play his fiddle. Daniel was alone too, but not lonely. James thought he might learn from Daniel how to be alone and yet not lonely, how to be self-sufficient. One must not become selfish of course (Daniel was not selfish) but it would be a useful lesson to learn how to find happiness inside oneself.

The last time James had walked up to the cottage he had found it all shut up, empty and silent, but tonight he was lucky. Daniel was sitting at a table studying a book about the anatomy of sheep. He rose when James appeared and welcomed him warmly.

"Come away in, Mr James," said Daniel. "I was wondering if you'd come tonight."

"I came two nights ago but you were out," James told him.

"M'phm. I'm sorry about that. I was on the hill."

"You were on the hill!"

"Just that. Maybe you'll have heard Mr Johnstone mention that we've lost some sheep? I'm a wee bit worried about it."

James was aware that this was an understatement. Daniel looked worried to death. "Perhaps there's a hole in the dyke," suggested James.

"There's not," replied Daniel. "I've been round every dyke on the hill. I've been over to Crossraggle and I've been over to Tassieknowe. No, they've not gone over the dyke."

"Couldn't they have fallen into a hole or a bog, Daniel?"

"It's not often that happens. You'll maybe lose a crone or two that way—they're old and not so nippy on their legs—but it's shearlings that have gone. That means last year's lambs, Mr James."

"What could have happened to them?"

"That's what I've got to find out, and I'll find out no matter how long it takes me. There's nobody going to lift my sheep and get away with it!"

"You mean they've been stolen!"

"Just that," nodded Daniel. "There's no other way of it that I can see. Listen, Mr James. Isn't there plenty of folk that would give good money for a nice gigot of mutton and ask no questions about where it came from? Isn't there, now?"

"Yes, but—"

"I've no proof, mind you. It's proof I'm wanting," declared Daniel with vehemence, pounding the table with his closed fist. "It's proof I must have, Mr James. I've been out the last few nights on the hill but I've had no luck so far."

"What are you looking for?"

"A car," replied Daniel. "I've been thinking about it a lot and this is what I thought: they couldn't lift sheep without they had a car and maybe a trailer, and they couldn't lift sheep on the road for there's always the fear of a lorry coming along when it's not wanted. What they need is a nice quiet place where they can take a car and not be disturbed."

"Sherlock Holmes!" smiled James.

"I like yon other fellow better," Daniel said. "The wee Belgian fellow that uses his brain and thinks things out first and then proves he's right. That's what I'm trying to do—in fact I've done a bit already."

"What have you done?"

Daniel hesitated for a moment. "Well, Mr James," he said. "If you're really wanting to know—but mind this, I'm not wanting other folks to get wind of it. The whole thing'll get spoiled if it's talked about. Now, listen: about two miles up the valley there's a turning off the road, it's an old cart-track leading up to the quarry. Alexander and Jed and me used to have picnics in the old quarry when we were lads."

"So you know it well."

"Every stone of it," nodded Daniel.

"That's the quarry where the pool is—where the sheep come down to drink?"

"That's it, Mr James. The pool is maybe a hundred yards from the quarry, no more. Well, it seemed to me that if I was wanting to lift a sheep from Mureth that would be the place I'd choose, so I went and had a look and I found tyre-marks. A big car had gone up to the quarry and turned and I'm pretty certain there was a trailer to it. Now what would it be doing there?"

"The people were having a picnic," suggested James gravely. Daniel looked taken aback. "A picnic!" he exclaimed.

"I was only teasing you," said James smiling. "I think you've worked it out admirably—Poirot couldn't have done it better— and I agree it's fishy. We'll go up to the quarry together."

"Together!"

"Of course. You don't suppose I'm going to be left out of the fun."

"But, Mr James—"

"When do we start, Daniel?"

"If I go myself I can slip away quietly and—"

"Now listen, Daniel, just get this into your head. I'm coming with you. We're going together. Got that?"

"Mr James, I'm not wanting folks to know."

"I won't tell anybody. I often come in when my uncle and aunt have gone to bed. They leave the door unlocked, in fact quite often the door is never locked at all."

"Well, we'll see."

"Daniel, if you don't promise faithfully to take me with you I'll—I'll—I'll tell Mrs Dunne the whole thing."

Daniel smiled. "It's threats, is it? You'll send round the Town Crier. Very well, Mr James. I'll tell you when I'm going. I'm not saying I wouldn't like to have you with me if it comes to the bit."

James wanted to know more about the expedition, when it was likely to take place and various other details, but Daniel was uncommunicative. "It'll not be for a wee while," Daniel declared. "I'm keeping my eyes open."

The subject was shelved meantime. Daniel got out his fiddle and played "Loch Lomond" and "Auld Robin Gray" and "The Nut-brown Maiden" and various Hill Billy songs which he had picked up when he was ranching in the wild and woolly west. He did not play like Mamie, rambling on from one tune to another, he played each tune separately. James listened and smoked —but not Daniel's tobacco—and presently he went home to bed.

10

MAMIE DECIDED to make a fruit-cake. She had plenty of eggs and butter from the farm and she had received a parcel that morning from her sister Jean in America, so all the ingredients were ready to her hand. Mamie's cakes were a feature of tea at Mureth; Jock liked them better than anything and now there was James—who liked them too—so although they were large and solid they did not last long.

Lizzie was in the kitchen, ironing. She suggested that she should put away her ironing and help, but Mamie preferred to have the place to herself.

"Why don't you go out?" said Mamie.

"Where should I go?" asked Lizzie dubiously.

"To the cottages," suggested Mamie. "Go and see Mrs Couper or Mrs Bell. You haven't been there for ages, have you?"

Lizzie considered the matter. "I might," she agreed. "There's that new young man that Daisy's walking out with. Mrs Bell could tell me the latest about that."

"What is he like?" asked Mamie.

"He's a nice enough fellow if it wasn't for his squint," said Lizzie thoughtfully. "I couldn't fancy a man with a squint but there's no accounting for tastes. I said that to Daisy and she said it made him more interesting, but if you ask me I think it's his motor-bike Daisy's interested in and not the man at all."

"I hope you didn't say that to Daisy."

"I did, then—why not? She didn't need to mind."

"Did she mind?"

"Not her," replied Lizzie cheerfully. By this time Lizzie was quite pleased to go and was taking off her apron which was all the preparation necessary for her expedition.

Mamie took out the flour bin and as she did so she marvelled. How curious these people were! How different from herself! Daisy did not mind outspoken remarks about the appearance of her latest young man nor the suggestion that she was encouraging him for the sake of his motor-bike, but she fiercely resented other remarks or actions which seemed perfectly harmless. For instance only the other day Mamie had bought some strong cotton aprons for use in the dairy and had offered two of them to Daisy, thinking that they would keep her dresses from getting soiled and would save her the expense of buying aprons for herself. They were particularly nice aprons—so Mamie thought— but Daisy thought otherwise and instead of being grateful for the gift had received it as a mortal insult. Maybe Mrs Johnstone thought she was dirty, declared Daisy with flashing eyes. If she wanted new aprons she could buy them herself—nice print ones, not ugly coarse things like that. She had been so "affronted" that it had taken all the eloquence and tact at Mamie's command to prevent her from giving notice on the spot. Perhaps an extremely clever psychologist might know what you could say and what you could not say to the Daisies of this world; Mamie had wrestled with the problem for nearly twenty years and was no nearer a solution.

When Mamie made a cake she always made two, one for Jock and herself and the other for Lizzie and her children. Sometimes Mamie worried about Lizzie's children. She felt responsible for the two young, fatherless creatures growing up in Mureth House. She felt she ought to know them better, to know what they were thinking and doing, but the fact was she scarcely ever saw them. Lizzie conspired to keep her children hidden from view and the children seemed unwilling to be seen or spoken to. They were shy—or sulky—they fled at Mamie's approach. If she asked for them they were produced, of course, but what use was that? If she tried to talk to them the conversation was made up of questions and answers—slow reluctant answers which got no further towards an understanding of their mentality. Jock was of the opinion that Lizzie's children were "not all there" but for once Jock was wrong. They were "well above the average" said the Headmaster of Drumburly School.

It would not have mattered so much if Lizzie had been different herself (if Lizzie had been an intelligent woman Mamie could have left the matter in her hands) but Lizzie was a curious creature, rather foolish and completely devoid of humour and (worst of all, in Mamie's opinion) her whole life was ruled by superstitions, by the struggle against unseen powers which she placated in strange ways. Lizzie never used salt without throwing a pinch in the fire; she never crossed the burn without muttering some strange rhyme; she never walked under a ladder; her whole day was poisoned if she happened to see a black cat. She would gaze into her empty tea-cup, trying to read her fate in the disposal of the leaves, and she always made a curious pattern in white chalk upon her newly scrubbed doorstep.

There were many more spells and superstitions which Lizzie believed in and which tormented her and took all the pleasure out of life.

Jock was interested in Lizzie's curious beliefs and especially interested in the pattern of whorls and circles which decorated the back doorstep and would have decorated the front doorstep also, if Mamie had not been firm about it. Jock asked Lizzie where she had learnt the pattern and what it meant, but Lizzie could not—or would not—answer either of these questions. She had always known the pattern. It was a nice pattern. The step looked queer without it, said Lizzie with a secret sort of look.

Afterwards Jock told Mamie what the pattern meant. "It's a pagan spell," said Jock. "It really is very interesting. Of course Lizzie has always known it; her mother knew it and her grandmother and their grandmothers and great grandmothers. The first woman who made that pattern upon her doorstep made it to keep evil spirits from crossing the threshold of her cottage and turning the milk sour or laying a spell on her baby or doing some other mischief to her family."

Mamie was amazed and incredulous but Jock assured her that it was absolutely true.

"But Jock, we ought to stop it," exclaimed Mamie, who was by no means in favour of having a pagan spell upon the back doorstep of Mureth House.

"Och, leave her alone," said Jock, smiling. "If she never does anything worse she'll do no harm."

So the spell was woven every morning by Lizzie down upon her knees.

All very well, thought Mamie, as she measured out the ingredients of her cake. All very well for Lizzie—it doesn't matter so much for her—but what sort of rubbish is she teaching the children and how am I to help it if I can't get near them and speak to them? If only they would accept me as a friend . . . but they think of me as an enemy. I know they do.

It is curious how quite often when one happens to be thinking of a person that person will appear. Mamie was beating her
cake and thinking about Duggie and Greta when the door opened
and Greta sidled in. She would have sidled out again when she
saw Mamie, but Mamie called to her.

"Come in, Greta," said Mamie. "Come in and shut the door."

Greta entered reluctantly. She was a small, thin child with a
sallow complexion and lank black hair—not an attractive-looking
child and even less attractive by reason of her expression which
was sulky and somewhat furtive. Mamie had known Greta all her
life, she had been present when Greta was born, but she had
no more idea of what Greta was really like, inside, than the man
in the moon.

"What do you like doing best?" asked Mamie, pausing in her
activities and looking at Greta earnestly.

"Nothing," said Greta, gazing at the floor.

"Nothing?" exclaimed Mamie in surprise. "You like doing
nothing?"

Greta did not reply.

"You like helping Mother, don't you?" suggested Mamie.

"No," said Greta, after a short pause.

"Do you like reading stories?"

"No," replied Greta.

"Playing games?"

Greta shook her head.

"Perhaps you like dolls," said Mamie with dogged perseverance.

Greta hesitated. She opened her mouth to reply and then
thought better of it. There was a short silence, a slightly uncom-

fortable silence, but it was something not to have received a
direct negative and Mamie was hopeful.

"I used to like dolls too," said Mamie cheerfully. "I had a
black doll called Topsy and I loved her dearly. She was so nice
and soft—I took her to bed with me every night. Other people
thought she was rather ugly but I thought her absolutely perfect."

Greta was showing a little interest now. She did not speak
—that would have been too much to expect—but she gazed up
at Mamie with her dark beady eyes. She looks foreign, thought
Mamie suddenly. She looks like an Italian child. Why didn't I
notice that before? Who on earth was her father, I wonder.

"Topsy went everywhere with me," continued Mamie. "I had
other dolls of course, but I didn't like them half as much. I used
to talk to Topsy and tell her everything. I used to sit and cuddle
her."

"I'd like that," said Greta.

"You'd like a doll?"

Greta nodded.

"You shall have one," said Mamie joyfully. "You shall have
a doll exactly like Topsy."

"Tomorrow?" asked Greta, struggling to dissemble her pleasure at this news.

"Tomorrow or the next day. I shall have to make her, you
see. You can't buy dolls like Topsy in the shops. They're *very*
special."

Greta actually smiled.

"What will you call her?" asked Mamie.

"Topsy," replied Greta without the slightest hesitation.

"Good," nodded Mamie. "That's a lot easier for me because

I shall know exactly how to make her, and Topsy is the very best name for a black doll. There's a story about a little girl called Topsy who had no father or mother."

Greta was leaning on the table now. "I'll be Topsy's mother," Greta said.

There was no music that evening in Mureth drawing-room and no cribbage either. Mamie had ransacked her "piece-bag" and was hard at work. She had found an old black woollen stocking which was exactly what she needed for Topsy's skin; she had found a piece of black astrakhan which had once been part of a collar on a driving-coat and would do admirably for Topsy's hair. Topsy's eyes would be black boot-buttons, her mouth could be embroidered with scarlet thread, her body stuffed with rags and an odd piece of scarlet flannel would make her a nice warm dress.

"What on earth are you doing?" Jock wanted to know.

Mamie explained.

"It's a good idea," said Jock. "It's clever, too. I'll help you shall I, Mamie? I could cut up the rags into small pieces, couldn't I?"

"Oh, do help!" exclaimed Mamie. "Perhaps if you help we could have it ready by tomorrow. Come and tell me where you think I should put her mouth."

Jock laid aside his paper and settled himself beside Mamie on the sofa with the scissors and the rags.

"You see," said Mamie earnestly. "It would be better if I could embroider her mouth *before* we stuff her—but then it's difficult to know exactly *where*."

"Let me see," said Jock.

James observed them. They were intent upon their task, discussing gravely where exactly Topsy's mouth should be placed and how large it should be. Perhaps it was slightly comical but James did not feel inclined to smile. How good they were—and how unconscious of their goodness! If only there were more people in the world like Uncle Jock and Mamie the world would be all right.

James rose and went upstairs to his room. He was not needed and he had some letters to write.

11

$\mathcal{T}$HE HOLIDAY which James had been granted was still in progress but in spite of this there was plenty to do. He helped Jock to fill in forms of one kind and another; he took messages across the river to Mr Mackenzie who was managing Boscath Farm, and sometimes he bicycled into Drumburly and did Mamie's shopping. On one of these occasions he met Holly Douglas and they had coffee together at the Steele Arms, sitting in the old-fashioned lounge and talking and laughing cheerfully.

Holly was friendly and James decided that he liked her a lot. He talked about all he was doing and all he hoped to do and Holly listened with flattering attention.

"You really like it?" she asked.

"Yes, and I seem to be getting on all right with everybody —except Mr Mackenzie. He's Uncle Jock's manager at Boscath Farm, you know."

Holly had not known, but now that she knew she enquired further into the matter and James was glad to tell her. He did not intend to bother Uncle Jock with his difficulties in getting on with Mr Mackenzie, but Holly was different. It was perfectly safe to tell Holly how unpleasant and obstructive the man had been.

"He's jealous of you," said Holly thoughtfully. "He's a farmer and has had to make his own way and then you come along and walk into a good position straight off. That's his point of view. I

don't say it's the right point of view, but I'm sure it's the explanation."

"Yes, I see that," agreed James. "But I'm not in a good position. I haven't any position at all."

"You give him orders."

"Not orders—messages," objected James. "I do what Uncle
Jock tells me, that's all."

"Yes, of course. I understand that," declared Holly, smiling.
"But does he? Some people are awfully silly, aren't they?"

"Frightfully silly," nodded James.

They finished their coffee and agreed to meet again. James
wanted Holly to come over to Mureth, he would take her to see
the river, and Holly promised to come when she could manage
it. She hated bicycling but perhaps she might persuade Aunt
Adela to lend her the little car . . . Oh yes, she would manage
it somehow.

On Sunday Jock and Mamie and James drove over to Drumburly Kirk. James had hoped to see Holly at the kirk but none
of the Drumburly Tower party were there so he was a little disappointed. Plenty of other people were there, of course, and after
the service they chatted to one another in the kirk-yard. It was
like Sundays at home, thought James, Sundays at Ashbridge, for
at Ashbridge the same thing happened. The congregation lingered
in the church-yard after the service and talked, enquiring for
absent friends and making plans for future meetings. The two
ceremonies were different but the social gatherings were alike,
which showed that beneath superficial differences human nature
was much the same.

Mamie introduced James to Cathie Duncan and her brother
Henry, who was at present serving in the Army but was destined

to farm Crossraggle whose boundaries marched with Mureth. The young Duncans were pleasant and friendly and James was chatting to them happily when Mrs Duncan bore down upon them with a beaming smile and began to gush! James must come over to Crossraggle; he must come any day that suited him, to any meal he liked. When would he come? Monday? Tuesday? Wednesday?

The Young Duncans looked embarrassed and distressed and James had a feeling they did not want him.

"Not *this* week, I'm afraid," said James with a charming smile. "Perhaps *next* week if you will leave it open."

Mrs Duncan was only too delighted to leave it open. James must ring up when he had a free afternoon. "Any time," said Mrs Duncan. "Any time you like. Cathie and I will be delighted to see you, won't we, Cathie?"

"I shall probably be out," murmured Cathie turning away.

Curiously enough James liked Cathie a good deal better for this extremely rude remark.

"If you're out I shall come and look for you," said James to her retreating back. "I'm rather good at hide-and-seek."

She turned and smiled; the incident was closed, but as he climbed into the Mureth car James could not help chuckling. If Mrs Duncan had been aware of his uncertain future she would not have been so effusive in her offers of hospitality; she would not have been so anxious to offer him her daughter upon a silver plate.

"It's funny, isn't it?" said Mamie as they drove home. "I mean I'm never very sure if it's right to talk to people after the service."

"Surely there could be no harm—" began James, but Mamie was looking at Jock, it was Jock's verdict she wanted.

"No harm at all," nodded Jock. "A man's got two duties, one to God and the other to his neighbour, and a nice friendly crack is a neighbourly affair."

"Of course!" exclaimed Mamie in relief.

"*A nice friendly crack*," repeated Jock. "But mind you there are limits. Ferguson asked me if I'd any cross-bred shearling lambs for sale. I told him he could ring me up tomorrow morning."

"But Uncle Jock—"

"Och, I daresay there was no harm in the question," allowed Jock. "I might have said yes to the man but would that have ended the matter? He would have asked how much I wanted for them—and maybe Duncan would have chimed in—and before the thing was finished the kirk-yard would have been like a market. With the scarcity of petrol there's a temptation to talk business after kirk, but it's a temptation that ought to be resisted."

At first James had thought his uncle ridiculously narrow-minded and old-fashioned but now he saw there was a good deal of truth in what Jock said. Many farmers drove in to Drumburly Kirk on Sundays and if they once started business transactions in the kirk-yard there was no knowing where the matter would end. This view struck home all the more forcibly because the portion of Scripture to which they had listened that morning was the story of Christ driving out the money-changers from the Temple and overturning their tables. It was a story that appealed to James tremendously for it showed Christ was not always meek and gentle—as depicted in stained-glass windows. He could be strong and courageous when He chose. The fact that Christ was capable of rage seemed to make Him more real and understandable to James.

Mamie was wondering whether it had been all right to give

Mrs Ferguson that recipe for a chocolate cake, but after a little thought she decided that it was perfectly all right for Jock had said one should be neighbourly . . . and of course she had got nothing in return for the recipe, except gratitude, so one could not possibly call it a business transaction.

Jock (one regrets to say) was wondering if Mr Ferguson would ring up tomorrow morning and, if so, what price he would give for the lambs. They were fine, healthy lambs and unless Ferguson was willing to give a good price for them he could get his lambs elsewhere.

With so much thought going on it should surprise nobody to hear that the drive home to Mureth was accomplished in silence.

One golden sunshiny day succeeded another and when hay-making began James was to be seen in the field with the men, helping to load the carts. But there was not much hay at Mureth; soon it was safely gathered into the barn, and, this having been completed, Mamie suggested that James should have a day on the river and catch some fish. James was by no means averse to the idea; he looked out Jock's rod and tackle, borrowed Jock's waders and got Lizzie to make up a packet of sandwiches for him.

James had completed his arrangements and was just starting out when he saw his uncle riding up the path. He was aware that Jock had been over to Boscath.

An old ford crossed the river just above Mureth House and this was the usual means of communication between the two farms. In summer it was a convenient means of communication, for the ford had a gravel bottom and the water was never more than two feet deep (carts could cross quite easily and Jock could ride through on his horse) but in winter, or when the river was in spate, it was a very different story. Then the ford became impassable. The nearest bridge was at Drumburly, so, if the ford could not be used, the two farms were separated by ten miles of road. Jock often regretted that he had not built a bridge, when building a bridge had been a less costly performance, even a foot-bridge would have solved his problem. Two farms separated by a temperamental river were a serious problem indeed, and the shortage of petrol added considerably to his difficulties.

Today, however, there had been no trouble. The river was low. Jock had been over to Boscath and had a talk with Mackenzie and come back. He stopped his horse and looked down at James.

"You seem to have fallen out with Mackenzie," he said.

"I know," replied James. "I'm awfully sorry, Uncle Jock. He never liked me much. I think he thought I was snooping—and on Saturday I had rather a—"

"Snooping!" exclaimed Jock. "If Mackenzie had nothing to hide he didn't need to care, did he? What do you think of Boscath?"

"It isn't as tidy as Mureth, but perhaps—"

"Perhaps tidiness doesn't matter, eh?"

"I like things tidy," said James.

"So do I—and it *does* matter. Take Denmark, for instance," said Jock, dismounting from his horse so that he could speak to James more comfortably. "The Danes are good farmers; they haven't a great deal of land but they make the most of it. I went over there one summer and had a look round. Their efficiency is amazing. Their farms are models of neatness (no broken implements lying around, cluttering up the place), their fields are neat, too. No weeds, no hedges—"

"No hedges!" echoed James in surprise.

"A hedge takes up six feet of good land, and good land is valuable. They tether their cows with long ropes and lead them home for the milking. You might see a man walking along the road with eight or ten cows behind him. They've exterminated every rabbit in the country. How's that for efficiency?"

"It certainly sounds—"

"I don't go so far as that," declared Jock in a thoughtful voice. "I like hedges, they're pretty, but I keep them well trimmed and the ditches properly drained. I like my cattle to have liberty to stray about the field—and I like rabbit-pie—but all the same I learnt a lot from the Danes." He paused and added, "It would do Mackenzie good to go for a visit to Denmark."

"Uncle Jock," said James. "I think perhaps I'd better tell you how I fell foul of Mr Mackenzie."

"It might be as well," agreed Jock drily. "I've had Mackenzie's version of it, so now I'll have yours."

"Yes," said James rather uncomfortably. "It was on Saturday. I went over with a message, you'll remember, and when I got there he was out and the men were knocking off work. There was still some hay left out and a couple of hours overtime work would have cleared the field. I didn't like the look of the weather much and I knew the glass was falling; we'd got all the Mureth hay in on Friday of course."

"The hay was dry?" enquired Jock.

"Beautifully dry. Gosh, I *was* fed up! When I saw the men knocking off I felt I wanted to go and gather in that hay with my own hands."

"Did you speak to the men?"

James nodded. "As a matter of fact I did. I said I'd help

if they'd stay on and do overtime, but they wouldn't. Apparently they had done that before in much the same circumstances and Mr Mackenzie had refused to pay them overtime because he hadn't sanctioned it. So that was that. I was mooching about, wondering what I could do, when Mr Mackenzie arrived back in his car so I said something to him about it and perhaps I wasn't as tactful as I should have been. He was as sick as mud," said James frankly.

"He was, was he?"

"Yes, he muttered something about 'amateur farmers' and went into the house. I'm sorry about it. I mean I know I shouldn't have interfered, but it seemed all wrong."

"Of course it was wrong!" cried Jock furiously. "The man went out in his car and left the hay lying on the ground! It was like a surgeon leaving his patient on the operating table and going out to have a drink. A man who can do that is no use. He hasn't the right mentality to be a farmer."

"It was Saturday," said James who was beginning to feel a little sorry for Mackenzie.

"Saturday! What's that got to do with it! Rain is just as wet on Saturday as any other day. By heaven, I'll have that man out of Boscath before he's much older!"

James would have liked to hear Mr Mackenzie's version of the affair but this did not seem the right moment to ask for it. He hesitated and then said, "Is there anything you would like me to do this morning, Uncle Jock?"

Jock smiled, his anger was short-lived and in any case he was not angry with James. "It looks to me as if you intended to catch some fish," said Jock. "Away with you, James! There's nothing I like better than a trout fried in oatmeal to my breakfast."

12

*J*AMES WAS no stranger to the river. Uncle Jock had taught him to fish when he was quite a small boy and every time he had come to Mureth on a visit he had fished. There were salmon in the river but James had come out after the wily trout.

He had seen many rivers but never one that he liked better than this. It was a small river—as rivers go—neither very wide nor very deep. Perhaps its charm lay in its varied character. *Here* you had high rocks from which the water cascaded into deep pools, leaping from ledge to ledge in glassy waves. *There* you had shallow stretches where the water splashed and rippled over its bed of stones. Big black boulders did their best to block its passage but the water slid between them or curled round them and ran on. Further down, nearer Drumburly, the speed of the river lessened and it dawdled along between grassy banks, mirroring trees and willows in its quiet surface. It was deeper here, as still waters often are, and its bed was of silted mud, deposited through thousands of years, so it was less interesting to fish and more dangerous to wading fishermen.

James had no intention of going down to the slow-flowing reaches. There were plenty of good places for trout within a mile of Mureth House. He made up a cast and knotted it to the line. Rod in hand, he wandered down to a pool he knew of, where the river made a bend.

There was a nice westerly breeze, James had it behind him

as he cast across the pool, but for all that his cast was exceedingly bad. The line fell with a splash in the water, the gut was hopelessly tangled. James had not fished for years and his hand had lost its cunning. He drew in his line, cursing himself for not having practised a bit on the lawn before coming down to the river; at this rate he would frighten every fish in the pool. After a few casts, however, he began to get into it; the line flew out smoothly, the flies landed upon the rippling surface of the pool as sweetly as a kiss . . . Gosh, it was fascinating! He drew the flies slowly across the pool and cast again. Nothing rose. There was no sign that any trout existed—or ever had existed—in the pool.

James tried there for a while and then wandered on. He fished another pool where a hill-burn came tumbling into the river. There was usually a trout here, but today there was no trout, or, if there were, he was not tempted by James's flies.

James did not mind. He was enjoying himself. Even if he caught no fish—even if he *saw* no fish—it was worth while. He revelled in the sunshine, the gentle breeze, the bright ripple of the water, he lifted his eyes and saw the white clouds moving slowly across the blue sky. He felt soothed, rested, refreshed.

The river was so lovely, so perfectly beautiful . . . he wondered what Rhoda would think of it. He had told Rhoda about the river but no amount of telling could convey its charm. If only he could show it to her! Perhaps she would paint it. James did not know a great deal about pictures but he felt pretty certain that the river was "paintable." That was the word. Rhoda had painted the Roman Well at Ashbridge but had refused to paint a picture of some trees on Cock Hill above Vittoria Cottage. "Not paintable," Rhoda had said.

James still thought of Rhoda, though perhaps not quite so
constantly as before. She was as far out of reach as the moon,
and how foolish it was to keep on crying for the moon! Rhoda
had refused him definitely; she had told him she was very fond
of him but she had made it quite clear that her painting came
first. She could not be his wife and continue as a professional
painter. James had accepted that . . . he accepted it with the
vague idea that perhaps she might change. Later on, when he was
settled, he would write and ask her again—or perhaps go to London and ask her—but since coming to Mureth he had realised
that farming could not be quickly learnt, it would be ages before he could embark upon a farm of his own. He was not settled,
nor likely to be settled for years, so he had nothing to offer any
girl. This being so he had written a pleasant, friendly letter to
Rhoda, telling her some of the amusing things that had happened,
and he had received a pleasant, friendly letter in reply.

Having fished assiduously all morning without a single rise
James decided to knock off for lunch. He climbed the bank, took
off his waders and sat down with his back against an enormous
stone. Lizzie had made a tempting assortment of sandwiches and
James was extremely hungry. It was not until he was halfway
through his lunch that he realised he had chosen the old Stone
Circle for his picnic ground. Uncle Jock had shown it to him and
told him about it when he was here before.

The circle had been here in the days of Moses, when the
Children of Israel were wandering in the wilderness on their way
to the Promised Land. It was a place of worship, like Stonehenge.
It was an open-air temple where men gathered to worship the
sun, to hail its rising above the rounded hills and make sacrifices
of blood and fire. James had not been interested in it when he

was a boy and had had a vague sort of feeling that Uncle Jock was a bit too keen about the Stone Circle . . . but, now that he was older, James understood. Odd, thought James, here am I leaning against a stone which was erected by a sun-worshipper something like three thousand years ago. I wonder what those Stone Circle men looked like, I wonder what sort of lives they led, what sort of things they did and thought. It must have been a terrific job collecting the stones and setting them up without cranes or tractors or anything.

James started upon his last sandwich, which he discovered was full of dates. Dates, thought James, that's queer. Uncle Jock said that if you stood in the middle of the Circle at sunrise on the first day of summer you could see the sun come up through a gap in the hills, so the Circle was not only a temple of the sun, it was also a calendar to tell the seasons of the year. They must have been intelligent fellows to have worked it all out.

When he had finished his lunch James wandered round looking at the stones and marvelling at their size. Half the Circle had vanished, for the river had changed its course and washed some of the stones away, but twenty-two remained—big clumsy stones set firmly in the soil. Somebody had planted a ring of thorn trees round them, perhaps as a gesture of respect; the trees were old and gnarled but they were covered with green leaves. It was a peaceful place, but it had not always been peaceful. Long ago it had been the scene of wild excitement, of fanaticism and religious fervour . . . and who could tell what sort of blood sacrifices had been offered upon the sacrificial stone!

It was now time to make a move. James decided to fish up the river to Mureth. He had little hope of catching anything for obviously this was one of those days when the trout were not taking. It seemed a perfect day for fishing but it was not. All the same there might be one trout willing to be caught, and James was extremely anxious to catch one so that Uncle Jock might have his favourite breakfast. James put a butcher on as his tail fly and began to fish.

His second cast rose a trout, but unfortunately James was so surprised that he failed to strike at the right moment and it disappeared. Almost immediately another trout came at him and this time he struck too soon. He fished on, but more carefully, and presently hooked and landed an extremely nice fish, probably about a pound. There were trout rising all over the pools and James had an hour's first class fishing, he caught five good fish and lost three others (much larger of course) through being too excited.

When James got home he was wet through, so he changed his clothes and washed and went down to tea. It annoyed him considerably to hear voices coming from the drawing-room for he had expected to find Mamie alone and had been looking forward eagerly to telling her about his adventures. He paused with his hand upon the doorknob. He was in no mood to make polite conversation, but he wanted his tea. Oh well, said James to himself and with that he opened the door and went in.

"There you are, James!" exclaimed Mamie in tones of relief. "We thought you were lost. Here's Holly!"

"I came over with a message from Aunt Adela," said Holly, smiling at James. "Mrs Johnstone asked me to stay to tea."

"Good," said James cheerfully. He was glad the visitor was Holly for she was friendly and easy to talk to. There was no need to make polite conversation for her benefit.

"Come and tell us all about it," Mamie said.

"How many did you catch?" asked Holly.

James sat down and accepted a cup of tea. "It was lovely," he declared. "It was perfectly marvellous. I've decided fishing is the best form of sport in the whole world. There's nothing to touch it."

"I know. It's frightfully exciting," Holly agreed.

"You're keen on fishing?"

"Oh yes, rather. Of course I don't get much of it, you know."

Thus encouraged James began to talk. He found himself talking a good deal, talking and eating, drinking large quantities of hot, sweet tea. He found himself telling the story of the big trout that got away and telling it amusingly, telling it against himself. It was fun to make Holly laugh.

Mamie had withdrawn into herself (it was a habit of hers to withdraw into herself when other people were talking) so that it almost seemed as if she were not present, or as if she were present only to pour out tea and see that her companions were doing justice to the scones and honey and the chocolate cake. After a little James noticed her withdrawal and tried to include her in the conversation but Mamie would not be drawn.

The subject of the conversation had now changed from fishing to mutual friends. Holly had stayed at Oxford and, whilst staying there, had been taken by her hosts to a bathing-party at an enormous house called Bendersleigh Manor.

"The Brights'!" exclaimed James.

"Yes, do you know them?"

James had never met the Brights but he had heard of them, of course. Rhoda's brother, Derek Ware, had married Valerie Bright. "What is she like?" enquired James.

"Rather marvellous in a Bright way," replied Holly mischie-
vously. "Big and Bright and Beautiful—that's Valerie."

"Doesn't Mr Bright make toothpaste?" asked Mamie suddenly.

"Gallons of it," nodded Holly.

"Yards of it, you mean," said James. "Toothpaste is always
measured by length. You're told to put half an inch on your brush
—surely you know that, Holly."

They laughed.

"Tell us about the bathing-party," urged James.

Holly was only too willing to oblige; she gave a most amusing
(if slightly malicious) account of the bathing-party at "Toothpaste Palace." Everything had been done regardless of expense.
Even the bath-towels, with which the guests had been provided,
were larger and fluffier than ordinary bath-towels. The party had
been ornamented by a galaxy of film stars, male and female (not
stars of the first magnitude, but sufficiently glamorous), who lay
about the terrace in elegant attitudes and showed little inclination
to take to the water.

Having finished with the bathing-party Holly proceeded to
discuss a play which she had seen in London, a play called *Eve's
Dilemma* with Harriet Fane in the name part. "It was an idiotic
play," said Holly. "It was an absolute flop."

"Harriet Fane is my aunt," said James laughing. "Better to
warn you before you say any more."

"But she's wonderful!" cried Holly. "Surely you didn't think
I meant *she* was a flop! The play wasn't worthy of her, that's all.
Harriet Fane is a gorgeous person, I admire her more than I can
say. But how does it happen that she's your aunt?"

"Because she's my sister," said Mamie.

"Harriet Fane is really Harriet Armstrong," explained James.

They talked some more about Harriet and then Holly rose to go. "It's been lovely," she declared. "I may come again, mayn't I?"

Mamie said she might, but she did not say it with much enthusiasm. She was incapable of gush.

"What about the dance?" asked James significantly.

"Oh yes," said Mamie. "We're having a little dance. I'm afraid it's just a dance in the barn for the farm-people, but if you would like to come . . ."

"Of course I should *love* to come!"

"We have it every year," explained Mamie. "We have it when the big barn is nearly empty, before the harvest. Jock and I always go, of course, but I'm afraid you might find it rather—I mean it's really for the farm-people, so—"

"I'd love to come," repeated Holly. "Honestly, I should *adore* it."

"And Eleanor must come," said James.

"Eleanor!" exclaimed Holly in amazement.

Mamie was surprised too. "But James—" she began.

"We must ask Eleanor," said James firmly. "You could write a note to Lady Steele, couldn't you? If you wrote it *now*, Holly could take it back with her. That would be a good plan, wouldn't it?"

Neither Mamie nor Holly agreed with James. Holly had no desire to be burdened with the task of looking after her young cousin at the dance and Mamie was averse to writing the letter of invitation because she was certain that Lady Steele would refuse to let the child come, but James was adamant. He opened Mamie's desk and placed a chair for her. "It won't take long," he said.

Mamie sat down somewhat reluctantly and wrote to Lady Steele, explaining about the dance and saying that they would be very glad if the young people, including Eleanor, could come over to Mureth on Tuesday and join the party.

13

IT was cribbage that evening after dinner. Jock and Mamie played as usual and James sat and watched them. He discovered quite suddenly that he loved them dearly. He had always been very fond of them of course, but in the last few weeks he had begun to understand them, and with understanding had come love.

"Fifteen two, fifteen four, fifteen six and a pair makes eight and a double run of three is fourteen and one for his nob is fifteen . . . that puts me out, Jock," announced Mamie.

"Good for you!" said Jock.

They gathered up the cards but did not start another game. James saw a look pass between them.

"We wondered," said Mamie, "we wondered whether you had been here long enough to make up your mind whether—"

"Whether or not you want to take up farming?" said Jock, finishing the sentence for her.

"There's no hurry," said Mamie hastily. "If you haven't quite decided there's no hurry."

"Yes," said James. "I do. I like it immensely. The only thing is . . . well, I've got to earn my living. The point is whether Uncle Jock thinks I would ever be any good, and if so how long it would take me to learn enough to be any good."

"How about you taking over Boscath?" suggested Jock.

"Taking over Boscath!" echoed James in bewildered tones.

107

"Running it for me, with me behind you," explained Jock. "Mackenzie is leaving in the autumn."

"How could I?" asked James. "It would be simply grand of course, but I don't know anything. I might let you down."

"I'll tell you what to do and you'll do it. I daresay you'll make mistakes, but it'll be good for you to take some responsibility." He hesitated and looked at Mamie. She nodded. "You see, James," continued Jock in a slightly embarrassed manner. "It's like this, you see. We've decided that if you really like farming you're to have Mureth when I'm dead."

James was speechless. He gazed at Jock helplessly.

"Would you like that?" enquired Jock.

"Like it!" gasped James. "Uncle Jock, it's—it's marvellous. Goodness, I don't know what to say! Mureth!"

"I told Caroline about it."

"You told Mother?"

"Years ago," nodded Jock. "Of course she didn't say much. She couldn't say much because we didn't know whether you'd like the life. But Mamie and I made up our minds that if you showed a liking for farming you were to have Mureth."

"It's simply—staggering," declared James in a dazed voice. "I never thought for a moment—it's simply—staggering. Mureth! Goodness!"

"Go on, Jock," said Mamie. "Tell him about the name."

"Och, Mamie, could we not leave that till another time?" She shook her head.

"Well, maybe you're right," said Jock with a sigh. He looked down at the board and began to fiddle about with the cards in an uncertain manner. "It's like this, James," he said. "We wondered if you could see your way to taking the name. There have been

Johnstones at Mureth for two hundred years and somehow it would seem queer if—if there wasn't a Johnstone of Mureth. But it's for you to decide. There's nobody going to press you if you'd rather not. It was Mamie's idea in the first instance. Mamie thought you might—might think of it."

"Uncle Jock!" exclaimed James. "Yes, of course I would! I'd be proud to take the name. I mean it's a tremendous honour for you to want me to take it. But I hope it'll be a hundred years before . . . I mean you're as fit as a fiddle, aren't you? Goodness, I don't know what I'm saying!"

"Johnstone Dering or Dering Johnstone," said Jock. "Mamie thinks Dering Johnstone sounds best."

"Uncle Jock," said James in desperation. "I can't thank you properly. It's so absolutely staggering. I feel as if I were dreaming or something. It isn't only Mureth, it's you. I mean I know how you and Mamie love Mureth, so if you think I'm the right person to—to have it—well, it means you must like me a lot, and of course—"

"I think you may take it we like you quite a lot, Jamie," said Jock laughing.

Mamie took up the cards and shuffled them and they started another game as if nothing had happened. Just as if nothing had happened, thought James, looking at them in bewilderment. The conversation had taken place between two games of cribbage; it had lasted about ten minutes and had completely changed James's life.

James felt stifled, as if he couldn't breathe. "I think I'll go out," he said. "I might walk up the hill and see Daniel Reid."

"Good idea," agreed Jock. "Gosh, Mamie, that's two for his heels—the second time this game!"

It was still light when James opened the front door and
looked out. The sky was cloudless, it was a pale primrose colour
shading to amethyst, the hills stood up against it as if they had
been cut out of black cardboard. James sat down upon the steps
and looked at Mureth. He decided not to go and see Daniel. He
did not want to see anybody, nor to speak to anybody, until he
had got used to himself in his new circumstances. He was quite
dazed. Half an hour ago he had been wondering what the future
held in store for him. Now he knew. The future held Mureth.

James heard the hoot of an owl and the faint, far-off tinkle
of the burn.

Of course it would be years and years before Mureth came
to him (Uncle Jock was as strong as a lion, thank goodness) but
all the same he found himself looking at Mureth differently; the
hills, the river, the animals, even the people in their little cottages
seemed to take on a new significance. He envisaged them in a sort
of rosy glow. For a while James sat there without thinking at all
—just woolgathering—and as he sat there the sky darkened and
the light faded. It was almost dark except for a gleam in the sky
behind the hills, a sort of unearthly radiance . . . moonrise. At
first the moon was a thin sliver of gold; and then, as it rose higher,
it was for all the world like the golden dome of a temple set
upon the hill-top. Gradually the dome became a sphere, enormous,
glowing, poised upon the ridge of Winterfell. The ball rose slowly,
majestically, it cast loose (as it were) and floated in the sky . . .
and all the valley was filled with the brightness of it, with bright
moonlight and dark shadows, and away in the distance there was
the crowing of a cock.

James still sat there on the steps but now his thoughts began
to move. He thought of the immediate future and of what he

would do. He must learn all he could, understudy Jock, read every book about farming that he could lay his hands on; he must talk to other farmers and observe their methods . . . so he would prepare himself for the day when he would be master here. It was good to see his way ahead, to feel settled with his future assured. It was good to feel Uncle Jock at the back of him, solid as a rock. James had been feeling like a rudderless ship, buffeted by the waves, but now the ship had come to anchor in a secure harbour. Jock and Mamie wanted him, they wanted him as an adopted son—that was what it came to—and James loved them dearly.

His thoughts turned to Rhoda (the moon was as golden as Rhoda's hair); he had something to offer Rhoda now. He could write to her and tell her what had happened and ask her . . . but could he? James put his arms round his knees and thought about it. No, he couldn't do that, for, although this new and quite unexpected development made all the difference in the world to him, it would make no difference to Rhoda. If Rhoda loved him enough to marry him she would marry him supposing he had not a penny to his name—that was Rhoda. She had not refused him because his future was uncertain, she would not accept him because his future was assured. It would be an insult to write to her on those lines, to write and say, "You refused to marry me before, but now I'm going to have Mureth some day, so . . ."

No, thought James, it's no good. Rhoda is as far away as ever. Better to put Rhoda right out of my head and get down to some hard work.

When James had gone out Jock smiled at Mamie. "You were right," he said.

"I was sure he would," nodded Mamie. "You're pleased, aren't you? What made you suddenly decide to ask him tonight, Jock?"

"I wanted to be sure before I asked him. It's not everybody that's cut out to be a farmer. I was not absolutely sure about James until this morning."

Mamie waited.

"He had been over to Boscath on Saturday," said Jock. "Mackenzie had gone off in his car and left some hay lying out in the field. James said to me, '*I felt I wanted to go and gather in that hay with my own hands.*'"

Mamie nodded understandingly. She had been a farmer's wife for nearly twenty years.

"Mackenzie had told me a long, garbled tale," continued Jock. "He said James had been interfering with the men, putting the men against him and undermining his authority. But then I heard James's version of the affair."

"There was nothing in it, of course," said Mamie.

"There *was* something in it," replied Jock smiling. "There was enough in it to send me back to Boscath in a towering rage and give Mackenzie the sack," and he proceeded to tell Mamie the whole story.

"That's what's been worrying you," said Mamie when the tale was told. "You never really liked Mr Mackenzie, did you? So now you don't need to worry any more."

"Not about that," agreed Jock. He took up the cards and shuffled them in an absent-minded way. "I'm worrying about my lambs. Some more of them have disappeared. You know, Mamie, I wish I'd taken the other man."

"I like Daniel Reid," said Mamie with conviction.

"I know that, and I trust your judgment, but the man's not straight."

"I'm sure he's straight!"

"I was sure of it, too. I'm disappointed in Reid. The fact is I saw him at the Show on Wednesday; he was talking to a couple of nasty-looking individuals—goodness knows where they'd come from! Flashy sort of fellows in blue suits."

"But Jock!"

"I know," nodded Jock. "His friends are his own affair, but you see we'd arranged that Reid was to go over to Silverbeck that afternoon and have a look at the ewes, and instead of that he went to the Show, so he was neglecting his duty. But the worst thing of all, to my mind, was the next morning—he talked as if he had been over to Silverbeck."

"He said he had been there?" asked Mamie incredulously.

"Not straight out," replied Jock frowning. "He just talked as if he *had* been there."

"Are you sure you saw him at the Show?"

"Of course I saw him."

"Why didn't you speak to him about it?"

"Och well," said Jock uncertainly. "I just felt . . . I mean I didn't mind the man going to the Show. If he'd asked me I'd have said he could go and welcome. What I mind is deceit. I don't feel I can trust the man, that's the truth of it."

Part 2

$\mathcal{T}$HE DANCE at Mureth was an annual affair, it was really for the farm-people (as Mamie had said) but this year Mamie had asked a few of the young people in the neighbourhood so that it would be more fun for James. She had asked the young Steeles of course and, having asked them, Mamie decided she must ask the young Duncans from Crossraggle and the new doctor and his sister from Drumburly. She warned her prospective guests that it was "not a real dance," but in spite of her warning all the young people were coming—all except Eleanor Steele. Mamie was not surprised when Lady Steele rang up and refused the invitation on Eleanor's behalf.

"She's much too young," said Lady Steele. "Andrew won't hear of it. But Ian will be here and will bring a friend if he may and of course Holly will be delighted. She told you that herself."

"I'm sorry about Eleanor. I was afraid—" began Mamie, but she was interrupted by James.

"Let me speak to Lady Steele," said James. "Please, Mamie. It's really rather important—"

"What did you say, Mamie?" enquired Lady Steele's voice in Mamie's ear.

"I said I was sorry," replied Mamie. "Don't, James. No, you can't. Lady Steele says she's too young."

"Tell her it isn't a proper grown-up dance," urged James.

"Tell her we'll look after Eleanor and send her home early."

"I can't hear what you're saying, Mamie," declared Lady Steele. "There's something the matter with the telephone. A man's voice keeps breaking into the conversation."

"It's James," explained Mamie. "James, I wish you wouldn't."

"Tell her," urged James. "Tell her what I said."

Mamie told her, but Lady Steele was adamant. Eleanor was too young.

The barn, in which the dance was to be held, had been built in the good old days when men took pride in the work of their hands. The walls were of stone from the quarry on the hill; the timber was from Mureth trees, sawn and shaped upon the estate. Great beams crossed the building, holding up the roof; they were dove-tailed into one another and built firmly into the walls. Jock kept the winter food for his stock in this barn, so by now it was almost empty and it was easy to clean it out and polish the wooden floor. The men set to with a will, they decorated it with branches of green leaves and hung strings of bunting and paper lanterns across the building from hook to hook. When Mamie went down at tea-time she was surprised and pleased beyond measure.

"It's really splendid," she said to Willy Dunne who was in charge of the work. "It's even better than usual."

"Umphm, it's no bad," agreed Willy Dunne complacently. "We were wanting to make a good appearance this year when there was gentry coming."

Mamie could not help smiling. Willy Dunne was by way of being a Socialist, but surely these were not the sentiments one expected from a man with a red tie.

"Well, you've certainly put your best foot foremost," Mamie

told him. "The old barn looks lovely. You won't forget the band, Willy."

It had been arranged that two fiddlers and a man with a piano-accordion were to be fetched from Drumburly for the occasion.

"I'll fetch them, never fear," replied Willy Dunne. "And Daniel Reid will give them a hand, too. He's a real good fiddler, is Daniel."

Mamie nodded. She wondered how many guests there would be, for the Mureth people were allowed to ask their friends from neighbouring farms. Not too many, she hoped. The barn was apt to become extremely hot and stifling if it was over-filled.

"There'll be about fifty," said Willy, as if he had guessed her thought. "That's not counting the party from the big house."

"We shall be ten," Mamie told him.

"There's one thing," said Willy, looking a trifle embarrassed. "I was just wondering if you'd give me a turn, Mistress Johnstone. You'll be leading off with Mr Mackenzie from Boscath. That's right and proper. But I'm the auldest inhabitant. No the auldest in years, ye ken, but what I mean is nobody's been in Mureth as long as me, barring auld Mr Couper and he'll be in his bed."

"I'd like to, Willy," replied Mamie with becoming gravity. "And as a matter of fact Mr Mackenzie isn't coming, so how would it do if we led off together?"

"It would be fine!" exclaimed Willy Dunne, beaming all over his face. "Och, that would be fine!" He hesitated and said thoughtfully. "I wonder now. You'll not have any idea why Mr Mackenzie's not coming to the dance?"

Mamie had a very good idea as to the reason for Mr Mac-

kenzie's refusal of the invitation, but she was not particularly
anxious to disclose it, because it was Jock's prerogative to inform
his men of changes in policy and Mamie never interfered in Jock's
affairs.

"Maybe he's leaving," suggested Willy Dunne, gazing up at
the paper lanterns in a ruminative manner. "Maybe Mr Johnstone's
not overpleased with the way Boscath's managed. It wouldn't surprise me—nor any other body in the place—if Mr James was to
have Boscath Farm."

"I expect Mr Johnstone will be telling you himself."

"Just that," agreed Willy. "We'll all be pleased, too. Mr
James is the right sort. He's not afraid to take off his coat and
he's got a pleasant word for everybody."

It was curious, Mamie thought as she walked back across
the steading. It really was very curious indeed how things got
about. You chatted quietly, in the privacy of your own drawing-
room, and in half no time the matter you had discussed was common knowledge. Mamie knew enough about these people to be
certain that every cottage in the place was seething with rumours
and conjectures—rumours about Mr Mackenzie's departure and
conjectures about James. As she looked back upon her conversation with Willy Dunne she realised that he had led her on. He
had shaped the conversation to obtain the information he wanted
and she had walked blindly into the trap. Not that it mattered, of
course, thought Mamie smiling a little at her own stupidity. They
would have to know sooner or later.

"Mistress Johnstone, could I speak to you for a moment?"

Mamie stopped and looked round and her smile vanished, for
this was a sinister request and all the more so when it fell from
the lips of Mrs Dunne. Mamie knew well that the request to

speak to her for a moment meant trouble, nobody ever wanted to
speak to her for a moment about pleasant things—and Mrs Dunne
was the snake in the Eden of Mureth Farm. She *looked* so nice,
thought Mamie, looking at her. She was small and plump with a
rosy, smiling face but for all that she was at the bottom of any
trouble in the cottages.

"Yes, Mrs Dunne," said Mamie, with a cheerfulness she did
not feel. "I've just been looking at the barn, they have decorated it
beautifully and it's going to be a lovely fine night so everybody will
enjoy the dance."

"I'm sure I hope so," said Mrs Dunne smiling in a very
amiable manner. "There's been enough work put out on it, and
those that work hardest get the least thanks. I was saying so to
Mr Dunne this very morning. You needn't expect thanks for all
your work, I said."

Mamie had just thanked Willy Dunne; and she was trying to
find words to explain this to his wife without offending her, but
Mrs Dunne did not wait for her to find them.

"But that's not what I wanted to speak to you about," continued Mrs Dunne, still smiling but lowering her voice a little.
"It's about yon new shepherd. Maybe you and Mr Johnstone like
the man, but he's not all he might be—and that's the truth. Mr
Dunne and me saw him, reeling drunk, in Drumburly Hight Street
the other night."

"Oh, Mrs Dunne! But—"

"We all have our faults, and the man's pleasant spoken, I'll
admit . . . perhaps just a wee bit *too* pleasant spoken. It's an awful waste of a nice wee house, too," said Mrs Dunne thoughtfully.

"You mean because he isn't married? Mr Johnstone and I
think that's Reid's own affair—"

"Married! I'd be sorry for his wife!"

"Perhaps it's just as well he hasn't got one, then. He does his work well and the house is beautifully clean."

"He's never in it," said Mrs Dunne, smiling delightfully. "The house is empty most nights. I've made it my business to go up and have a look and he's more often out than in."

Mamie gazed at her in silence.

"It's none of my business where he goes," continued Mrs Dunne. "I've never been one for gossip. I may have my suspicions, but I'd rather keep them to myself."

But you wouldn't, thought Mamie, looking at her in distaste. The *last* thing you want is to keep your suspicions to yourself.

"Maybe he goes to Drumburly," said Mrs Dunne, beaming all over her plump, rosy face. "It would be dull for him alone in the cottage. Or maybe he finds company nearer home. There's folks here in Mureth that isn't *all that* particular about their friends and thinks little harm in breaking the ten commandments."

Mamie could find nothing to say. There might be truth in the accusation or there might not. She was distressed at the thought that there might be truth in it for she felt responsible for the morals of Mureth.

"Daisy's a nice-looking girl," added Mrs Dunne kindly.

"Yes, isn't she," agreed Mamie, pretending to be dense. "She's as pretty as a picture and she's very good at her work. We've never had a better dairy-maid."

No more was said. Mrs Dunne had dropped her poison and was quite content. Mrs Johnstone might pretend to be dense, but she was not as dense as all that, and even if the poison did not work very quickly its effect would not be entirely lost. Someday something might happen and Mrs Johnstone would remember what she had said.

Mrs Dunne hated the Bells. Nothing would please her better than to see the Bells discredited, to watch them packing up and leaving Mureth. If she could accomplish that she would be happy, or so she thought. She hated all the Bell family but Daisy was the worst for Daisy was not only young and pretty, she was clever too. Daisy had discovered Mrs Dunne's vulnerable points and enjoyed pricking her where the pricks would hurt . . . and Mrs Dunne, who liked hurting other people and making them squirm, disliked being hurt herself.

It is curious but true that those who make a habit of saying unkind things are often the most easily hurt and offended when their victims retaliate.

15

$\mathcal{J}$OCK AND Mamie and James had supper early and walked over to the barn. It was a fine evening, cold for the time of year, and it was still quite light, of course. It seemed odd to go to a dance in broad daylight. But the daylight was dimmed in the barn and the coloured lanterns were lighted and the place had a delightfully festive appearance.

Although it was only a quarter to eight the barn was full of people. The guests had been asked for eight o'clock but Mamie was not in the least surprised to find that so many had arrived already. (In this part of the world people always arrive at parties long before the stated time; and Mamie, having lived here all her life, was aware of this peculiarity. Perhaps it is because there are not many festivities and they are unwilling to lose a single moment of pleasure or perhaps they allow the extra time for fear of being delayed upon the road.) Many of the guests had walked over the hills from the other farms in the neighbourhood, some had come even further in carts or upon bicycles. The party from Drumburly Tower had not arrived, nor had the Duncans from Crossraggle.

Jock did not enjoy parties but he hid his feelings well. He went round talking to everybody, asking after fathers and mothers and children—who were either too old or too young to be present —asking after the hay and agreeing that it had been a fine year for hay—though a bit too dry for the roots. He was popular and deservedly so for he was kind and friendly, talking as man to man without false heartiness or condescension.

"Uncle Jock is in his element," said James to Mamie.

"Not really," Mamie replied. "Jock is in his element amongst animals or in the hay-field. He doesn't like parties."

"But they all love him," James said. "I wonder if I shall ever learn to talk to the people like that."

"You do," she told him. "I mean you don't talk to them like Jock, but you talk to them like yourself, which is the best way. It's no use at all putting on *special* sort of talk, if you know what I mean. Special sort of talk may be all right for society people, but people who live and work on the land see through it at once and hate it. I've never learnt to talk," said Mamie sadly. "I've tried very hard but I'm shy. I always wonder whether they *want* me to talk to them and that's fatal. You shouldn't think of yourself at all of course. It's silly to be shy."

"If you're made like that you can't help it."

"Shyness makes you stiff and awkward and then people think you're stuck-up. If they only knew!"

By this time it was eight o'clock and the other guests were drifting in: Holly Douglas, Ian Steele and his friend from Edinburgh, Cathie and Henry Duncan. All exclaimed in surprise and admiration at the beauty of the barn and the magnificence of the decorations.

"I wish we had a barn like this," said Cathie. "Our barns are tumbling down and Daddy can't get wood to mend them. Our barns are all ratty and batty."

The others laughed, but not very heartily, for most of them knew that Crossraggle was going downhill fast and *that* was no laughing matter.

The next arrivals were Dr Forrester and his sister. Dr Forrester had come as assistant to Dr Black (who was getting too old for his widely scattered practice) and his sister had come to keep house for him. They had bought a tiny house in Drumburly High Street and had just got settled in. Mamie had not met them before and had wondered what they would be like; she decided that she liked them. They were young and rather shy and they knew nobody, so it behoved her to put them at their ease and to introduce them to the other members of the party. When there was a job like this to be done Mamie forgot her own shyness. She enquired about the house and whether they liked it.

"We like it awfully," Nan Forrester said. "It's so lovely to be together—neither of us has ever had a house of our very own before. It's tiny, but that's all the better because of course I shall have to do everything myself . . . and we like our neighbours too. I can't tell you how kind they've been."

The band was tuning up and an air of excitement pervaded the barn. Willy Dunne approached Mamie and bowed a trifle sheepishly.

"It's a waltz," said Willy. "I knew fine you liked waltzing so I told them to start with it."

She smiled and put her hand on his arm and off they went. At first they had the floor to themselves (for this was the usual custom) and then other couples joined in. Jock was dancing with Mrs Dunne, James had chosen Mrs Bell, the others paired off in a haphazard manner.

Mamie loved dancing and Willy Dunne was a competent if somewhat uninspired performer. There was no need to talk to Willy, he did not want conversation. When he danced he danced and gave all his mind to it, gripping his partner tightly and steer-

ing her carefully round the room. Mamie began to enjoy herself
and her anxieties as hostess vanished. She saw numerous friends
amongst the whirling couples and a good many strangers and she
was relieved to notice that they all looked happy . . . they were
happy in a serious sort of way, but later they would warm up
and the gravity would disappear.

Having taken the floor with Willy Dunne it was imperative
to dance with the other men. Mamie knew this. She knew that
if she did not there would be all sorts of unpleasantness in the
Mureth cottages. She danced the Circassian Circle with Willy
Bell, and then she danced with Joseph Couper and with Daniel
Reid. Wilson, the second shepherd, who lived in the cottage on
the hill above Reid's cottage was a shy young man with a nice
little wife and two small children. He hovered about, looking at
Mrs Johnstone and then looking away, advancing and retreating,
but quite unable to speak. It was rather funny, really, but Mamie
was sorry for shy young people so she was not amused. She
went up to him and took his hand and led him onto the floor.
It was "Strip the Willow," a somewhat boisterous affair; they went
through the whole performance without exchanging a syllable.

After this Mamie found herself standing beside Mrs Wilson,
who was not as shy as her husband but was equally difficult to
talk to, except upon one subject. Fortunately Mamie knew Mrs
Wilson's subject so she enquired for Charlie.

"He's fine," said Mrs Wilson smiling happily. "He's growing
so big you'd scarcely know him. It's the extra milk that's doing
it. It's awful good of you to give us the extra milk, Mrs Johnstone."

Mamie said she was glad.

"And he's getting so clever, too," declared his mother. "You'd
never think he was only just five years old. He's made great friends

with Mr Reid. Mr Reid's awful good to Charlie and they have
jokes together. He's got a way with bairns, Mr Reid has. Last
week Mr Reid came up to the cottage and Charlie was going off
to bed, so Mr Reid said he'd tell him a story, and he told him an
awful funny story about two farmers called Big Klaus and Little
Klaus. It's an old story, Mr Reid was saying. Maybe you've heard
of it."

Mamie said she knew it well.

"Is that so?" exclaimed Mrs Wilson. "Well, you'll know all
about it, then . . . how Big Klaus loaned Little Klaus his horses
for the ploughing and Little Klaus was so proud of ploughing
with five, fine horses that he kept on shouting 'Gee up, all my
five horses!' Well, would you believe it, Mrs Johnstone, Charlie's
been playing he was Little Klaus ever since. He's been going
round the place shouting, 'Gee up, all my five horses!' That's what
he's been doing. And he watches for Mr Reid coming down the hill
and runs after him and shouts, 'Good morning to you, Big Klaus!'
just like the story. He's awful smart for just five years old, Charlie
is."

Mamie was about to congratulate Mrs Wilson upon the extraordinary intelligence of her son when James appeared and
asked Mrs Wilson to dance with him and snatched her away. It
was nice of James, thought Mamie smiling. James had believed
her to be in need of help and had come to the rescue, but as a
matter of fact Mamie did not mind listening to people; it was
talking that bothered her, and she had been quite interested in
Mrs Wilson's story. It showed Daniel Reid in a new and very
pleasant light. Mamie was still drawn to Daniel Reid (she could
not help liking him in spite of Mrs Dunne's accusations and in
spite of Jock's assertion that he was not straight). She still felt

that Jock must have made a mistake about seeing Reid at the Show when he ought to have been doing his rounds upon the hills . . . and yet it was very unlike Jock to make mistakes.

When James had danced with all the people he should, he decided it was time he had some fun. He saw Holly standing beside Ian Steele and asked her to dance with him.

"You said you'd dance this with me, Holly," Ian reminded her.

"I know, darling, but I've changed my mind," replied Holly, smiling at her cousin engagingly. "Poor James has been doing his duty nobly and if he wants to dance with me he can."

"Of course I want to," said James. "Haven't I just told you I want to dance with you—and it's a waltz."

"Thank goodness it's a waltz!" exclaimed Holly, who was of the opinion that Country Dances were a waste of time.

It was pleasant to dance with Holly; she was an accomplished dancer, polished, easy and intuitive, she melted in his arms and smelt delightful, (perhaps James would not have noticed this so much if his last partner had not been Mrs Dunne, who was fat and tightly corseted and smelt of camphor balls). They talked a little as they danced, but not too much.

"This is fun," said Holly. "The floor is wonderfully good and the music has a swing. Why don't you have lots of dances in this gorgeous barn? You could have one at Christmas, couldn't you?"

"No."

"Why not?"

"Because it's a barn," smiled James. "A barn is for corn, not for dancing. It can be used for dancing when it's empty, that's all."

"What a pity!" said Holly with a sigh. "Christmas is even

more special for me than for other people; it's my birthday, you
see."

"Holly!"

"Yes, that's why. Daddy wanted me to be called Noelle but
Mother knew a girl called Noelle and disliked her intensely, so
they decided I was to be Holly. Nasty prickly stuff," added Holly
with a smile in her voice.

"Not all hollies are prickly."

They danced for a little while in silence.

"This is fun," said Holly again. "It's far more fun than an
ordinary dance. There's something very special about Mureth."

"You feel that?"

"I love Mureth, James."

"Really and truly?"

"Really and truly," declared Holly with a sigh.

When the dance was over James suggested they should go
outside. He had been out before, with Daisy, and it was not too
cold. Daisy had taken him round to the side of the barn where
there was a wooden fence to lean upon; she had expected James
to kiss her in a friendly way, but James did not want to kiss Daisy.
He decided to take Holly to the secluded corner by the wooden
fence; it would be very pleasant indeed to kiss Holly. Holly was
sweet, she amused him and intrigued him and he liked her a lot.
He was aware that Holly would marry him if he asked her . . .
James had made up his mind that he would like to marry Holly.

They went out together. It had been dark before (when he
was here with Daisy) but now the moon had risen and all the
valley was filled with its light. James and Holly leant upon the
fence and looked across the valley at the hills.

"What a gorgeous moon," said Holly softly. "It's gold, isn't it?"

"Yes," agreed James.

"It's like a bent sovereign, James."

The moon was waning, of course. It was a queer shape—not a perfect sphere as it had been last week when James had watched it rise from behind Winterfell and balance on the hill-top.

"Have a cigarette," said James producing his case.

Holly accepted one gratefully, but all the same she was a little surprised for it was not what she had expected. She had given James his cue ("I love Mureth," she had said) and James had brought her to this secluded corner. She had known exactly what James would do; he would kiss her and say, "Come and live at Mureth—with me." But it hadn't happened like that. Something had gone wrong at the last moment and James had offered her a cigarette. It didn't matter, thought Holly. She could wait. When you are certain of something you don't mind waiting.

They smoked companionably. They talked about various unimportant matters.

James was not at his best. He felt shaky and uncertain of himself. He made up his mind to ask Holly to marry him but he could not ask her now. He could not ask a girl to marry him when his mind was full of another girl, even if the other girl was as far out of his reach as a golden moon sailing in a dark blue sky.

The dance went on until nearly two o'clock, which is late for country dwellers who are not used to late hours and have to be up and doing early. Jock and Mamie discussed the evening's entertainment as they prepared for bed.

"It was a success," said Mamie. "I wondered if it would be a success, having the Steeles and the Duncans, but it was. Cathie looked sweet, didn't she?"

"She's a pretty wee thing," agreed Jock.

"It's sad about Crossraggle. Why can't Mr Duncan make the farm pay?"

"He leaves too much to chance. Maybe the man's not well, he was looking pretty wretched the last time I saw him . . . he was looking sort of miserable," said Jock thoughtfully. "If I had not known Duncan I'd have said it was drink but Duncan is a teetotaller and quite crazy on the subject. There's never a drop of strong drink to be seen at Crossraggle, he even grudges the men their beer."

Mamie nodded. Mr Duncan's principles were common knowledge. One was bound to respect him for them, of course, but they were uncomfortable things to live with and life was sufficiently complicated without having to battle with a complex on the subject of strong drink. Men liked a glass of beer and occasionally a glass of spirits and Mamie could not see that it did them any harm. Indeed there was remarkably little drunkenness in the district except at the New Year when it was the time-honoured custom to drink not wisely but all too well. An unfortunate custom, no doubt, but so deeply rooted in tradition that nothing short of an atom bomb would be likely to uproot it and all one could do was to turn a blind eye upon the celebrations and wait until they were over and sanity returned.

Mamie's thoughts had wandered quite a long way from the dance, but Jock was still thinking about it.

"I don't like the Douglas girl," he said suddenly.

"Why?" asked Mamie in alarm. She herself did not like Holly, but she had been trying to tell herself that she was prejudiced and old-fashioned.

"Does it matter?" asked Jock, smiling down at her as she sat at the mirror brushing her soft brown hair.

"Yes, it does," said Mamie earnestly. "Please, Jock, why don't you like Holly Douglas?"

"I didn't like the way she was dressed for one thing."

"But Jock, it was a beautiful dress—and you never notice women's clothes anyway. I don't believe you know what I was wearing."

"I don't believe I do," admitted Jock laughing. "The fact is I don't seem to notice clothes if they're right—it's when they're wrong I notice them—and it may have been a beautiful dress, but it was not right for dancing in a barn."

"She *was* over-dressed," agreed Mamie thoughtfully, "but she looked very pretty. Cherry colour suits Holly."

"That's cherry colour, is it?"

"Jock, I wish you'd tell me, *really*."

He thought for a moment and then he said, "She wears a disguise. It's a pleasant disguise, I'll admit, and there may be pleasant things below it, but I can't be doing with people that are not exactly what they seem."

Mamie was silent.

"What's worrying you?" asked Jock. "The girl is nothing to us. She'll be away back to London next week or the week after, for she's a Londoner through and through. She's happiest when she hears yon high heels of hers tapping on the pavement and can glue her pretty nose to the shop-windows."

"How do you know?" asked Mamie in amazement.

"I danced with her and talked with her . . . Och, I'm tired!" declared Jock yawning. "I'm getting too old for late nights."

16

IT SEEMED to James that he had only been asleep for about five minutes when Lizzie came in to waken him. As a rule she put down his cup of tea and went away, but this morning she lingered.

"Is it late?" asked James sleepily.

"It's just gone half-past six."

"Too early," mumbled James, turning over and burying his head in the pillow.

"Mr James," said Lizzie. "It's yon man. I told him it was too airly, but he'll not take no for an answer."

"Who? What?" asked James, trying to wake up.

"He'll not take no for an answer," repeated Lizzie in aggrieved accents. "It's too airly, I said. You'll not get Mr James out of bed at this hour—and after the dance, too—he'll want to sleep in, I said. But d'ye think he'd listen to me!"

"Who was it?"

"Och, he's cheeky!" said Lizzie disgustedly. "I've no use for the likes of him, the wee, brown, skinny creature—"

"Is the cow calving?" asked James, sitting up and rubbing the sleepiness out of his eyes.

"He was here at the back o' six if you please," continued Lizzie. "And me scrubbing out my kitchen. Away and get Mr James, he says. I'll do no such thing, I says. So then—"

"Lizzie, who was it?" demanded James.

"It was the new shepherd, the wee—"

"Daniel Reid!" cried James, thoroughly awakened. "Gosh, of course! I know! Tell him I'll be down in two minutes."

James leaped out of bed as he spoke and proceeded to dive into his clothes in record time, but it was more than two minutes before he was ready and when he got down to the kitchen Daniel had gone.

"You're to go up to the cottage," said Lizzie. "He said it's urgent, but maybe not what you think."

This cryptic message puzzled James considerably, he pondered it as he strode up the hill. He had thought it was the "sheep-lifters" (as Daniel called them) so presumably it was not. But, if not, what on earth *could* it be? Daniel was not the man to say it was "urgent" unless it was very urgent indeed. All sorts of fantastic ideas came into James's head, but none that satisfied him, none that held water.

The cottage looked very peaceful. Smoke was lifting lazily from the chimney in the still morning air; the windows were bright and shining in the morning sunshine.

James ran up to the cottage door, pushed it open and entered. He saw Daniel kneeling on the hearth-rug making up the fire, and in the big chair at the side of the fire he saw—Eleanor Steele.

"Eleanor!" exclaimed James incredulously.

She sprang up and rushed at James and flung herself into his arms.

"Eleanor," cried James, holding her tightly. "Eleanor, my dear, what on earth . . ."

Eleanor was shaking all over, sobbing soundlessly, clinging to James with all her might. How light and frail she was! She had buried her face against his shoulder so all he could see of her was the top of her head with its silvery, silky hair.

"Eleanor," he said. "What's happened?"

She clung to him and sobbed.

Daniel had risen and was standing by the fire. "I found the wee lassie on the hill," he said quietly. "It seems she walked over from Drumburly and lost her way. It's easy to lose your way among the hills. She was sleeping beneath a rock when I found her—well, by rights it was Gyp that found her. She said she was wanting to see *you*, Mr James, so I brought her in and gave her a wee drink of warm milk, it was all she'd take. Somehow she put me in mind of a lost lamb," added Daniel apologetically.

"On the hill all night!" said James in dismay.

"Umphm," nodded Daniel. "And now I think I'll just go and feed the hens."

He vanished discreetly as he spoke.

"Eleanor, what happened?" asked James. "You got lost. You were frightened, weren't you? It's all right now. Come and tell me all about it." He picked her up and carried her over to the fire and sat down with her in his arms. "Here's a hankie," said James in comforting tones.

Eleanor blew her nose and wiped her eyes. "I'm sorry," she said. "I didn't mean to be silly. I walked and walked, but the hills looked all the same and it was so cold and dark. When I got to the top of one hill there was another one in front."

"There always is," James told her.

"And I heard a fox," said Eleanor with a shudder. "It's a horrid thing to hear a fox . . . in the dark."

"Horrid," agreed James.

"Oh James, I *do* love you," said Eleanor raising her eyes to his.

James had not noticed Eleanor's eyes before. They were grey eyes, dewy with tears. He was surprised at the beauty of Eleanor's eyes but somewhat dismayed to see that they were full of adoring love.

"I think you're a verray parfit gentil knight," said Eleanor softly.

James could find nothing to say, and, even if he could have found the right thing to say, it is doubtful if he could have said it. There was a lump in his throat the size of a marble—or so it seemed to James.

"I love you awfully much," said Eleanor. " I love you as Clare loved Ralph de Wilton."

There was a little silence.

"I suppose you don't love me, do you?" asked Eleanor in a very small voice.

"Of course I do," said James huskily. "I love you like a little sister." It was perfectly true. He loved Eleanor as he loved Bobbie. In some ways she reminded him of Bobbie but he could not, for the life of him, see why; for Bobbie was bouncing and cheerful like a large, clumsy, affectionate puppy, and Eleanor was a fairy creature.

"Oh James!" said Eleanor in disappointed tones. "I don't love you like that at all."

James had been afraid of it. He said with more confidence than he felt, "Yes, you do, darling. You love me like a big brother."

She snuggled against his shoulder; it was rather pleasant, James found, for she was warm and soft and her silky hair had a faint scent of violets. He put his cheek against her hair.

"You'd better tell me about it," James said. "What were you doing on the hills all by yourself?"

"You asked me to the dance," explained Eleanor. "You asked me three times; once that day in the garage and once in the letter and once over the telephone. They wouldn't let me come, so it was no use, you see. I put it out of my head and I didn't think of it much until Holly came up to the nursery in her new frock. It was a lovely frock, wasn't it? Holly came to show me her frock and say good night. It was nice of her but it made me awfully miserable. It made me so miserable I couldn't bear it."

"You thought you would come!" exclaimed James in amazement.

"You asked me," she said with a little sob. "You wanted me to come . . . it's only four miles over the hills . . . I've walked over before. I put on my best frock and brought my shoes in a bag. I thought I would look in at the door and perhaps you'd see me and I'd say I'd come after all. You *did* ask me, didn't you? It was light when I started, but then it got dark . . . and I lost the bag. Oh dear, do you think it was awful of me, James?"

"Darling," said James, hugging her, "not awful at all. Of course you wanted to come to the dance. The only thing is . . ." The only thing was, what on earth was he to do?

"I wanted to dance with you."

"Everything's all right now," he told her. "Daniel found you, thank goodness. It isn't a terrible disaster. In a few weeks you'll have forgotten all about it."

"I don't think so. I think I shall always remember and be sorry about it. Not sorry that I tried to come, but sorry I got lost. It would have been a nice thing to remember . . . dancing with you."

There was a little silence. James knew the whole story now, and understood exactly what had happened. He could understand her feelings too. Somehow he could see her changing her frock and putting her shoes in the little bag and slipping quietly out of the house. He could see her running up the hill-path, hurrying along, a tiny fairy figure in the waning light. And then it got dark and she lost her way and the hills all looked the same and she was tired and frightened and cold! Poor little girl, thought James tightening his arms about her.

But it was no good thinking about it—the night was past and she was safe; it was the future that must be thought of. What was he to do with Eleanor? Could he possibly take her home in the car and explain the whole thing to her parents? That was the obvious course. Then he thought of Sir Andrew, with his sarcastic sneer, and of Lady Steele who was so immersed in Good Works that she had no time to spare for her daughter. They would think Eleanor was mad (perhaps they wouldn't be far wrong in that—but whose fault was it?); they might think she was bad, but in that they would be very far wrong, thought James. They might even think that he had . . . that he had . . . well, that he had tampered with her affections, thought James in dismay. It was not likely that anybody would believe he had only spoken to her once in his life . . . even Mamie (thought James desperately), would Mamie believe the story? Could he take the child to Mamie and explain?

James formulated one plan after another and rejected them all. The more he thought about it the worse it seemed. Whichever way he turned there were pitfalls. Eleanor's escapade was innocent and childish, but people might not see it in that light. The Steeles might not see it in that light. Somehow he must save her from the unkindness of people who did not understand, because the unkindness would harm her and destroy her innocence.

She was just a child, her head was full of all the stories she had read, full of romance and poetry, so that she was living in another world and not in this world at all.

How on earth am I to cover it up, thought James helplessly.

"Eleanor," he said at last. "What are we going to do?"

Eleanor was sleepy. She had been cold and frightened but now she was warm and safe. She said softly, "I thought perhaps we could be married."

"No," said James hastily. "No, Eleanor, honestly—"

"People can get married at Gretna Green."

"No," said James. "People can't get married at Gretna Green, now."

"Well, somewhere—"

"No, you're too young, darling. Honestly, you are."

"I'm nearly fifteen. Girls can be married when they're fourteen."

"You're too young," said James firmly.

"Perhaps you don't want to marry me."

"We couldn't," said James. "People can't be married without their parents' consent until they're twenty-one. That's the law, so you see it's no good thinking about it."

"I could come and live with you," suggested Eleanor, snuggling her head against his shoulder.

"No, I'm afraid not. I'm afraid you'll have to go home."

He had expected tears and lamentations but there were none. "We would be so happy," she said with a little sigh. "I don't think Shelley and Emilia bothered to get married and they were very, very happy together."

"But that's poetry," James told her. "It's different in real life."

She sighed.

"You'll have to go home," repeated James, giving her a little squeeze to mitigate the brutality of his words.

"Not yet, please," whispered Eleanor.

17

*J*AMES AND Eleanor were still sitting there when Daniel returned. Daniel looked somewhat abashed when he saw his lost lamb curled up in Mr James's arms and turned to go out again.

"Come in, Daniel," said James. "We want your advice. Miss Eleanor was tired and frightened, but she feels better now. The only thing is we don't know what to do."

"We'll need to ring up the Tower," said Daniel sensibly. "They'll be wondering what's happened to the young lady."

"Yes," agreed James in doubtful tones. "But the only thing is . . . you see, Daniel, it would be better if we could get her back without—er—"

"Umphm," agreed Daniel.

"It would save—er—bother."

Daniel nodded.

"You see," said James. "You see the fact is Miss Eleanor's parents wouldn't let her come to the dance, so she thought—well, I mean she wanted to come to the dance."

"To see *you*," put in Eleanor softly.

"She was coming over to the dance," said James, stressing the point. "You understand, don't you, Daniel? She was coming to the dance and she lost her way. It's quite simple, really."

"Quite simple," agreed Daniel gravely.

James sighed with relief. "So the whole thing is to get her back without—"

"That's right, Mr James. And it's early yet. Maybe they'll not have missed her."

"They won't miss me," said Eleanor. "I often go out for a walk before breakfast and I'm often late. Of course there's a row when I'm late but that doesn't matter . . . but I don't want to go back."

"I know," James said. "But I'm afraid you must." He hesitated and then added, "You wouldn't like to get me into trouble, would you?"

"Trouble?" she exclaimed in amazement.

"There's no saying what people might think," put in Daniel.

James was not over-pleased with this remark. It was intended to be helpful but it raised a point which James was anxious to avoid. He felt he was on thin ice and the best thing to do when the ice is thin is to hurry on to safer holding. But Eleanor, though foolish in some ways, was no fool. She sat up and looked at James.

"What would people think?" she asked with a puzzled frown.

"Nothing," said James hastily. "At least—well, they might think I had persuaded you to come over to the dance, and of course they would be very angry with me. That was what Daniel meant, wasn't it Daniel?"

"Aye, that's it."

"The best thing to do," continued James, "the best thing will be for Daniel to take you over to the Tower on his motor-bike and leave you at the gate. Then I shan't come into it at all."

She looked at him. He saw her sad grey eyes, and he knew that she was bewildered and disappointed not only because her plans had all miscarried but because he had failed her. Of course, seeing it from her point of view, he had failed her badly. He must seem to her a cowardly hound, trying to save his own skin. It was dreadful, but what could he do?

"Aye, that's best," nodded Daniel. "It'll save a deal of trouble all round. I'll away and get the bike. The sooner we're on the road the fewer folk we'll meet. I'll see Miss Eleanor safely home."

"I'm trusting you with a good deal," said James significantly.

"You can trust me, Mr James," declared Daniel as he left the room.

Eleanor got up. She pushed back her hair and arranged her dress. It was the party frock which she had put on for the dance, but now it was crumpled and stained and dirty.

"I'm sorry," she said with a pathetic little quiver in her voice. "I've been—a bother. I've behaved—like—a baby."

"It's all right. I think you've been splendid," James told her. But what use was this? It was no use at all. What could he say to comfort her? "Darling," said James earnestly, taking her hand in his. "Darling little Eleanor, don't worry about it. Someday when you're older you'll understand."

"It's always—when I'm older."

"If you were three years older I'd marry you—and nobody on earth should prevent it," declared James.

"I wish I was three years older—or dead," said Eleanor with a little gasp. She turned and went to the door.

Daniel was waiting.

"So you see," said James, walking up and down the drawing-room as he spoke, "so you see, Mamie, something must be done. We can't sit back and do nothing. She'll go raving mad if something isn't done."

"It sounds as if she were mad already," said Mamie in dismayed tones.

"She isn't mad," declared James.

"What did you say to her that day at lunch?"

"Hardly anything. We scarcely spoke at lunch. Afterwards I met her in the garage and I suppose we must have talked for about five minutes."

Mamie gazed at him. They had talked for five minutes and the unfortunate child had fallen crazily in love with him! He was very attractive of course. Nobody could deny that. Mamie herself had felt his attraction, but still . . . "James, she *must* be a little queer in the head," said Mamie uncertainly.

"She isn't," declared James, prowling up and down. "She's just unhappy and half-crazed with shadows . . . like the Lady of Shalott. She's rather like the Lady of Shalott."

(And you're like Lancelot, thought Mamie, looking at him.)

"Yes," said James thoughtfully. "She's like the Lady of Shalott. She doesn't see this world except through a mirror; she reads and reads until her head is full of romance. She's lonely and neglected. She's unhappy. She isn't having any proper education. Something must be done about it and you're the person to do it."

"Me!" cried Mamie in alarm.

"Yes, you. You must go and see Lady Steele. Of course you mustn't tell Lady Steele a word about—about what I've told you, but just tell her she's neglecting Eleanor. Tell her Eleanor ought to be sent to school."

"James, I can't!" cried Mamie. "How can I? It's impossible."

"You must," James told her. "If you don't I'll do it myself. I'll go over and see Lady Steele and tell her the whole story."

"James, listen—"

But James was not listening. He was standing at the window now, tying knots in the blind-cord. "Perhaps, after all, that will be the best way," he was saying. "It will create a bit of a scandal of course, but that can't be helped. I shall go over and see Sir Andrew and Lady Steele and make a clean breast of the whole affair and tell them exactly what I think of them. It will be rather —rather exhilarating in a way," added James with a little chuckle.

"No!" exclaimed Mamie in horrified accents. "No, it wouldn't *do*."

"I shall tell them—"

"No, honestly! They might think—no, James, you mustn't come into it at all."

"Will you do it then?"

Mamie hesitated, but only for a moment, the alternative was so appalling that she really had no choice. "Yes, if you really think —yes, I'll do it," said Mamie.

18

*M*AMIE HAD promised to tackle Lady Steele about Eleanor's future; she was not looking forward to the interview so the best thing to do was to get it over as quickly as possible. She tried to fix a date on the telephone but her ladyship's engagement book seemed pretty full.

"Tuesday is the Blood Donors," said Lady Steele. "I shall be busy all day, of course, and on Wednesday I have to go over to Dumfries for a Girl Guide Meeting. Thursday? Oh yes, I knew there was something. I'm speaking to the Mothers' Union in the afternoon. Friday is hopeless, it's the Nursing Association in the afternoon and the Women's Rural Institute in the evening."

"What about Thursday morning?" Mamie enquired. "I could look in and see you about eleven."

"Is it about the W.R.I.?" asked Lady Steele. "You know we've got to choose a new Vice President in place of Mrs Duncan, don't you? Yes, I *could* see you on Thursday morning, but it had better be ten-thirty because I'm having lunch early."

Mamie let it go at that. It was easier. She could listen to Lady Steele's ideas about a new Vice President for the W.R.I. and agree with them (as long as she doesn't choose *me,* thought Mamie in trepidation) and then she could broach the subject of Eleanor.

On Wednesday afternoon Holly came over in the little car, bringing with her some papers from Lady Steele.

"Aunt Adela wants you to have a look at these," explained Holly. "They're all about the W.R.I. and there's a list of members. She wants you to make up your mind who to vote for, but I wouldn't bother if I were you. I mean Aunt Adela has made up her mind about the new Vice President."

"Yes, but still . . ." said Mamie who had uncomfortably high principles. "I'd better do it, I think." She hesitated and then asked Holly to stay to tea. It was nearly four o'clock and the laws of hospitality made the invitation unavoidable.

"Oh, I'd love to," declared Holly. "But as a matter of fact James said he would be fishing today. I thought I would go down to the river and watch him."

"Why not come in and have tea?" urged Mamie. "We'll have it at once. I'm sure you want tea after your drive. Do come in, Holly, I'm all alone."

"It's very kind of you, Mrs Johnstone, but I'd rather go down to the river," Holly replied. "James told me about the river. He loves it, doesn't he? He loves everything about Mureth. He's very happy that he's going to be settled here. And of course it *is* a lovely place. I mean it isn't as dull as most country places, there's quite a lot going on."

Mamie opened her mouth to declare that Mureth was not in the least dull, that Mureth was an earthly paradise, but she changed her mind before the words came out. "It depends on what you like," said Mamie soberly. "If you like the country and country occupations Mureth is nice, but some people don't, do they?"

Holly smiled in rather a curious way, but did not reply.

"I mean—" continued Mamie, "I mean anybody who was fond of town and parties and theatres and things like that would find Mureth very dull."

Holly was still smiling. She said, "But anybody who felt like that need not stay at Mureth all the time."

Mamie said no more. She watched Holly take off her coat and throw it into the car and walk off to the river. There was defiance in Holly's walk. She swung her hips . . . almost as if Mureth belonged to her.

The afternoon seemed endless to Mamie. She could not settle to anything. She had tea by herself and several times during the meal she got up and looked out of the window. Where were they? What were they doing? Why didn't they come back?

Jock came in about five o'clock, he had been over at Boscath and was full of rage and fury over the delinquencies of Mackenzie but very soon he realised that Mamie was not listening to his grievances with her usual attention.

"What's the matter?" he enquired.

"Nothing," said Mamie hastily, for she had decided that Jock must not be told of her anxieties.

"There *is* something," declared Jock.

"No—honestly."

"It's Mrs Dunne again, I suppose."

Mamie did not reply. She felt guilty and miserable for she hated to keep anything from Jock and now she had two secrets on her mind: one was her fears about Holly and the other was her prospective interview with Lady Steele. Neither of these secrets were her own and neither could be divulged.

"That woman is the limit," declared Jock. "I wish we could get rid of her but Willy Dunne is such a decent chap—it wouldn't be fair."

"Goodness no! We couldn't do without Willy," agreed Mamie. "And as a matter of fact it isn't Mrs Dunne. It's just—I feel a bit —a bit unsettled."

"Unsettled!" exclaimed Jock in consternation. "Good heavens, Mamie, you're ill! I'll ring up Dr Black—"

Mamie laughed. She laughed quite heartily for the idea of ringing up Dr Black amused her a lot; and Jock, watching her, was reassured, for there couldn't be much the matter with a person who laughed like that.

"Tell me more about Boscath," said Mamie, changing the subject. "What are you going to do about Boscath when Mr Mackenzie leaves?"

"What should we do?" asked Jock. "If James were married he could live there of course—that would be ideal—but it would be dull for him living alone. I want somebody there during the winter when I can't be certain of getting across the river."

"I know," agreed Mamie. She hesitated and then added, "Perhaps you had better wait and see."

"You said there was a girl he was fond of."

Mamie nodded. " He told me about her when he came but he hasn't mentioned her lately."

"Oh well," said Jock doubtfully. "We'd better wait. It's nice having him here—we'd miss him in the house, wouldn't we?"

They were still talking about James when the drawing-room door opened and he walked in. He was wet and dirty but smiling cheerfully and he held up a string with four nice trout upon it.

"Four!" he exclaimed. "One each for breakfast and one for Lizzie. I've had a grand time."

"Good work," nodded Jock.

Mamie said nothing. She gazed at him anxiously. He was pleased and happy but the fish might account for that.

"Holly has gone home," continued James. "I gave her a lesson. She doesn't know the first thing about fishing, but I daresay she would learn with a little practice."

"Was Holly Douglas with you?" asked Jock in surprise. "I wonder you caught anything. Women are all right in their proper place but I'd rather have their room than their company when I'm fishing. What was she doing here, anyway?"

"She came over with some papers for me," explained Mamie.

James was still smiling. He said, "Yes—well—if you really want to fish seriously it's better to fish alone, but all the same it was rather fun having Holly. She's friendly and amusing."

Mamie heaved a sigh of relief. It was all right. Nothing whatever had happened.

19

$\mathcal{T}$HE FOLLOWING morning Mamie drove over to Drumburly Tower and was shown into Lady Steele's business-room at
precisely ten-thirty. She found her ladyship seated at a large
table covered with papers and letters and typewritten documents.
There was a typewriter upon the table and a telephone and a
large silver inkstand with an inscription upon it which commem-
orated the fact that it had been presented to Lady Steele by the
Children's Welfare League in recognition of her long and valued
services as President.

"Sit down, Mamie," said Lady Steele kindly. "I'm so glad
you were able to come. Just wait a moment until I finish these
notes for my address to the Mothers' Union . . . There now,"
said Lady Steele, gathering up the papers and clipping them together neatly. "That's finished. Holly can type them out for me
presently. She types quite well, I wish she could stay here longer,
it's most useful."

"Is she going away soon?" asked Mamie hopefully.

"She was to have gone home yesterday, but she changed her
mind and she's staying on. She won't stay *long* of course because
she hates the country. Holly is an attractive creature, isn't she?"

"I suppose she has lots of admirers," ventured Mamie.

"Oh my dear!" said Lady Steele laughing. "I can't keep track
of Holly's affaires. Holly gets around—as the Americans put it.

Of course there's no harm in it. Why shouldn't she have a good time while she's young?"

"Yes, but—"

"I know what you're going to say and you're perfectly right. A good time is all very well, but it can't go on for ever. I was telling her so only the other day and I could see that she was considering it quite sensibly. The fact is she and her mother don't get on at all, and they've very little money, so unless Holly finds a husband soon she'll have to find a job; and she won't like that much. I can't see Holly sticking to anything for long—but you didn't come here to talk about Holly, did you?"

"No," said Mamie, "I came to—"

"You've looked at the list, I suppose," said Lady Steele, scrabbling amongst her papers. "You've gone over it carefully and made up your mind who to vote for."

"Yes," said Mamie. "I think—"

"We can't do better than Mary Wood, if she'll stand. If not it will have to be you."

"But I couldn't—"

"Mary Wood—or you," said Lady Steele firmly. "There isn't much to do and you could do it perfectly well. It's high time you began to take an active part in public affairs. But there's no need to worry, I expect Mary will stand. Mrs Duncan can propose her and you can second her."

"I thought of Mrs—"

"That's settled then," declared Lady Steele. "If Mary consents to act as Vice President you can take over the magazines."

"It would be rather difficult for me to deliver them," objected Mamie. "Honestly, Lady Steele—"

"If you can't manage it yourself you can send that boy of

Lizzie's. Children like doing that sort of thing—playing at post-man!" said Lady Steele, smiling at the idea of giving so much pleasure to Lizzie's son. "He'll love it if you put it to him the right way."

"Yes," said Mamie doubtfully. "I suppose—"

"It's splendid that we've had this talk," continued her lady-ship. "And I'm so glad we see eye to eye about everything. Of course I disapprove strongly of arranging things before meetings, but there's no harm in talking things over. Andrew calls it making unilateral agreements," declared Lady Steele laughing. "What I find is unless one *sounds* people beforehand, and finds out ex-actly what they think, things are all settled in quite the wrong way and it takes a great deal of time and trouble to put them right."

"Yes," said Mamie, "but don't you think perhaps—"

"Thank you so much for coming," said Lady Steele, her eyes straying to the clock. "Was that all you wanted to discuss with me?"

Mamie knew that she was intended to say, "Yes, thank you," and get up and go away, and the temptation to do so was almost irresistible; but she had promised James . . . and if she did not keep her word James would keep his.

"No, there is something else," said Mamie.

"About the competitions? There's no need to bother any more about *that*. The whole thing is settled, and quite pleasantly settled. I had a little talk with Mrs Black and she sees she was mistaken, so—"

"It isn't about that," said Mamie, breaking in with the courage of desperation. "It's about something quite different. It's about Eleanor."

"About Eleanor!" echoed Lady Steele in amazement.

Mamie nodded. "I hope you won't think it very interfering of me but I've always taken a great interest in Eleanor. She's so pretty and clever, isn't she? I think she ought to go to school."

Mamie paused, but for once Lady Steele was dumb.

"I know she has a governess," continued Mamie, who had been through this interview so often, in her own mind, that she had memorised every word she was going to say. "I'm sure the governess is very capable, and it's nice for you to have Eleanor at home, but Eleanor ought to have the companionship of other girls—girls of her own age. You said so, didn't you, Lady Steele?"

"I said so?" asked her ladyship in surprise.

"At the Youth Club," Mamie reminded her. "In your opening address. I remember you said what a good thing it was for young people to have lots of friends of their own age."

Mamie had said what she had intended to say, so she paused again, but Lady Steele was silent. Somehow the silence was unbearable. Mamie was frightened . . . and because she was frightened she went on.

"It's a pity, isn't it," said Mamie. "I mean if Eleanor were the butcher's daughter she could join the Youth Club and have lots of friends, but as it is she has no friends at all. She would be happier at school with other girls to talk to. You're so busy, aren't you? You haven't time to talk to her. It's lonely for her to be so much alone."

There was another silence.

Mamie knew that she had said too much—far more than she had intended. She wondered what would happen. It would not have surprised her if Lady Steele had risen in wrath and told her to be gone and never again to darken the doors of Drumburly

Tower. But Lady Steele did no such thing, she sat and stared at
Mamie with a bewildered expression. It was such a bewildered
expression that if Mamie had been in the mood to appreciate
humour she might almost have laughed.

"Mamie," said Lady Steele. "What's all this about?"

"It's about Eleanor," said Mamie helplessly.

"But there's something behind it."

This was what Mamie had feared. She gazed intently at the
silver inkstand so that she need not meet the bright-brown eyes
of Lady Steele.

"What's behind it?" urged her ladyship. "I mean why—why
have you suddenly—"

"Because Eleanor isn't happy."

"Happy?"

"She's miserable," said Mamie frankly. "I know it isn't my
business, but—"

"But she has everything she wants!"

"I don't think so—not really. It isn't enough to have plenty
of food and nice clothes. Children need—need more than that,
don't they? I've heard you say so, often."

"Yes," said Lady Steele doubtfully. "Yes, I never thought—"

"You're so busy."

Lady Steele took up a glass paperweight and moved it. Then
she looked at it and moved it back again.

"No business of mine, I know," murmured Mamie, rising as
she spoke. "It was only . . . I thought I would just . . . just
mention it. I mean I haven't got a little daughter, you see. I would
have liked to have a little daughter . . . so very much."

Mamie groped for the door handle, her eyes were full of
tears so she could not see very well, but she found it and opened

the door and went out. Lady Steele remained sitting at the table, gazing into vacancy.

After a little while her ladyship sighed and pulled herself together and her eyes fell upon the notes she had written for her talk to the Mothers' Union. She took up the little sheaf of papers and looked at the headings . . . and then quite slowly and deliberately she tore it up into little pieces and dropped them into the wastepaper basket. Lady Steele had decided she could not address the Mothers' Union. They would have to find somebody else. It was very short notice, and they would be annoyed and surprised beyond measure, but that could not be helped.

Meanwhile Mamie was driving home. Her state of mind was unenviable, for the reaction had set in and her conscience was pricking her uncomfortably. She ought to have been pleased with herself for having made Lady Steele listen to what she had to say (it was a feat few people managed to accomplish), but Mamie was not pleased with herself for she had begun to wonder whether she had done right. Perhaps school was not the best place for Eleanor. The child was delicate and unusual; she might get ill; she might hate school; she might be even more miserable at school than she was at home. In addition to this, Mamie was aware that she had hurt Lady Steele very badly; she had said too much (it was because she was frightened, of course). She should have accomplished her object by gentle hints instead of using bludgeons. That's me all over, thought Mamie sorrowfully. I knew I wasn't the right person to do it.

The third thing that worried Mamie was the worst worry of all. It was the information she had received about Holly. Lady Steele had spoken quite affectionately of Holly, but every word

she uttered had confirmed Mamïe in her opinion that Holly was
not the right wife for James. Mamie wanted the very best for
darling James. She knew how wonderful married life could be,
but she knew it could be wonderful only if two people were absolutely right for one another and could share all their pleasures
and interests.

Jock had said he did not like Holly. Mamie did not like her
either, but she tried to put prejudice aside and be perfectly fair.
She tried to see Holly as a farmer's wife . . . but she couldn't.
Holly was not cut out for a quiet life, she would be discontented
and miserable in the country, miles away from all the fun and
gaiety to which she was accustomed.

Long ago, soon after her marriage, Mamie had discovered
that she could not have a child. It had been a bitter disappoint-
ment, an almost unbearable grief, not only on her own account
but because she had failed Jock in not giving him an heir to
Mureth. For years Mamie could hardly speak of it—could hardly
think of it without tears—but gradually the bitterness faded, only
the sadness remained, and when she and Jock got over the dis-
appointment they had set their hearts upon James. They were
both convinced that if they had been blessed with a son he would
have been exactly like James . . . and lately, while James had
been living with them, this conviction had been strengthened,
James was almost perfect. Mamie had prayed fervently that James
would like Mureth and settle down, for she could not bear to
think of Mureth going to a stranger when she and Jock were dead
(going to somebody who would not understand it and love it
and take care of it) and now her prayer was answered. James
would have Mureth and would take the name of Johnstone, so
there would still be a Johnstone of Mureth in spite of her failure

to provide a natural heir. And James would be happy here for he loved the place and he had a flair for farming (so Jock said and who could know better?). Yes, James would settle down and be happy, but not if he had a discontented wife.

By this time Mamie had arrived home, she had also arrived at a desperate decision. She left the car in the drive and, without stopping to remove her hat and coat, she went straight into the drawing-room and sat down at her desk.

As a rule it took Mamie quite a long time to write a letter; it was difficult for her to put her thoughts on paper and spelling was not her strong point. A dictionary lay upon her desk and she referred to it frequently; she was particularly shaky upon the subject of double letters in the middle of a word. She would spell probable with double letters—probbable and decide it looked queer (which it certainly does) or she would spell possible with two s's and decide it didn't look right (a decision with which most people would disagree).

Today, however, Mamie wrote her letter straight off and without any reference to Messrs. Chambers's admirable lexicon, for she was aware that if she paused a moment for thought or reference the letter would not be written at all. She wrote it at white heat, sealed, addressed and stamped it and running through to the kitchen she called Duggie and sent him off on his bicycle to the post.

Duggie had no sooner gone than Mamie regretted her action and would have given quite a lot to have retrieved the letter and thrown it into the fire.

20

$\mathcal{J}$AMES WAS hard at work now and he was enjoying it all thoroughly. His duties were varied for Jock wanted to give him a bird's-eye view of farming as an introduction to the life. James helped Willy Bell in the byre and learned to milk a patient cow; he gave a hand in the dairy, took the horses to be reshod and performed a dozen other seasonable tasks. Sometimes when Daniel was raking the sheep, James went with him. "Raking," he discovered, consisted in moving the sheep about the hills to new pastures. "They go up to bed at night and come down to their breakfasts, just like Christians," Daniel told him with a smile.

With the other men James found he had to watch what they were doing and ask questions in order to learn from them, but with Daniel it was different, for Daniel was able to put himself into the position of a learner and explain. He told James all sorts of interesting things about his sheep.

It was fascinating to see Gyp at work. A word from Daniel and she would be off like an arrow from a bow to carry out his wishes. She would get behind the sheep and move them slowly and gently without alarming them. She would run backwards and forwards until they began to stray in the right direction and then she would crouch in the heather, watching her master with bright eyes and responding to his whistle and the gestures of his arm. Daniel would send her to round up a little group of sheep and bring them down to him. He would wave and whistle and she would single out one sheep from the others and herd it into a pen. This manoeuvre was called "shedding" and James thought it the cleverest thing he had ever seen. When the sheep had been shed and penned Daniel could examine it at leisure; he might find that it was lame, and discover a small lump of hardened mud between its toes and remove it with the knife which he always carried in his pocket. Foot-rot was unknown upon the hirsel of Mureth, for Mureth lay high and the ground was dry and healthy, but Daniel dreaded foot-rot more than any other disease to which sheep are heirs and was always on the watch for it.

The Mureth sheep had black faces and black legs; they looked alike to James but to Daniel they looked different and already he was getting to know them and to know their characteristics and peculiarities.

"There's yon two-shear ewe with the sprained fetlock," Daniel would say, wrinkling up his eyes and gazing up the hill. "She's going quite sound this morning, but we'll have a wee look at her all the same," and he would send Gyp streaking off to fetch her.

When James asked him how he could tell the sheep apart, Daniel smiled. "How do you tell humans apart?" he enquired. "They've all got two eyes and a nose and a mouth, isn't that so, Mr James?"

"Yes, but they *are* different, Daniel," said James. "Take you and me, for instance. Even a sheep could tell us apart."

Daniel laughed delightedly. "That's one up to you," he declared.

One particularly fine afternoon James and Daniel went up the hill to take a look at the dyke which separated the hirsel of Mureth from Tassieknowe. The hills were tawny-coloured, with here and there a black scree or a patch of heather. The bell-heather was in bloom, it blooms earlier than the true heather, and every patch of it was full of murmuring bees. As one walked through it the yellow pollen rose in clouds and the scent of it was sweet and heady in the sunshine.

"It'll be a fine year for honey," said Daniel. "But it's bad for sheep. I never saw the hills so dry and there's scarce a drop of water in the burns. If it goes on much longer we'll need to do something about it, and that's the truth."

"What could you do?" asked James.

"Bring the sheep down and cart water up to them," said Daniel with a sigh. "But that's only half the trouble; there's little or no grass on the hills. The draw-moss is like tinder. Three days soft rain is what we're needing and there's no signs of a break."

The dyke which they had come to see was a very fine specimen of its kind. It was about four feet high and ran for miles, straight as a bow-shot, over hills and valleys. The building of these dykes is an art which has been handed down for generations from father to son. The stones are fitted together without cement or clay, and wedged so neatly and tightly that the wall can withstand the wind and rain and driving snow of long and boisterous winters.

At one place the land had subsided and the dyke was breached. It was in process of repair. Two dykers were at work upon it when Daniel and James arrived upon the scene—two strong burly men, as they had need to be, for some of the stones were large and heavy.

"It's very clever," declared James as he watched them. "It's like a jigsaw puzzle on end. I made a crazy path last winter; that was difficult enough, but this is a hundred per cent more tricky. It has got to stand up."

"That's the idea, Mr James," agreed Daniel with his usual dry humour.

The two men smiled. It was the sort of joke they appreciated.

"Maybe you'd like to have a try," suggested one of the men.

James was always ready to try his hand at anything, so he took off his jacket and rolled up his sleeves and got to work, carrying the stones and helping to wedge them firmly. It was interesting but back-breaking in the extreme. Meanwhile Daniel was prowling about and examining the fallen stones.

"It's a biggish gap," said Daniel. "You'll not have seen any sheep go through, I suppose."

"We've not," replied the elder man. "If there's any sheep gone through they've gone before we were here."

James climbed upon the wall and looked down the hill towards a little burn in Tassieknowe property. "I think I see a Mureth sheep," he said. "It's got our red mark on its back—yes, I'm almost sure."

"Good for you," said Daniel approvingly. "Where there's one there'll be others. They'll have gone down to the water, most likely. I'll take Gyp and have a cast round."

James watched him go. It was very hot. The sun poured down upon the bare hillside in a golden flood. There were hills all round—rolling hills and shallow valleys—and there was not a sign of human habitation in sight. The only unnatural feature of the landscape was the wall, and even that was so old and grey and weathered that it did not look as if it had been built by men's hands, but rather as if it had always been there from time.

immemorial. The dykers had knocked off work and were having
a well-earned rest and James offered them cigarettes and lighted
one himself. It was peaceful and quiet, the only sounds were
the singing of a lark and the far-off whinny of a curlew.

Daniel and Gyp had found some sheep and were rounding
them up and James watched them, for there was nothing he
liked better than to see Daniel and Gyp at work . . . and then,
quite suddenly, he saw a group of people coming up the little
valley by the side of the burn.

The sight was quite startling in this solitary place and all
the more so because the people themselves looked completely
out of place in their surroundings. The party consisted of three
men and two women all of whom were attired in bright, smartly
tailored tweeds (the sort of garments which might have been
seen in a London shop, labelled "For Sport" thought James, smiling to himself at the idea). For a moment he wondered who on
earth they were and where they could have come from and then
he remembered the Big-Business Magnate who had bought Tassieknowe. Mr Heddle was his name, and obviously this was Mr
Heddle, walking in front of his friends and carrying a gun. What
did he intend to shoot, James wondered.

Mr Heddle was a large man but in spite of his bulk he moved
easily and lightly. He was hatless and his black wavy hair gleamed
in the sunshine with an oily sheen. His friends looked jaded; they
were tagging along behind their host in a dejected manner as if
they had quite enough and wished themselves safely at home.

Mr Heddle caught sight of Daniel and Gyp. He hastened his
steps and waved. "What are you doing with those sheep!" he
shouted.

Daniel stopped and looked round, but Gyp knew no law but

her master's; she carried on, herding the sheep up the hill towards James, running backwards and forwards to keep them on the move.

"Call off that dog!" shouted Mr Heddle, advancing upon Daniel with an air of importance.

Daniel said nothing. Perhaps he was too surprised for speech.

"Are you deaf!" shouted Mr Heddle waving angrily. "Call off that dog. Can't you see it's chasing my sheep!"

The two dykers had risen to get a better view of the scene. They were chuckling over it, for it was a pretty good joke to hear a shepherd being rebuked in this extraordinary way. James was amused too. It was like a scene in a comedy: the tall commanding figure in the checked plus-fours confronting Daniel in his patched jacket and faded corduroy trousers. And Daniel was so utterly amazed at the insults which were being heaped upon him that he could find no words to refute them.

"Call off the dog!" bellowed Mr Heddle. "If you don't call it off I'll shoot it."

James could hardly believe his ears; but all the same he realised that the thing had gone beyond a joke and that it was time he took action. He leapt off the wall and ran down the slope. "Wait!" he shouted. "I can explain!"

But Mr Heddle was far too angry to listen. He raised his gun and fired.

It was a frightful moment and James felt quite sick with horror. He stopped and looked round, expecting to see the dog lying upon the hillside dead, or dying; but Gyp was unharmed, she was not even alarmed, and it was obvious that Mr Heddle had missed her completely. Perhaps he had not intended to shoot the dog but only to frighten its owner and James was ready to give him the benefit of the doubt. Daniel was not. Daniel was roused to fury. He had turned to rush to Gyp, for she was his first thought, but seeing her unharmed he wheeled round and advanced upon Mr Heddle instead.

"You dirty swine!" yelled Daniel. "I'll learn you—"

"Daniel, stop!" cried James, tearing down the slope as fast as his legs would take him. "Wait! Gyp's all right. Wait, for heaven's sake! Gyp's all right, I tell you!" He caught Daniel's arm and turned to face Mr Heddle. "I can explain everything," he declared breathlessly.

"Let me get at him!" cried Daniel.

"Wait—listen!" cried James, shaking his arm. "The whole thing is a mistake. Mr Heddle doesn't understand—"

"I understand the dog is chasing my sheep," declared Mr Heddle furiously. "I'm within my rights to shoot a dog when I see it chasing my sheep."

"They're Mureth sheep," declared James.

"That's nonsense. I bought this place with the sheep on it. All the sheep on this hill belong to me."

Daniel gasped. "Did you ever hear the like!"

"They're Mureth sheep," repeated James firmly. "There's a gap in the wall and they've come through onto your ground."

"How can you tell one sheep from another?"

"Your sheep have blue markings and ours have red."

Everyone turned to look at the sheep. By this time Gyp had succeeded in getting her charges up to the wall and was herding them carefully through the gap.

"You see," urged James. "She isn't chasing them. She's a sheep-dog. She's putting them back through the gap."

"That's damned clever, y'know," said one of Mr Heddle's

friends, a youngish man with a light tweed cap which was tilted at a coy angle upon his sleek black hair. "That dog would do for a circus, y'know. And I believe this feller's right, Nestor. I noticed your sheep have blue dabs on their behinds."

The rest of the party laughed.

"It's a wise farmer that knows his own sheep," remarked one of the women *sotto voce*.

These remarks and the slightly malicious laughter were not calculated to soothe Mr Heddle, for no man likes to look a fool and Mr Heddle was used to adulation. James could imagine him in a sumptuous office, giving orders to obsequious secretaries. He looked like that, thought James. There was something rather alarming about the man, one had a feeling he might do anything.

"I'm very sorry, sir," said James, hoping that a soft answer might turn away wrath. "The whole thing has been a mistake, but fortunately there's no harm done."

"If he'd harmed Gyp I'd have had him up for it," growled Daniel. "Folk should stay where they belong—and not come where they're not wanted."

"Mr Heddle fired in the air," declared James. "You fired in the air, didn't you, sir? You never intended to shoot the dog."

"The man and the dog were on my property—trespassing."

"Trespassing!" cried Daniel. "There's no such thing in Scotland."

James wondered what to do. Should he explain who he was and try to smooth things over? But he was so dirty and untidy (he had not thought of his appearance before, but now he suddenly realised what he must look like to Mr Heddle and his friends). His grey flannel trousers had a jagged tear in the knee; his shirt was dirty from carrying the stones for the dyke; he had no hat and no tie! Gosh, I better get out of this, thought James.

"I'm awfully sorry," he repeated. "It has been a mistake—a misunderstanding all round. Come on, Daniel." He bowed to Mr Heddle and walked back up the hill, dragging Daniel with him.

Gyp was sitting in the gap, smiling at them. She had done her part in the business and was pleased with herself as she had every right to be. Daniel seized her and began to examine her thoroughly; he was still seething, grumbling like a volcano which is about to erupt.

"The black-hearted villain!" growled Daniel. "I'll learn him to shoot at my dog. If there's so much as a scratch on her I'll have him up. It's a scandal! If I find a pellet in her I'll go straight to the police no matter what you say. A circus!" exclaimed Daniel in tones of scorn. "Did you ever hear the like! Yon ignorant loon said Gyp ought to be in a circus! Gyp in a circus! Standing on her hind legs with a petticoat and a red jacket, I suppose!"

James said nothing. He was incapable of speech for he was trying desperately not to laugh. Perhaps the laughter which he was trying to suppress was slightly hysterical . . . it was swelling and bubbling within him. He rocked helplessly.

"Aye, you may laugh," said Daniel. "But I tell you if Gyp had been hurt it would have been no laughing matter. I'd have gone for yon stuffed owl and laid him out on the hillside and neether you nor any other body would have stopped me."

"I know," agreed James. "And I wouldn't have blamed you. But Gyp hasn't been hurt, and honestly I don't think he meant to hurt her."

"I wouldn't put it past him. The scum of the earth—that's what he is—with no sense and no decent feelings."

"I wish we hadn't fallen foul of the man," said James, whose desire to laugh had suddenly vanished. "He's—he's a dangerous man, Daniel, there's something about him—"

"He's dangerous all right."

"And he's a near neighbour," added James with a sigh. "It's been a bad afternoon's work, Daniel."

21

WHEN JOCK was told of the scene upon the hill he agreed that it was a bad afternoon's work and in spite of all that James could say he was inclined to blame Daniel Reid for the misunderstanding.

"Reid should have explained to Mr Heddle," declared Jock. "He should have gone forward at once and explained the whole thing before the matter got out of hand. I don't blame Reid for being angry with Mr Heddle for shooting at his dog, anybody would have been angry, but if he had had the sense to explain at the very beginning instead of standing there like a dummy—"

"He was so surprised at Mr Heddle's ignorance."

"Oh, I daresay Mr Heddle made a fool of himself, but that was because he was out of his own place. When I go to London I feel a complete fool. What with revolving doors that bash me on the heels when I try to get through them, and moving staircases that trip me up when I try to get on and off; what with the traffic and the noise and everybody pushing and shoving as if their very lives depended upon getting onto a bus before their neighbour I'm just left gasping. So you see I can't blame Mr Heddle for making a fool of himself here."

"No," said James, smiling at the picture Jock's words had evoked. "No, I see what you mean, but you take revolving doors and staircases in a humble spirit. You wouldn't try to throw your weight about in London, and that's what he was doing—throwing his weight about."

Jock saw that this was true, but he still blamed Reid. He decided that Reid would have to go . . . not at once, of course, but later on. Meantime it would be as well if James did not see too much of Reid. James must be given other work to occupy him.

It had been in Jock's mind for some time to drain a meadow not far from the Stone Circle. The meadow was low-lying and swampy, reeds and king-cups grew upon it in profusion, but Jock knew that if it could be properly drained it would grow good grass for his cows. It would be interesting for James to learn how to do it and it would keep him busy. He could not do it himself of course but Couper could be spared to help.

The three of them went down to the meadow together and Jock showed them what he wanted done, they measured the ground carefully and put in pegs and then Jock went away and left them to it.

The work was hard but James was interested in the job, it was constructive and worth while. He and Joseph Couper measured and dug the trenches and laid the red-clay pipes which would carry off the surplus water. Couper was very slow to work with and it was no use trying to hurry him. The work went forward steadily, peacefully, thoroughly—it was the Mureth tempo.

James discovered that Couper knew quite a lot about the Stone Circle. He referred to it as "The Stanes" and informed James that he had come out at sunrise on the fifth day of May and had seen the sun rise in the correct position: in a direct line with the biggest stone in the circle.

James was interested in this, not only because the sun still continued to behave in the time-honoured manner in spite of the

fact that no band of worshippers assembled to hail its rising, but
also because he had always thought Couper a bit "dim." (Very
nice, thoroughly trustworthy but a trifle dim, would have been
James's verdict upon Couper if anybody had happened to ask him
for it.) So naturally he was surprised to find Couper historically
minded and imaginative as well. By dint of questioning, while
they rested from their labours, James found out a good deal from
Couper. He had known before that "The Stanes" was in reality a
gigantic sundial, telling the days of the year instead of the hours
of the day; but he had not known, until Couper told him, that
the fifth of May was the Great Day of the year to sun-worshippers, marking the beginning of summer when the long dark winter
lay behind and the time of warmth and light and fertility lay
ahead.

At first James had some difficulty in understanding what
Couper said and apparently Couper had almost as much trouble
in understanding James (not quite, of course, for Couper occasionally listened to radio programmes in which James's manner of
speech was the fashion), but working and talking together they
gradually learnt one another's language and after that it was all
plain sailing.

"What did you feel at the Stanes?" asked James. "I mean
when you saw the sun rise behind the hill."

"I felt kind o' queer," replied Couper thoughtfully.

"You felt as if time had gone back and you were one of those
long ago Stone Circle men?"

"Eh?"

James repeated his suggestion in different words.

"Just—kind o'—queer," said Couper vaguely.

Obviously he had felt something but equally obviously he

could not put his feeling into words. James gave up the struggle.

One evening a very curious incident disturbed the peace of Mureth. James found it necessary to go to Couper's cottage to alter the arrangements for work upon the following day. He had promised to help Couper with the draining operations as usual but Uncle Jock wanted him for something else. James walked down to the cottage and found it deserted, it was lightless, bolted and barred. He was surprised because the Coupers were a stay-at-home family. Old Mr Couper scarcely ever went out at all, certainly never at night, and the Couper children were too young to go to the pictures. James was further surprised to discover the Bells' cottage empty—the Bell baby was not yet six months old! The Dunnes were out too. Not a creature was left in the place.

Of course there was no reason why the Mureth cottagers should not go out at night when the day's work was over; some of them made a habit of it. Daisy frequently hied off to a dance at Drumburly; Mrs Bell was a faithful member of the Women's Rural Institute, and would not have missed a meeting for a good deal, and the others sometimes went out to parties at the houses of friends in the neighbourhood, but it was unprecedented for the whole community to disappear—and that was what had happened.

James mounted a knoll and looked up the hill to the two shepherds' cottages, Daniel Reid's and the Wilsons'; it was difficult to make sure at this distance but he felt pretty certain that they were empty too. He returned to Mureth House with the news.

"How funny!" said Mamie. "Lizzie has gone out, too. She asked if she could go today instead of tomorrow and she's taken the children with her."

"They'll have gone to a dance at Drumburly," said Jock comfortably. "There's no reason why they shouldn't, if they want to."

"To a dance!" exclaimed Mamie. "Old Mr Couper and the Bells' baby—"

"And the three little Couper children!" added James.

Mamie and Jock and James looked at one another doubtfully.

"Reid hasn't gone," said Mamie after a little silence. "He came in a few minutes ago and said he had shut up the hen-houses. The Coupers usually do it, of course; I thought he'd just done it to oblige them. Reid says there's a fox on the hill—several foxes, he thinks—and he asked if you would lend him your gun. The Wilsons have lost two ducks so something had better be done about it."

"They'll be in that old den on the scree near the rowan," nodded Jock. "But I'm not lending my gun to Reid. James and I'll go up one of these days and see what we can do."

No more was said about the mystery of the empty cottages, but James could not take it so easily. He disliked mysteries and this one was a trifle sinister—or so it seemed to him. The Bells and the Dunnes were barely on speaking terms, and Lizzie was usually at loggerheads with both families, so what could have induced them to go out together on an evening expedition? It would be too extraordinary a coincidence if they had all gone out separately to different places. They *must* have gone together, thought James.

James did not go to sleep for quite a while and he wakened early with the mystery still on his mind. He was wide awake, still brooding upon it, when Lizzie appeared with his morning tea.

"Lizzie," said James. "What happened last night? Where did you all go? There wasn't a soul in the place."

"There was Mr Reid," she replied. "Mr Reid said somebody better stay and he'd stay. He's not such a bad wee man when you get to know him."

"What did you do?"

"We hired a bus. We shared it, ye see. It was not that dear when it was all shared out, but they made me pay full price for Duggie and Greta and the wee ones got taken for half. It's yon Mrs Couper," declared Lizzie in aggrieved accents. "She wanted half fares for hers and Mrs Wilson wanted half fare for Chairlie and Mrs Bell said wee Mary could go free—*she would*."

James knew Lizzie's little ways. Any information required of Lizzie had to be extracted by main force. "Where did you go?" he enquired.

"It was Willy Bell's brother told us. He works on the railway so he knew all about it, ye see."

"I wish I did!" cried James. "Can't you tell me about it? Where did you go?"

"In the bus," replied Lizzie. "Willy Bell got the bus in Drumburly from the man at the garage, ye see. It all had to be fixed in a hurry."

"You chartered a bus in a hurry and you all went off to pick dandelions," nodded James.

Lizzie smiled. She did not smile often, but, when she did, it was rather a pleasant sight. "Och, away!" exclaimed Lizzie. "You know quite well it was the King we went to see."

James gazed at her in astonishment. It seemed incredible, but as Lizzie was incapable of such a flight of fancy he believed her information to be true. "Listen—" he said, "listen to me. If you don't tell me all about it here and now I'll go and ask Mrs Bell. She'll be glad to tell me."

Thus goaded Lizzie pulled herself together and unfolded her tale.

Mureth's expedition to see the King had been planned in haste for it was only yesterday morning that a message had been received from Willy Bell's brother—via the milk lorry—to say that the Royal Train was on its way north and that it was to be shunted onto a local line for the night. This manoeuvre was to take place at a small country station less than twenty miles away. Willy Dunne communicated with his friend at the garage in Drumburly and managed to charter a bus. Everything was arranged.

It was suggested that old Mr Couper was too old to go, but Mr Couper refused to be left behind. He wanted to see the King. Nobody had as much right as he, for had he not seen Queen Victoria? (Nobody but he had seen Queen Victoria, nobody in Mureth.) It was thought by some that wee Mary Bell was too young to go, but Mrs Bell was determined that her daughter should see the King. Mary would not remember the occasion (one could hardly expect it at five months), but when she was older she could be told about it, and perhaps, long years hence, she would talk about it as old Mr Couper talked about seeing Queen Victoria. Only her mother thought this a good reason for taking Mary, and Mrs Dunne remarked with a charming smile that if wee Mary became a nuisance like old Mr Couper she was likely to remain single all her life. This was one of Mrs Dunne's most successful sallies for it insulted the Bells and the Coupers at one blow, but by this time the excitement was so intense that neither family retaliated.

Everybody put on Sunday garments, each family packed sufficient food for its own members; the bus appeared at the appointed hour and Mureth set forth.

Quite a number of people had heard, in one way or another, of the plans for the Royal Train; so the country road, which was usually deserted, was thronged with cars and carts and bicycles and other conveyances and with people of all ages and both sexes wearing expectant smiles. Some of these people took up their position in the tiny station, others on the bridge. Willy Bell's brother conducted the Mureth contingent to an excellent place in a shallow cutting and left them there to sit upon the bank and eat their supper and await the arrival of the train.

They had not long to wait. In fact they had scarcely finished their picnic meal when loud cheering from down the line told of the train's approach. Willy Dunne was so excited at the prospect of seeing his sovereign lord that he lost his footing upon the bank and would have fallen if Daisy had not had the presence of mind to fling her arms round his waist and so restore his balance; but Mrs Dunne, far from being grateful, bent a gaze of hatred upon Daisy for saving her husband's life. "She would rather have had him crushed to pulp beneath the wheels," said Lizzie with relish.

The train passed slowly, so slowly that everybody had an excellent view of His Majesty, standing at the window in the corridor and smiling at the cheering throng. Everybody waved. Little Mary was shaken out of a blissful sleep and held up to get a good view; fortunately she was still too dazed to resent this unprecedented treatment. "I seen your great-grandmother, sir!" yelled old Mr Couper in quavering tones. Alice Couper, a sensitive child, burst into floods of tears. The others cheered loudly.

The Queen, standing at another window, waved and smiled. Somebody called out, "God bless your bonny face!" (Lizzie had a feeling it was Willy Bell, but she could not be sure of this.)

The train moved on. The great moment was over. Mureth had seen its King and Queen.

Coming home in the bus everybody talked at once and nobody listened. Every man was convinced that the King had looked at him, personally, and had smiled at him alone; every woman was perfectly certain that the Queen had waved to her children and to nobody else's. Mr Couper kept on saying, "I seen the King. I seen his great-grandmother, too. Nobody but me has seen them both, nobody in Mureth." Only Mrs Dunne was silent—though perhaps silent is not the right word; she had gone to sleep with her hat over one eye and was snoring peacefully.

Of course it took some time to get the whole story out of Lizzie, but James managed it by dint of persuasions and searching questions and threats to go straight to Mrs Bell. He thought it over while he dressed, chuckling delightedly, and it gave him enormous pleasure to retail it to his uncle and aunt over the breakfast table.

Mamie laughed quite a lot, but Jock looked rather cross. "Isn't it just like them, the silly fools," said Jock in disgust. "If they'd told us about it we could have taken the car and gone ourselves."

22

*J*AMES HAD promised to take Daniel Reid a book about sheep; a new book for which he had written to Edinburgh. Daniel could have written a book about sheep himself—so James thought —but he was never tired of reading about them and he had told James that however much you knew about sheep there was always more to learn—a statement which James found slightly depressing. The evening was misty but that did not matter for James had been up to Well Cottage so often he could have trodden the path blindfolded. As he approached he saw Daniel come out and lock the door behind him. Obviously Daniel was going out.

"Hi!" shouted James, running forward. "Hi, Daniel, I've brought the book!"

Daniel waited for him and welcomed him and asked him to come in.

"But you're going out," objected James.

Daniel did not answer that, and they stood for a moment in silence.

It was difficult for James. He did not want to appear inquisitive; he was not sure whether Daniel wanted him or not. Daniel might be going to Drumburly on his bike or to one of the other cottages . . . and then he looked more closely at Daniel and noted that Daniel was not dressed for "company"; he was in his

usual working clothes and he had a haversack upon his back
with a waterproof strapped onto the top of it.

"Daniel!" exclaimed James. "You're going after the sheep-
stealers! You were going without me!"

"Well—" said Daniel uncomfortably, "well, Mr James, I
thought I'd go and have a look. I've been out a good many times
and seen nothing and I couldn't ask you to go on a wild goose
chase, could I? If I knew I'd be seeing them it would be different
. . . and it's misty tonight. It'll be mistier before long. You're not
familiar with the hills like me, and you see—"

"Och, away!" cried James laughing.

Daniel laughed too. "You're learning the language," he said.

They debated the question of whether or not James should
partake in the expedition. Daniel was against it and brought out
every argument he could think of to persuade James to go home
to his comfortable bed, but James was determined to accompany
Daniel. He promised to obey orders, to stick closely to Daniel so
that he should not get lost and finally to "keep a still tongue in
his head" about the whole affair.

"Och well, if you must," said Daniel with a sigh.

A few minutes later they were going up the hill, Daniel leading and James following closely.

Daniel's gait upon the hill was peculiar and distinctive. He
stooped forward with his hand grasping his shepherd's crook and
his legs bent at the knee, but in spite of his ungainly appearance
his legs went over the uneven ground at a steady pace and it was
all James could do to keep up with him. Uphill or downhill seemed
the same to Daniel, his pace neither quickened nor slackened; it
seemed to James that Daniel could go on all day and half the
night without turning a hair or pausing for a breather.

They went in silence. James was reminded of his campaigning experiences in Malaya, and yet how different it was! Instead of the hot steamy jungle he was on a bare hillside with a cool, wet mist all about him and a stony path underfoot. He had a thick stick, provided by Daniel, instead of a more lethal weapon in his hand. Last but not least James reminded himself that although he was out after bandits he must not deal with them quite so ruthlessly as he had dealt with the bandits of Malaya. If there were to be a fight it must be a kid-glove affair. You couldn't lay out a sheep-stealer upon a Scottish hillside and get away with it —or could you? wondered James.

Daniel stopped and looked round. "Mr James," he said. "You'll remember you're not in Malay?"

James chuckled.

"All right," nodded Daniel. "Just as long as you keep it in mind. Yon stick is loaded."

"It's a nicely balanced weapon."

"Aye, it's a good stick. I've had it a long while."

"How many notches on it, Daniel?"

"Never you mind. We're not wanting any notches on it to-night."

They went on. They had been climbing steadily but now they began to descend. Obviously Daniel knew exactly where he was going. He led James down a path beside a little tinkling burn and halted in front of a ruined cottage.

"We'll wait here," said Daniel. "It's a shelter, and it's close by the road and about twenty yards from the track that leads up to the quarry. I've been spending a good few nights here lately. Mind your feet, Mr James, there's stones and nettles by the door."

The cottage was in a ruinous condition but part of the roof

still remained and beneath this exiguous shelter Daniel had made
his camp. The nettles were cleared, a few stones had been built
up to make a fireplace and there was a couch of dry grass. Daniel
unpacked his haversack and produced a packet of sandwiches, a
thermos flask and an electric torch. He spread his waterproof
upon the couch and invited his guest to be seated.

"You know how to look after yourself," remarked James.

" 'All the comforts of the Salt-Market!' " said Daniel chuckling, "but maybe you're not acquainted with Baillie Nichol Jarvie?"

"It's some time since I met him, I'm afraid."

"Och, it's a grand book, *Rob Roy*, and the Baillie's one of
my best friends. He's so natural and true to life. He's so pawky.
Well, that same gentleman liked his comforts and so do I when
I can get them. Mind you, I can thole discomfort—nobody better
—when I have to."

"Yes," agreed James. He had "tholed" a good deal of discomfort in his time.

"I daren't kindle the fire," said Daniel regretfully. "They
might see the lowe from the road. It's a pity but there it is."

They each had a large sandwich, and a cup of coffee out of
the thermos, and while they were thus engaged Daniel was pre-
vailed upon to reveal his plan of action. James knew most of it
already but he wanted to have it clear in his mind. They would
wait in the cottage until they saw a car stop at the turning and
go up the track to the quarry, then they would leave the cottage
and follow the burn up the hill. The burn ran out of the pool
near the quarry where the sheep came to drink. It was the habit
of hill sheep to spend the night high up on the hill and come down
in the early morning; the sheep-lifters, knowing this, would lie
in wait for them.

Daniel was strangely reluctant to give James all this information and it was only by searching questions that James obtained it.

"It's better for me to know the plan in case we get separated," James pointed out.

"But we'll not get separated," declared Daniel, and he reminded James of his promise to obey orders and to stick closely to his superior officer during the campaign. "Now mind, Mr James, there's to be no stravaigling and there's to be no rushing on and leaving me behind."

"All right, keep your hair on," said James smiling.

Several cars and lorries passed while they were talking; the headlights flared through the aperture, which had once been a window, and wheeled round the ruined walls. None of the vehicles stopped but their passage showed the strategical value of the cottage for the task in hand. James said so and Daniel agreed, adding that he wished there were fewer vehicles upon the road at night. He had slept here more times than he liked to remember and had been awakened by everything that passed.

"They'll come tonight," said James with conviction.

"I've been saying the same thing every night," Daniel told him. "The fact is I'll be so surprised when they come, if ever they do come, that I'll not know where I am or what I'm doing."

"I'll show you how to deal with them!" laughed James.

"Now mind, Mr James. We're here to watch what's doing, that's all."

"But if we see them taking a sheep! Good lord, there's two of us! We could knock out four of them easily if we took them by surprise."

"And be had up for manslaughter?"

"Not kill them of course. I don't mean . . ." he stopped. Another car was passing and this one seemed to be slowing down.

James had risen. "There they are!" he cried. "The car has stopped. It's turning up the track."

"Gosh, I can hardly believe it!" exclaimed Daniel. He seized his torch and his waterproof and followed James out of the cottage.

James was in front this time, he was tense with excitement (much too excited to wait while Daniel collected his belongings). He leapt over the stones and set off up the burn as quickly as he could; but before he had gone far he remembered his promise to stick to his leader. He had given his word not to "rush on" and that was exactly what he was doing. He stopped and waited. There was no sign of Daniel, no sound but the tinkling of the burn. He would have to go back. It was the last thing he wanted to do—every instinct urged him to go on—but a promise was a promise. Reluctantly James retraced his steps.

He found Daniel sitting on a large stone not far from the cottage door.

"Hullo, what's up?" he enquired.

"I've hurt my foot," growled Daniel. "I've waited for this night for weeks and now it's come I must go and get crocked up through carelessness—just danged carelessness—not looking where I was going. I tripped over yon piece of barbed wire and measured my length on the ground. Did you ever hear the like! Och, it's sickening! It's too sickening for words," and he proceeded to explain to James just how sickening it was in very unparliamentary language.

"Have you hurt it badly?" asked James anxiously.

"I've twisted my ankle, that's what I've done. I've done the same thing before once or twice. It's not that bad, but it's bad enough to spoil our plans. I could no more climb the hill than I could fly and that's the truth."

"No, of course you couldn't."

"It's sickening, Mr James. I'm afraid there's only one thing for it, you'll need to go back to Mureth and fetch my bike."

"Your bike!"

"For me to get home," Daniel explained.

"I will, later," said James. "Not now, old chap. I've got a job of work to do first. I'm going up to the quarry, myself."

"Mr James, you'll do no such thing!" cried Daniel.

"I'll go and see what they're doing and come back to you—"

"You'll get lost! As sure as I'm here you'll get lost in the mist. Now listen, Mr James, you promised to obey orders. I wouldn't have brought you with me if I'd thought you'd go back on your word."

James agreed that he had promised, but asserted that this unforeseen accident had changed everything, it absolved him from his promise. He was absolutely determined to go up to the quarry and see what was happening there. He would not tackle the sheep-stealers single-handed, that would be foolish. He would just watch. He would see what the men were like and take the number of the car. Nothing that Daniel could say would stop him. He left Daniel sitting upon the stone, still protesting, raging, pleading, threatening all manner of disasters, and once more took the path up the side of the burn.

23

*J*ULY NIGHTS are short and when James reached the quarry a greyness had become visible in the air, the first faint glimmer of dawn, but this advantage was offset by the thickening of the mist which seemed to rise from the ground. James went carefully, for the ground was rough and he had no desire to sprain his ankle, and it took him some time for he did not know the terrain; but presently he saw lights, like faint glowworms in the mist, and knew that he had reached his objective. James knew a bit about stalking so he made a detour and found a place at the side of the quarry, between the quarry and the pool. It took more time to find a position that satisfied him but at last he found an admirable hiding place amongst some loose boulders. This would do.

The mist was his friend now, but not a very trustworthy friend for there were little eddies in it, made by the faint morning breeze. Every now and then the blanket of mist was stirred so that it cleared for a moment and closed down again. But James was near enough to see the car with its sidelights, standing in the quarry, and to see three men beside the car, clad in waterproofs. Two of the men were big and burly and the third was small and thin. It struck James that this third man was of much the same build as Daniel. Unfortunately James was not near enough to hear all they were saying but he heard a few words here and there and saw them pointing to the hill. Obviously the

small man was the leader of the expedition and was explaining
to his two companions what he intended to do. They were ob-
jecting that the mist was too thick but the small man was determined to carry on.

"We'll wait for you here, then!" exclaimed one of the big
men who had a louder voice than the others. "You can go up to
the pool yourself. I'm not wanting to get lost in this mist. If you
get one you can give us a whistle and we'll help you carry it
down."

The small man turned on his heel and came directly towards
James; he passed within a few yards of James and James crouched
low as he passed. The man had a cloth cap pulled over his eyes
and the collar of his waterproof was turned up. He had some sort
of weapon in his hand, it looked like a short thick club. The sight
of the club reminded James that he had no weapon—not even
the loaded stick—he had put down the stick during his argument
with Daniel and forgotten it. But he had two strong hands and
he would see to it that he had the advantage of surprise.

The man passed and went on up the hill and James emerged
from his hiding place and followed. It was not easy to follow
without being seen or heard for they were on a stony path, a
sheep-track presumably, and the mist was playing strange tricks.
James could see quite clearly for about five yards and beyond
that he could see nothing but a thick white blanket. It was as if
he were walking in a bubble of clear air which moved with him
up the slope. Fortunately the man had taken an electric torch out
of his pocket and was using it to find his way.

James had decided to watch and see what happened, but he
had forgotten that. His blood was up and he intended to catch
this man and hand him over to justice. He could catch him now,

of course. Nothing would be easier than to take him unawares,
to spring upon him and lay him out, but it would be wiser to
follow and watch him. If he could be caught in the very act of
killing a Mureth sheep, how much better that would be!

If only Daniel were here! Daniel knew the hills, he knew
the habits of sheep. Daniel was very angry with him (thought
James, smiling to himself at the recollection of Daniel's rage and
fury), but if James managed to catch the "sheep-lifter" Daniel
would change his tune; he would realise that James had been
fully justified in breaking his promise.

The glimmer of light moved on and James followed, keeping
as far behind as he could without allowing it to disappear from
view. Soon they came to a little pool and skirted it and climbed
further up the hill upon another sheep-track.

Until now it had been very quiet on the hill; James could
hear nothing at all but the occasional rattle of a stone dislodged
by his feet or by the feet of the man in front of him, but now
the silence was broken by the sound of a distant baaing. The sheep
were coming down.

Suddenly the glimmer of the torch disappeared and there
was nothing all round but the white blanket of mist. James paused,
undecided, and then he realised that he should have expected
this to happen. The right way to hunt a man was to put yourself
in his place and to think what you would do in like circumstances.
I should crouch by the side of the track, thought James. I should
hide behind a rock and wait for the sheep to pass, and that's exactly what he's doing.

Having decided this, James crept on quietly. He left the track
and trod upon the thick, wet heather, making for the place where
he had last seen the light. The sound of baaing was much louder

now and the sheep began to pass along the track on the way down to the pool. James could smell the strong odour of their wet wool; he could almost have touched them but they took no notice of him at all. It was a curious sight. It was like a dream. They passed in single file, one after another like beads on a string, grey and pearly in the morning mist. They moved down the track, jumping from rock to rock.

Here were the sheep, but where was the man? James began to think he had lost him. Perhaps he had come too far. He crept on slowly, straining his eyes, peering through the mist.

The plan of action was clear in his mind. He wanted to find the man and watch him. He wanted to take him red-handed. This meant that a sheep must be sacrificed but it was worth the sacrifice of a sheep. A dead sheep would be absolute proof of guilt —a dead sheep and the club which had killed it.

There was a big black boulder beside the track, James skirted the boulder and suddenly came upon his man. He came upon the man unexpectedly so that he had no time for thought, no time to withdraw and wait (as he had intended); he had only time to leap upon him and seize hold of him. The attack was violent and so utterly unforeseen that the victim was taken off his guard and offered no resistance. James managed to wrench the club from his grasp, to get two hands round his neck and roll him over. His cap had fallen off during the struggle so now James saw his face—a thin brown face with a big nose and bushy eyebrows and eyes that gazed up at James with a terrified stare. The sight of this face was such a shock to James that he loosened his hold on his prisoner. The man wriggled sideways, like an eel, rolled over and over amongst the heather and was gone in a flash.

"Daniel!" exclaimed James. He was so amazed and astonished

that he made no attempt to get up and follow. He sat quite still in the wet heather absolutely petrified with astonishment. "Daniel!" he said again.

He could not believe it was Daniel—and yet he had seen the man's face with his own eyes; Daniel's face, brown and weather-beaten, with the big nose and the bushy eyebrows. There was no mistaking Daniel's face. What on earth was the meaning of it? He had left Daniel at the cottage with a twisted ankle. How could Daniel be here, racing about on the hill?

There was only one explanation of the mystery and at first James shirked it for he simply could not believe ill of his friend . . . but what else was he to believe? He had seen Daniel in the quarry with the men and had followed him up the hill; had Daniel been bribed to kill one of his own sheep?

"Oh no!" cried James, burying his face in his hands. "No, it can't be true—not Daniel—I won't believe it."

James had become very fond of Daniel; he admired Daniel and trusted him absolutely. He would have trusted Daniel with his life. He had not believed Uncle Jock's story about seeing Daniel at the Show with two shifty-looking strangers (Uncle Jock had made a mistake, that was all), but now James saw that the story might well be true. The strangers were probably the two men with the big black car which was standing in the quarry at this very moment. These two had got hold of Daniel and per-suaded him to come in with them, had offered him a good rake-off, or perhaps they had some hold over him—that was possible.

But no, thought James. No, it simply couldn't be true; there *must* be some other explanation. If Daniel were in league with those men, and had arranged to meet them in the quarry, why had he brought James with him? James looked back over the

events of the evening and tried to make sense of them . . . and
sense began to appear. Indeed the more he thought about it the
more everything hung together and the case against Daniel became more circumstantial. Daniel's reluctance to bring James with
him, his reluctance to explain his plan, his insistence that James
must obey orders implicitly and, last but not least, his rage and
fury when James declared his promise null and void and went up
the hill himself, all these things could now be explained quite
easily. The twisted ankle was a ruse to get rid of James. James
was to be sent back to Mureth for the bike so that while he was
away Daniel could climb the hill and join his friends and carry
out his project. Yes, thought James miserably, yes it does make
sense. That must have been his plan, there's no other possible
explanation.

The only bright spot in the whole wretched business was the
fact that Daniel's plan had gone awry; there would be no Mureth
mutton in the Black Market this week. That was something,
thought James. It wasn't much, but it was something on the credit
side. Uncle Jock would be pleased that the mystery of the dis-
appearing sheep had been solved.

The sun was rising now and a little breeze was clearing
the mist. James got up and groped about in the heather for the
club, which he had wrenched out of his captive's hand during the
struggle. He picked it up and examined it with interest. Quite
obviously the club had been made for the purpose, designed by
the man who intended to use it. The thing consisted of a thin
steel bar about three feet long with a heavy knob at the end of it
—a deadly weapon, simple and well-balanced—you could kill a
sheep with it pretty easily if you knew the exact place to strike
. . . nobody knew better than Daniel the exact place to strike.

James sighed heavily and began to walk home across the hills, and as he went he thought it all over. What would happen next? Would Daniel be brought up for trial and imprisoned? James had no idea what the punishment for an offence of this nature was likely to be . . . but Uncle Jock would know. The first thing to do was to get hold of Uncle Jock and tell him the whole story from beginning to end. Uncle Jock would do whatever was to be done. Perhaps nothing much could be done (except to sack Daniel) for no sheep had been taken and James had no witness to back up his story; there was no evidence of the night's adventure except the steel club and, of course, the wheel-marks in the quarry where the car had turned.

24

*I*T WAS nearly dinner-time and little Charlie Wilson was playing in the garden of his father's cottage. He had a wooden horse which his fond mother had bought for him in Drumburly. Charlie was thrashing his horse severely, "Gee up, all my five horses!" cried Charlie. He was intent upon his game, but suddenly he heard the sound of footsteps on the stony path which led down from the sheep stell, and he saw a familiar figure passing the fence which surrounded the garden.

"Hullo!" cried Charlie, abandoning his horse and running to the gate. "Hullo, Big Klaus! Are ye coming in?"

Big Klaus walked on. He took no notice at all of Charlie, he did not even wave his hand and call out the usual greeting. Most certainly he was not coming in.

"Are ye going home to your denner, Big Klaus?" shouted Charlie.

There was no answer. The small thin figure in the waterproof walked on down the path.

Charlie opened his mouth to shout again, louder than before, and then he stopped suddenly with his mouth wide open. He was uncertain. It was Big Klaus, of course . . . or perhaps it wasn't . . . he looked different. Charlie could not have told you how he looked different; it was just that somehow or other he didn't look like himself.

The man went on down the hill at a good pace and when he

reached the door of Well Cottage he opened it and went in.

There was nobody in the room but it had the appearance of recent occupation as if its owner had just got up and gone out of it for a few minutes. A fire was burning in the grate with a bright glow, and a black kettle was sitting on the ledge at the fireside, singing cheerfully. The table was laid for dinner with a clean red-and-white check cloth, a knife and fork and spoon, a cup and saucer and plate and other paraphernalia for a lonely meal.

The man's eyes strayed round the room. He looked at the grandfather's clock, at the bookcase, at the two oak chairs standing one on each side of the fire. His eyes fell upon a china dog, standing upon the mantelpiece. Softly he walked across the room and took it from its place.

"That's not where I keep it, Jed," said a voice behind him.

The visitor spun round quickly with the china dog in his hands.

There was a little silence as the two men confronted each other across the room. They were very alike, thin and wiry with brown complexions; and their features were alike too; but, in spite of the likeness between them, nobody seeing them together like this could have mistaken one for the other. One face was pleasant, the lines upon it had been written by humour and kindliness; the other face wore a discontented, cynical expression. It was as if the two faces had once been alike and the two different natures had written different stories upon them.

"That's not where I keep it, Jed," repeated the owner of the room. "I'm not as trusting as Mother was. I keep my money—elsewhere."

He paused, but there was no reply.

"But maybe I'm doing you an injustice, Jed," he continued. "Maybe it was a fill of tobacco you were after. I'll not grudge you that."

Jed turned and put the china dog in its place. He said, "It's a funny way to welcome a fellow after all these years, Daniel." His voice was not like Daniel's, it was thin and whiny and, whereas Daniel had kept the Scottish turn of speech, Jed had lost it.

"Aye, it'll be about six years since we met," said Daniel in a conversational tone, "but there's no need to ask why you've come or what you're wanting. It'll be the same as usual."

"I wanted to see you, that's all."

"You wanted to see me," nodded Daniel. "It was a brotherly desire. Maybe you were wanting to see if you could still pass yourself off as Daniel Reid, it's been useful to you once or twice. You could, too," said Daniel thoughtfully. "We're not so alike as we were, but you could pass as me at twenty yards—or to a person in a hurry." He paused and then added thoughtfully, "It's not so much that you and me are alike, but more because we're unlike other folk—skinny and brown with big noses and bushy eyebrows—that's what does it. A person sees a big nose and bushy eyebrows and says to himself, that's Daniel Reid. It's a pity we both take after Mother's side of the family—a pity for me, that is. I'm just wondering what you've been doing, Jed. What have you been up to, eh?"

Jed did not seem pleased at the turn the conversation had taken. "I'm hungry, Daniel," he said. "I've been on the hills all night and—"

"You've been on the hills!"

"I started to walk over from Drumburly last night and I got lost."

"You got lost coming over from Drumburly?" exclaimed Daniel incredulously.

Fortunately for Jed the kettle boiled over and engaged its owner's attention, so there was no need to think up another lie.

Jed watched Daniel making tea, bringing out a second cup and saucer and plate from the cupboard, another knife and fork and spoon from the drawer; he waited while Daniel went away and returned with a piece of cold meat and a loaf of bread and various other eatables on a tray. When all was prepared the two men sat down at the table and began their meal.

"I thought you'd be pleased to see me, Daniel," said Jed in a complaining tone of voice.

"It's the china dog that's to blame. If it had not been for the china dog I might have welcomed you differently. I might have been taken in; I might have thought you'd turned over a new leaf and became a changed man. But you've not changed—not inwardly. You've changed quite a bit outwardly," said Daniel, regarding his visitor critically. "Aye, you've changed quite a bit. Nobody would think, to look at you, that you were younger than me. There's a dryness in your skin and the beginnings of pouches beneath your eyes and your hand's not as steady as it should be. You'll need to take care of yourself, Jed."

"Stow your gab!"

"It's brotherly advice, Jed, brotherly advice," declared Daniel, cutting off another helping of cold meat and filling his guest's plate.

"Haven't you got some whisky?" Jed enquired.

"Not for you. I've whisky in the house and I'd not be without it, for it's grand stuff when you come in soaked through and
your teeth chattering in your head; but you're over fond of it,
by the looks of you, and you're getting none here."

"Daniel, I want money. I'm in the devil of a hole. I'll tell you
the whole thing," said Jed, leaning forward and speaking urgently
and confidentially. "I came down here with a couple of pals, but
we had a bit of a row and they went off without me. I'm stranded.
I haven't got the price of my train-fare back to Glasgow. I need
money badly, Daniel."

"I never knew you in any other condition."

"Ten quid, Daniel. It isn't much to ask. You've got a good
job. Shepherds get well paid nowadays."

"I wouldn't give you ten pence."

"As a loan," pleaded Jed.

Daniel laughed mirthlessly. "It was a loan you got last time
—a loan to get you out of a hole—and I've never seen the money
yet. It's the same tale every time with you."

"All right," said Jed, changing the tone of his voice. "Here's
a different tale; perhaps you'll like it better. I saw you on Saturday morning with Miss Steele. She's a pretty enough piece if you
like them young. I like them a bit older, myself—"

"You dirty swine!" cried Daniel, raising his hand.

"Here, none of that!" exclaimed Jed and he slipped out of
his seat and backed towards the door. "You needn't get your back
up! I just thought you might be interested, that's all. If you
aren't interested there are people that might be: Sir Andrew
Steele, for instance."

Daniel had got himself in hand. "Come back and sit down,"
he said quietly. "Did you hear what I said? Come back and sit

down. You're no safer there than you would be sitting at this table, for I could catch you on the hill in two minutes and squeeze the breath out of you."

Jed came back reluctantly. He had gone a queer grey colour beneath his tan. "I don't know what all the trouble's about," he said in a shaky voice. "It was a joke, that's all. I didn't mean a word of it."

"Listen, Jed. I knew you were a fool, but I never knew you were as big a fool as that. You're crazy, that's what's wrong with you. Maybe you didn't hear there was a dance on Friday night —here, at Mureth. Miss Steele was at the dance."

"It was after eight o'clock when I saw you with the girl."

"It would be about that," agreed Daniel. "She went up to Mureth House with Mrs Johnstone and had a wee rest before I took her home. If you doubt my word you can ask Mrs Johnstone, but I'm not caring much one way or the other. If you choose to make a fool of yourself it's no affair of mine." He got up as he spoke and going over to the fireplace took out his pipe and filled it from the china dog. Perhaps he did not want Jed to see his face.

"It sounds funny," said Jed doubtfully.

Daniel was aware it sounded funny but he was not a liar by nature and he could think of no better lie on the spur of the moment. Daniel respected the truth, he considered truthfulness an important virtue (perhaps the most important virtue), but this was the second lie he had told Jed. Jed had believed the first (he had believed that Daniel could catch him on the hill, and had come back to the table and sat down as meek as milk); it was to be hoped he would swallow the second lie as easily.

"She went to Mureth House after the dance?" asked Jed. "What did she do that for?"

"How do I know?" enquired Daniel.

"Why didn't she go home with the others?"

"Maybe she was tired or something."

Jed hesitated. "You took her home on the back of your bike?" he enquired.

"That's what I did. Sir Andrew gave me five shillings for my trouble."

Oddly enough this seemed to convince Jed (he was the more easily convinced because he knew Daniel to be a truthful person. Habitually truthful people can get away with almost any lie if they tell it well). He said slowly, "There's no knowing what people like that will do. If they were working people, and had to earn their living, they wouldn't be so keen to turn night into day."

Daniel laughed. He was so relieved that his laugh was extremely cheerful. "Working people!" he exclaimed. "I wonder which works hardest, Mr Johnstone or you. He's up and about most mornings at the back of six, and he has papers and what not to keep him busy in the evenings, but he's not a working man by your way of it."

It was at this moment that the door opened and Mr Johnstone himself walked into the room, followed by his nephew.

There were now four men in the little room; four men who stood silent, looking at one another in blank amazement. Each was surprised in a different way, of course, and perhaps Daniel was the least surprised of the party; for, although it was not Mr Johnstone's habit to walk straight into his own cottages, unannounced, he doubtless had the right to do so. Jed's surprise was tinged with consternation. The visitors had walked in with the air of policemen . . . and Jed was not particularly fond of the police.

It was James who found his voice first, for James had a quick intelligence and had been trained to take rapid decisions. "Uncle Jock!" he exclaimed. "Uncle Jock, wait a moment. It was the other man."

"All right, James. Take it easy. We've got to get to the bottom of it, you know."

At these sinister words Jed rose and made a dash for the door, but James (who had come in last and was nearest the door) caught him by the arm and twisted it behind him.

"This is him!" cried James excitedly. "This is the fellow— what a fool I was! It wasn't Daniel at all!"

"Hold him, James."

"You bet I will!"

Jock looked across at Daniel who was standing by the fire. (Daniel's eyes had moved from speaker to speaker but apart from that he was motionless.) "Reid," said Jock. "This man's your brother, I suppose."

"That's it, Mr Johnstone," replied Daniel.

"Do you know what he's been up to?"

"I've no idea, but I'd be surprised to hear it was any good."

"When did he come?"

"Today," cried Jed. "I was with some pals—they'll tell you. I came to Drumburly this morning and I walked over the hills to see my brother. Is there any harm in that!"

"Is this true?" asked Jock, looking at Daniel.

"I wouldn't say so," replied Daniel with a sigh. "I've heard three different tales as to when he came and how he came, but if you ask me I would say he's been about the neighbourhood for some time."

"You can't pin anything on me!" cried Jed. "I tell you I came this morning. I've got witnesses. I've got two pals—"

"The two men you were talking to at the Show, maybe," suggested Jock.

Jed sighed and suddenly he went completely limp, sliding onto the floor. For a moment James thought the man had fainted and he relaxed his grip.

"Hold him!" cried Daniel.

The words came too late. Jed had pulled his captor onto the floor and, twisting sideways, he sprang up and was off like a bolted rabbit. James scrambled to his feet and pursued him with all speed.

"Mr James'll not catch him," said Daniel regretfully. "Jed's a slippery customer. He was out in Japan for a while and he learnt some queer wrestling tricks there. You need to know Jed to be up-sides with him."

"It's a pity, but it can't be helped," Jock said.

"Aye, it's a pity sure enough. I could catch him if it wasn't for my ankle. I twisted it on the hill last night." He pulled up the leg of his trousers as he spoke and displayed an ankle swollen to twice its usual size.

"That looks a bad sprain!" exclaimed Jock.

"It was sore at the time," admitted Daniel. "But it's a good deal better. I'll be as right as ninepence in a couple of days. Wilson is carrying on himself. He's a good chap and capable enough, it's just experience he lacks."

Jock, for once, was not thinking of his sheep, nor worrying for fear they should be neglected. There was something even more important at stake. He said impulsively, "Reid, I've done you a bad injustice. I see it now. I'm very sorry about it."

"Well, you couldn't say fairer, Mr Johnstone," declared Daniel with a bewildered air.

"I'm seeing daylight now," Jock continued. "But there's still a few things to be cleared up. Let's sit down and have it out."

Daniel agreed with alacrity. "It's what I'm wanting, Mr Johnstone. The affair is a mystery to me. I know fine you've not been satisfied with me lately and I was meaning to give in my notice and find another job . . . but maybe Jed's at the bottom of it?"

Jock nodded.

"It's Jed, is it?" said Daniel. "Och, well, it's not the first time I've borne the blame for Jed, nor the second time eether."

They sat down and began to talk, and when James returned, crestfallen, from the vain pursuit of his quarry, he sat down with them. Three pipes were lighted and the whole matter was thoroughly discussed.

Daniel's story was soon told. After Mr James had left him he remained sitting upon the stone, feeling very angry with himself, with Mr James, and in fact with the world in general; then his ankle eased a bit and he "hirpled along to the road-end," for it struck him that he could watch for the car. He had not long to wait. The car came down from the quarry sooner than he expected; it was a big car and it had some difficulty at the sharp turn into the main road. Daniel went up to the window and asked for a lift, explaining that he was a shepherd and had sprained his ankle; but his request was unheeded, the car drove off at high speed leaving him in the road. He was not surprised, of course; he had not expected his request to be granted but had made it in order to have a good look at the occupants of the car. There were two men in the car, big men in waterproofs with caps pulled down over their eyes. He could not possibly identify them but neither of them was Jed. As the car drove off he saw that the trailer was empty and from this he deduced that Mr James had frightened them away. Daniel waited about until the milk-lorry passed, he stopped it and got a lift home.

All this time (said Daniel) he had been worrying a good deal about Mr James, not only because Mr James was a stranger to the hills and might get lost in the mist, or fall over the edge of the quarry, but also because he was aware that if Mr James happened to see the sheep-lifters he would go for them with his bare hands without thought of the consequences. It was possible that this had happened and that Mr James was lying wounded upon the hill. But fortunately when he got to the steading he met Lizzie and she had told him that Mr James was safely at Mureth House.

James's story took a good deal longer to tell and it was nearly tea-time before everybody had had his say and everything, including Daniel's character, was perfectly clear.

25

$\mathcal{T}$HE TELEPHONE bell rang when Jock and Mamie and
James were at supper. They had been talking about the sheep-
stealers, of course, telling Mamie the whole story, and because
they were all so much relieved at the clearing up of the mystery
they were extremely cheerful, not to say merry, over it.

"That'll be the police," said Jock, rising as he spoke. "I put
a call through to them."

While he was away the conversation continued. "It's grand,"
declared James. "I feel as if a huge weight had been lifted off my
back. Honestly, Mamie, I don't know when I've felt so utterly
miserable as I felt this morning. It was horrible to believe that
Daniel could do such a thing—and it just shows you shouldn't
believe ill of people you trust. You should believe your instinct
rather than your eyes."

Mamie considered this. The idea was interesting, but all the
same . . . "I think everybody believes their eyes," said Mamie.
"Sometimes people say, *I couldn't believe my eyes,* but they don't
really mean it. Seeing is believing."

"I once saw a girl sawn in half," said James. "It was in Malaya. I saw it distinctly with my eyes, and several other fellows
saw it too. We were just wondering—and feeling a bit sick—
when the man stuck her together again and she got up and bowed
and kissed her hand to us."

"Goodness!" exclaimed Mamie. "You *have* seen a lot of queer things, haven't you? Tell me more about it, James."

James obeyed. They were still talking about the girl who had been sawn in half—or hadn't been sawn in half—when Jock returned.

"It wasn't the police," said Jock. "It was Mrs Duncan. The young Duncans have been invited to go over to Tassieknowe for an evening party and they want James to go with them. I told her James would ring up later. Mrs Duncan should know better than to telephone in the middle of a meal."

"They have their supper at eight . . ." began Mamie, who never liked anyone to be blamed unjustly.

"I'll tell them I'm too busy to go," declared James. "I don't want to go to Tassieknowe. I didn't like that man."

"You'd be better to go," said Jock. "It's a bad thing to fall foul of your neighbours and you might have a chance of putting the matter right. I wouldn't refer to the fracas on the hill but just make the man's acquaintance in a civilised manner and let bygones be bygones."

"Oh James, do go!" exclaimed Mamie. "You could see what they're like and ask Miss Heddle if she would come to tea or something."

James realised that he must go—all the more so because he felt that the "fracas on the hill" was his fault, or at least that he was partly responsible for it. He telephoned to Cathie Duncan and arranged that he was to be picked up at Mureth tomorrow night. It was a dinner-jacket affair, said Cathie, "a dinner-dance" was the description on the invitation.

He had no sooner rung off than Holly telephoned to invite him to go to Tassieknowe with the Drumburly Tower party which consisted of Holly and Ian and Ian's college friend. They had been asked to bring as many people as they liked and there was plenty of room in the car. Holly was annoyed when she heard James was going with the Duncans and suggested he should alter the arrangement.

"I can't do that," said James.

"Of course you can," declared Holly. "It would be much more sensible. We actually pass Mureth on our way. We'll call for you at half-past seven."

"I can't," said James firmly. "I'll see you there, Holly. You'll dance with me, won't you?"

"Oh James, do come with us. The Duncans are deadly dull, aren't they?"

"Are they?"

"Of course they are!" exclaimed Holly. "The whole Duncan family is as dull as ditch-water. They're teetotal into the bargain."

"That doesn't mean I can't have a cocktail tomorrow night— if I'm offered one," replied James chuckling.

"You'll be offered one," promised Holly. "It's going to be a slap-up show."

"How do you know?"

Holly laughed. "Everything that happens in the valley is known in this house. Uncle Andrew has his sources of information and Aunt Adela has hers. I tease them about their spies; Aunt Adela's are much the best value."

As James rang off he reflected that the party might be rather fun after all. It would be interesting to see the house, to see what sort of a job a rich magnate had made of an ancient Scottish farm, and what sort of entertainment he would provide. In most places in Britain the mere idea of giving dinner to an unlimited number

of people would have been preposterous, but here it was different
—there was always plenty of food on a farm.

The young Duncans called for James in good time; they were
excited about the party and full of chat. James discovered that
they knew nothing at all about the New People but they had
known old Mr Brown quite well and had often visited Tassiknowe
when he was there. Henry and Cathie both talked at once, so the
information they volunteered was slightly mixed. Mr Brown had
shut up most of the house and spent all his waking hours in a
small, dark "den." The house was illumined by lamps and smelt
of paraffin. It was always dark in the house because of the trees
and bushes which overshadowed it and hemmed it in. Mr Brown
refused to cut down trees or cut back bushes. Paper was peeling
off the walls in strips, but Mr Brown did not seem to notice. He
bred Highland cattle and crossed them with Ayrshires, hoping
to get the higher milk-yield of the Ayrshire combined with the
tough resistence to weather conditions of the Highland stock
(this was Henry, of course). His housekeeper was a marvellous
baker of scones and cakes and always walked off with all the
prizes at the local Show (this was Cathie's contribution). Mr
Brown was small and very old with a white beard and shaggy
white hair. He was an elder at Drumburly kirk and rode down
the valley to Drumburly every Sunday morning upon an ancient
mare which was stabled at the Steele Arms during the service.

By this time they had arrived at their destination. The gates
of Tassieknowe were standing wide open in a hospitable manner;
they were wrought-iron gates, painted peacock blue. The drive
had been newly laid with tar macadam and was smooth and shining, stretching up to the house which stood upon a little hill, open
to the four winds of heaven.

"I suppose this *is* the right place," said Henry doubtfully, slowing down as he spoke.

"Of course it's the place," replied Cathie. "The new man has cut down *everything,* that's all. Go on, Henry, there's a car behind."

"Mr Brown must be turning in his grave," murmured Henry in awed tones.

James had not seen the house before, of course, so he was not staggered by its metamorphosis. It was an old, square house, built of grey stone with a slate roof and squat chimneys; not a beautiful house, thought James, and somehow it seemed to wear an air of surprise, a slightly shamefaced air, but perhaps this was merely James's fancy. Perhaps it was merely chance that the curious old rhyme should come into his head—the rhyme about the old woman who went to the Fair and fell asleep on the road home. While she was asleep a mischievous boy came along and cut her petticoats short, so that even her own dog did not know her.

> *He began to bark and she began to cry,*
> *"Lawks a mercy on us! This is none of I!"*

James was reflecting how odd it was that the old rhyme (which he had not heard since he was a child) should spring into mind unbidden, when Cathie suddenly exclaimed in tones of distress, "Oh dear, it doesn't *like* it!"

"What doesn't like what?" asked Henry.

But James did not need to ask. He looked at Cathie and nodded his understanding and agreement.

As they went up the steps, the door was flung wide open by a man in a starched white jacket who ushered them into the hall and helped them to remove their wraps. Although it was still broad daylight the blinds had been drawn and the whole place was blazing with electric light. The floor was covered all over with a fitted carpet of peacock blue, the walls were white and shining, the furniture was of light unpainted wood of modern design. It was a type of décor which would have surprised nobody in a luxurious London flat, but in the heart of the hills it was unexpected and amazing. The two Duncans were stricken dumb with astonishment. Their eyes were round, like marbles. James noticed that they kept very close to him as if he were their one familiar friend in this strange new world.

The drawing-room was decorated and furnished in the same style as the hall; there were over twenty people in the room chattering gaily and drinking cocktails. Mr Heddle came forward and received them cordially and James was able to renew his former impression of the man: tall and perhaps a trifle too heavy for his age, with a curiously springy walk. He had dark-brown eyes and crinkly black hair: his clean-shaven face was wreathed in smiles. He was very good-looking, thought James as he shook hands with him, but good-looking in a foreign way . . .

"So nice of you to come, Mr Dering," declared Mr Heddle. "Of course I've heard all about your uncle—the best farmer in the district and our nearest neighbour!"

James murmured something noncommittal. He was glad to find that Mr Heddle did not recognise him. It was no wonder, really, for tonight James looked a very different person from the ragged, dirty, uncouth ruffian who had bandied words with Mr Heddle upon the hill.

"We're settled in now," continued Mr Heddle, looking round his drawing-room with a complacent air. "Anna and I are very anxious to know all our neighbours and to get to know them quickly so we thought a house-warming party would be a good idea. I hope people won't think we should have sat down and waited to be called on."

"I think it's very kind of you," replied James, accepting a glass of pale-green liquid which was being offered to him on a tray. "I'm sure other people will think so too. Calling is a bit out of fashion nowadays. My aunt isn't a good caller but she would like to meet you and Miss Heddle—so would my uncle of course."

"Here's Anna!" exclaimed Mr Heddle. "Anna, this is Mr Dering."

Miss Heddle was older than her brother, she was pale and composed, beautifully dressed. Somehow or other James did not think she and Mamie would have much in common (he could not imagine what they would find to talk about) and, this being so, he refrained from giving her an invitation to come to tea at Mureth. Wait and see, thought James.

The guests were a queer mixture. Some of them James knew —they were Drumburly people and people from neighbouring farms—but the others were Mr Heddle's friends: elegant women with carefully set hair and made-up faces, and men who looked like tailor's models, in dinner-jackets which fitted them with creaseless perfection. One would not have looked twice at these people if one had seen them dining at the Savoy but here they seemed as exotic as birds of paradise.

James sipped his cocktail. He discovered that it was exceedingly good and exceedingly potent. It had that smooth velvety taste which is dangerously deceptive. He was just savouring the taste of it and deciding that it might be wiser not to finish it (yes, much wiser, for he was out of training, so to speak, having par-

taken of nothing stronger than beer since he came to Mureth)
when he remembered the Duncans. The Duncans had been reft
from his side. Cathie was over near the fireplace, she looked like
a wild rose amongst orchids—thought James, changing his metaphor—but she looked as if she were enjoying herself; she was talking with animation, polishing off the remains of her cocktail and
holding out her glass to be refilled.

There was no time to be lost. James elbowed his way across
the room without ceremony and removed the glass from Cathie's
hand. Fortunately there was so much movement in the room and
such a buzz of conversation that his action was unnoticed by the
other guests—or at least he hoped it was.

"James!" exclaimed Cathie indignantly. "It's nice! I was enjoying it. I don't see why I shouldn't do as other people do when
I'm at a party."

"Nor do I," admitted James. "There's no reason on earth why
you shouldn't—except if you drink two glasses of that stuff you'll
be as drunk as a lord."

"But it's just like lemonade—"

"Not quite," James told her. "It's nicer than lemonade and
more inebriating. Honestly, Cathie."

She began to laugh. "Oh dear!" she said helplessly. "Oh
James, I believe I'm drunk already. How awful! Oh James, what
shall I do?"

"You'll be all right when you get something solid to eat," he
assured her. But he was slightly anxious about her all the same
and stayed beside her until dinner was announced and the guests
began to trickle into the dining-room.

26

JAMES FOUND himself sitting between Holly and one of the birds of paradise. Holly was in white with a silver girdle and silver flowers in her hair; she began to talk to him at once in a low, teasing voice.

"Something tells me this is going to be an orgy," said Holly. "I don't think Mummy would like it if she knew her innocent little poppet was here. Did you lap up all your beautiful cocktail?"

"No, did you?"

"One glass of the heavenly nectar was enough. My head's like a rock, but even I feel a trifle elated. What was in it, I wonder. Methinks our host has a puckish humour."

James looked round the table and noticed that the birds of paradise had been spaced out carefully between the local people and the whole party was animated and cheerful. If Mr Heddle had intended his potent brew to break the ice his aim had succeeded . . . all the same James felt angry. It wasn't fair. It was a trick. The sort of trick a Borgia might perpetrate . . . and with only a slight movement of imagination James could see Mr Heddle as a Borgia! He looked well in his conventional attire, but how much better he would look decked out in velvet and satin and hung with jewelled chains!

"I've been wondering about him, too," murmured Holly. "At first I thought he was Jewish, but he isn't. Look at his straight nose. He's beautiful."

"Beautiful!"

"Oh, men never admire that type. I don't really admire it myself but I can appreciate beauty when I see it. Think of him in a toga with a gold band round his head!"

It was odd that Holly should have the same idea: the idea that Mr Heddle would look better in exotic dress.

"The women are gorgeous, aren't they?" continued Holly. "They make me feel untidy . . . and yet I don't know . . . perhaps they're a little too *soignée*. What do you think, James?"

"Not one of them is half as lovely as you."

"Oh James!"

"It's true," said James seriously. "You and Cathie are ten times prettier than these painted dolls."

Holly turned towards her other neighbour at once, and turned so completely that she presented James with a view of her bare shoulder. He was rather surprised at the manner in which she had received his compliment but perhaps it was time to change over.

His other neighbour was a bird of paradise or an orchid or a painted doll—you could take your choice of metaphor. James really preferred the last for, after all, birds of paradise and orchids are real and natural but there was nothing real or natural about this woman. Her hair, her face . . . in fact everything about her was artificial. You could not tell what age she was. You almost expected her to move in jerks like a marionette; you almost felt it was clever of her to speak; you almost wondered who had made her. Somewhere about her there would be a little tag saying "Made in Paris". . . .

"We've met before," said the painted lady in a tired voice. "Oh yes, you look different tonight, but I recognised you at once.

I was surprised when I saw Nestor hadn't recognised you, he was very angry with you."

"It wasn't my fault."

"No, it was his. That's why he was so angry."

James realised that this woman was no fool. He was interested and amused.

"Nestor is charming when everything goes well," she continued, "but not quite so charming when he can't get his own way, or when things go bad on him."

"I should imagine he usually gets his own way," remarked James.

She did not answer that, but turned her head and looked at James appraisingly. "No woman would forget you," she said.

"Oh, really," said James uncomfortably.

"You looked like a young god," continued the tired flat voice. "Pan, I suppose. He ran about on the hills, didn't he?"

"I felt like a tramp," declared James.

"You were rather dirty but that doesn't matter here. Clothes don't matter here."

"You don't like Tassieknowe?" asked James with interest.

"No."

"Why not?"

She helped herself to a very small portion of strawberry ice. "Tassieknowe doesn't like me," she replied. "It doesn't like any of us. It's pushing us out. The only way you could live here is to surrender to it and I don't want to surrender. I'm going home tomorrow. I'm frightened."

"Frightened?"

"The silence and the loneliness . . . but there's something else as well."

"The house is your sort of place—" began James, looking round at the white shining walls, the heavy peacock-blue curtains and the polished table with its load of silver and glass.

"All this is on the surface," declared the painted lady. "Beneath the surface there's something very queer—something elemental and terrifying. Nestor is beginning to feel it. He's fighting against it, but he won't be able to stand it for long. I can't stand it a day longer. It's driving me mad."

"Why did he buy it?" asked James.

"Why do you buy things?" she wondered. "You think you want them; I suppose that's the reason. Perhaps Nestor wanted something different—something difficult."

Yes, that's the answer, thought James. Things come to friend Nestor too easily.

They danced after dinner. There was a very fine band on Mr Heddle's very fine radiogram. One had a feeling that Mr Heddle had arranged it—but how could he? There were limits to what money and power and charm of manner could accomplish . . . or weren't there? James danced with Holly and with Nan Forrester (the doctor's sister from Drumburly) and with his painted lady; and he danced with Cathie who had recovered and was enjoying herself immensely.

Miss Heddle was not dancing; James sat down beside her and talked to her, for he wanted to find out whether it was any use asking her to meet his aunt. He discovered that Miss Heddle was devoted to her brother and that her chief interest in life was to provide suitable food for him and his friends.

"It seems so unfair," said Miss Heddle in a complaining voice. "All those sheep on the hills actually *belong* to Nestor, but he isn't allowed to kill *one* of them—not even a *lamb*."

"We had some very good lamb tonight," said her guest smiling.

"It *was* nice, wasn't it?" agreed Miss Heddle. She lowered her voice and added, "We've been getting it every week from a MAN."

"From a man?"

"Nestor said just to buy it and not ask any questions," said Miss Heddle. "It's *frightfully* expensive, of course, but I think it's *worth* it, don't you?"

James gazed at her, speechlessly. So he had been eating Mureth lamb!

"He hasn't come this week," continued Miss Heddle. "I *do* hope he will come. It makes *all* the difference to housekeeping if you can depend upon getting *meat*. Nestor *needs* meat. He wasn't at *all* strong when he was a little boy and it's so *very* difficult to get the right kind of food for him. I don't mind telling you that's *one* of the reasons he bought Tassieknowe."

"Quite," nodded James. He wondered if he could ask what the other reasons were, but somehow he could not. Miss Heddle was rather foolish in some ways, but . . .

"You won't say anything about it, *will* you?" said Miss Heddle in sudden anxiety. "I mean about the MAN. Nestor said not to tell *anyone*, but somehow I felt it didn't matter telling *you*."

"I shan't tell the police," said James.

Miss Heddle laughed quite heartily at this joke. She would not have laughed if she had known that it was not a joke at all. Quite seriously James had weighed up the advantages and disadvantages of informing the police about the MAN, and had decided not to do so. There was no object in doing so, thought James, for the MAN had not appeared at Tassieknowe this week and it

was unlikely he would appear again. There would be no more
lamb for dear Nestor unless he could catch one of his own, unawares, and push it over the edge of a precipice.

". . . and butter and eggs and fowls," Miss Heddle was saying. "And rabbits and trout from the river. It all *helps,* you know.
In London, nowadays, it's so *very* difficult to get nice food. Of
course we're luckier than *other* people because Nestor has so many
friends."

"Friends in the Black Market, I suppose," suggested James.

"Oh no!" exclaimed Miss Heddle. "Not really Black Market;
just—just people who know how to get things they *want*, that's
all."

James nodded. He had made up his mind that Miss Heddle
was not a suitable acquaintance for his aunt.

The guests were now drifting back to the dining-room, but
not to eat. The long table had been cleared and was covered with
a green-baize cloth, in the centre of which stood a roulette board.
Each guest was provided with a handful of chips ("to play about
with" said their host) and several of the members of the house-
party began to explain to their less sophisticated fellow-guests how
the game was played.

There had been more drinks by this time and everybody was
slightly flushed and exhilarated, but James had drunk nothing and
was coldly sober. He enquired in a loud voice what the chips
were worth.

"What you like," replied his host suavely. There was a curious
glitter in his eyes as he surveyed his uncomfortable guest. James
had a feeling that Mr Heddle had suddenly recognised him.

"I'd just like to know, that's all," said James politely. "I expect we'd all like to know before we start playing."

"Pennies—or pounds?" suggested Mr Heddle, sitting down at the head of the table and putting his hand upon the rake.

There was a very uncomfortable silence. Nobody liked to suggest pennies and nobody wanted to suggest pounds. James looked round at his neighbours and wondered what they had thought. Dr Forrester and his pretty sister in her home-made frock—had they thought their host was providing this entertainment for fun, that they would win or lose their handful of coloured chips and then go cheerfully home neither richer nor poorer for their little flutter on the wheel? And there was Henry Duncan, with his flushed, boyish face and tousled hair; Henry could not afford to lose pennies, far less pounds . . . nor could Ian Steele (who was on a tight allowance if James knew anything about Sir Andrew). Holly was hard up—or said she was—but Holly could look after herself; he need not worry about Holly. He worried more about the two young Allens who were struggling to make ends meet upon a poor farm, and about the Kerrs who had four young children. None of these people could afford to lose much . . . and yet how difficult it was! All the more difficult because they were proud, because they did not want to plead poverty before their rich English host and his friends, and because of that preposterous legend that Scots were mean and looked at both sides of a penny before they gave it to a blind beggar. Scots were not mean—or at least James had never met a mean one—but they were thrifty, of course, and these people, who earned their living like Adam by the sweat of their brow, knew the value of money.

"Oh, I say, Nestor!" exclaimed a young man with black, shiny hair which looked as if it had been painted onto his skull. "Oh, I say—pennies! Not much fun in that! If pounds is too high we could split the difference—what?"

Cathie spoke next. She said, "I don't think I'll play. I'd rather look on if you don't mind. I've never played roulette before and honestly I couldn't afford to lose a lot of money. Daddy isn't very well off." She put her chips upon the table and they made a little rattling noise which seemed quite loud in the silence. Her face had gone very white and her lips were trembling.

Nan Forrester laughed. "That goes for me too," she said, putting down her chips as she spoke.

It was bravely done, thought James. In this sort of matter women were braver than men, or perhaps less bound by convention, less concerned with what others might think. Now that these two had opened the way quite a number followed their example —they put down their chips and stood back. James put his down with the others for he was no gambler and did not want to lose his money nor to win Mr Heddle's. Those that were left moved forward to the table and took their places.

Holly intended to play. She looked at James defiantly, as she drew in her chair, and he realised that she was a born gambler. She was certain that she was going to make a pile. James hoped she would. He felt flat, now. He felt miserable. He had spoilt the party and antagonised his host. I shouldn't have come, he thought.

"You understand, don't you," began Mr Heddle who was acting as *tourneur*. "Those who don't understand had better wait and watch how it's done. We play more or less the same way as they play at Monte Carlo, but of course we don't bother about *chefs de partie*, and the players make their stakes themselves."

There was a murmur of assent.

"Cut the cackle, Nestor," said the young man with the painted hair, whose pale face had assumed an expression of eager anticipation.

It was at this moment that James felt a touch on his arm and, looking round, saw Dr Forrester.

"I've got to go," said Dr Forrester in a low voice. "They've phoned for me from Drumburly. Nan's coming too—she's had enough of it—and she suggested you might like a lift home."

"Nothing I'd like better!" declared James.

"We'll slip away quietly, shall we? No good trying to say good-bye to our host."

"No good," agreed James. "I'll just tell the Duncans."

"We'll wait for you in the hall," nodded Dr Forrester.

Henry Duncan was sitting beside Holly, he had decided to try his luck, so James told Cathie he was going home with the Forresters.

"I wish *we* could," said Cathie. "I suggested it to Henry but he's going to play. Do you think he'll lose a lot of money?"

"He may win," James told her. "Somebody has got to win. Cheer up, Cathie."

But Cathie did not feel like cheering up.

"What about you coming with us?" suggested James. "Leave the car for Henry . . ."

She shook her head. "I'll wait for him," she said. "I may be able to stop him from losing too much." She paused and then added with a little catch in her voice. "It isn't *like* Henry to be silly. I mean he isn't a bit like himself. He was quite rude and horrid when I tried to persuade him not to play . . . and he said I had disgraced the family for saying what I did."

"That's nonsense," James said. "It isn't a disgrace to tell the truth. I thought it was very brave of you and so did lots of other people."

"I wish we hadn't come," declared Cathie miserably.

James hesitated. He wondered if he ought to stay and look after Cathie, but what good could he do?

"Don't worry about me," said Cathie, sensing his thought. "I'll be all right. It's much better for you to go home with the Forresters."

The Forresters were waiting for James in the hall.

"Sorry to hurry you but we'd better get a move on," said Dr Forrester. "It sounded a bit like appendicitis—either that or green apples, but you can't take a chance." He opened the big front door as he spoke and they stepped out of the stuffy, garish house.

"Why do we do it!" exclaimed James.

"I know," agreed Nan Forrester. "It seems absurd."

"We don't do it often, do we?" said Dr Forrester chuckling. "In fact I've never done anything the least like it before. It's been a completely new experience." He paused and then added gravely, "That's my only excuse for being such a fool."

"You weren't the only fool, Adam," said Nan hastily.

"Others will be making the same excuse. Others will be wanting to thank Mr Dering and not knowing how to do it."

"You should thank your sister and Cathie Duncan," said James.

James had not spoken to Dr Forrester before—or at least he had spoken only a few conventional words to him—but now he had time to look at the young doctor and size him up. He had a thin face and grey, steady eyes; his dark hair was somewhat ruffled by the night's excitements. There was a delicate air about him, as if he got too little sleep and too little nourishing food.

Nan was like him, but younger and less delicate. They were an attractive pair.

The car was old and shabby but well kept, and James noticed with approval that the engine sprung to life at one touch of the self-starter.

"It's not often I'm glad of a night-call," said Dr Forrester smiling as he spoke.

"You're busy, I expect."

"Far too busy. I don't know how we'll get through the winter. Dr Black is a rock of strength, but he's getting old. He can't do as much as a younger man. We need another assistant. The trouble is the practice is so scattered and there are so many older people who need a good deal of attention. The practice is not large enough numerically but far too large geographically. I'm hanging on, hoping the Government will do something about country doctors before they die of overwork or starvation . . . but never mind that," said Dr Forrester as he pressed the accelerator and sped down the drive. "Let's talk about the party."

Nan, who had insisted upon sitting in the back seat, leaned forward and said, "Was it *really* queer or did it only seem queer to the country bumpkins?"

"I think it was very queer," said James thoughtfully. "I suppose in London, amongst a certain set of people, parties like that might be quite usual, but this isn't London."

"What does the old house think of it all!"

James told them what the painted lady had said.

"Pushing them out!" echoed Dr Forrester. "How interesting! I don't know a great deal about psychosis, but that particular delusion is one of the recognised—"

"Delusion!" cried Nan. "Why should it be a delusion? You

and your psychosis! Tassieknowe doesn't like them—and neither do I."

The two men laughed.

"I wonder what he put in the cocktail," said James. "There was something pretty queer about *that*. Didn't you think so?"

"You mean some sort of drug," said Dr Forrester thoughtfully. "I must say I never thought of it at the time but now that you mention it I wouldn't be surprised if there was some sort of drug in it."

"Cocaine, perhaps," suggested James.

"More likely to be hashish. A very small dose of hashish would produce exactly the effect we saw—and felt," said Dr Forrester with a rueful smile. "Exhilaration and merriment."

"But that's crazy!" exclaimed Nan. "What on earth would be the idea of giving people dope?"

"It does sound crazy," admitted her brother. "But you know I think I can guess his idea. People here have been a bit stand-offish. Some of them are annoyed with Mr Heddle for having been able to carry out all those repairs and alterations. People here are not ready to bow and scrape before the great Mr Heddle and the great Mr Heddle doesn't like it."

Nan laughed. "So the great Mr Heddle said, 'I'll learn them!'"

"Could be that," said Dr Forrester quite seriously. "You can't judge a man like that by western standards. The mainspring of the Assyrian is arrogance."

"Assyrian!" exclaimed James.

"He looks like an Assyrian," Dr Forrester replied. "When I was in Babylon during the war I saw people just like Mr Nestor Heddle. I don't say he's a full-blooded Assyrian, but I'm willing to bet some of his ancestors were."

James said he was prepared to take Dr Forrester's word for it and added that he knew nothing about Assyrians except that once, long ago, they had come down like a wolf on the fold, their cohorts all shining with purple and gold.

"Their cohorts were *gleaming*," declared Nan, with an appreciative chuckle. "I must say it seems to prove the point. I can imagine Mr Heddle in the rôle without the slightest difficulty."

By this time they had reached Mureth Farm. James got out and thanked the Forresters and was invited to come and see them any day he happened to be in Drumburly. He stood and watched them drive off and reflected how curiously different people's lives were. He, himself, would soon be in bed, thank goodness; Adam Forrester would be in the sick-room, doing what he could to alleviate pain and to comfort fears and misery; Daniel Reid would be getting up and soon would be on the hill . . . and the party at Tassieknowe would still be in full swing, gathered round the green-baize table, under the glare of electric light, watching a little ball rolling round a roulette wheel.

27

ᴊ AMES DID not see his uncle and aunt till lunch-time, for they had left him "to have his sleep out" and he had slept like the seven sleepers; but at lunch-time he appeared looking none the worse of his adventures and proceeded to tell them the whole story and to apologise for his failure as as ambassador.

"I shouldn't have gone," said James ruefully. "I've made things much worse. The man hates me now, and I must admit I don't feel very kindly disposed towards him."

"It's amazing!" declared Jock. "The whole affair—the whole setup—it beats me."

"I needn't call or anything?" asked Mamie anxiously.

"Better not," observed Jock with dry humour. "You might get offered tea with opium in it. Mightn't she, James?"

James did not laugh.

"Don't worry, lad," said Jock. "You did what you thought right without fear or favour. If you've made an enemy you've made some good friends as well. The Heddles will soon get tired of the place—especially if the supply of Mureth lamb runs dry —and they'll be off back to London or Babylon or Timbuctoo."

"Anywhere except here," declared Mamie, giving Mr Heddle and his sister the freedom of the world.

"Anywhere except here," echoed James fervently.

Having settled the matter, more or less, they dismissed it from their minds. There was always plenty to do at Mureth, and plenty to think of, and gradually as the days passed (and James dug drains with Couper or helped Daniel to tend the sheep) the memory of the party at Tassieknowe faded from his mind as a dream fades at waking.

He had been so busy and so taken up with all the excitements that he had had little time to think of his own affairs, but now things settled down and he had time for thought. He began to think about Holly. Perhaps he ought to ring her up and ask how she had got on at the party and whether she had made a pile of money at roulette . . . or perhaps it would be better to go over and see her. He had not seen Holly properly since the afternoon they had spent together by the river—for the party did not count. He had *seen* her at the party, of course, and had admired her (she had looked perfectly lovely in that white dress with the silver flowers in her hair) but there had been no opportunity to talk to her about anything that mattered.

The afternoon by the river seemed quite a long time ago. It had been a curious sort of afternoon, a mixture of pleasure and embarrassment. James had enjoyed teaching Holly to fish, and they had had a good deal of fun over her efforts to throw a cast, but when they sat down to share the picnic tea he had suddenly become aware that Holly expected him to ask her to marry him. She had praised the beauty of the river almost too extravagantly; she had declared her pleasure in the delights of the country in general and of Mureth in particular, but in spite of all this ecstasy —or perhaps because of it—James had not uttered the fateful words. Somehow he was not quite sure, after all, that he wanted Holly as his wife. Somehow he could not imagine her as the wife of a farmer.

James thought about it as he went about his work. He wanted
a wife. Jock and Mamie were a good advertisement for matri-
mony and seeing them so happy together made James feel lonely.
He wanted a wife and here was Holly ready and willing to become his wife—why couldn't he be sensible and ask her? Because, thought James, because . . . Oh, I don't know! Perhaps
when I get to know her a bit better I shall feel more certain about
it.

But he was not getting to know Holly better and he would
never get to know her better unless he saw her more frequently.
He decided to go over to Drumburly Tower and call. Holly had
often asked him ("Come over any time," she had said). I'll go,
thought James. We can talk about the party. It will be rather
amusing to hear what Holly has to say about it. He borrowed
Daniel's motor-bike and went over quite comfortably in fifteen
minutes.

The maid who answered the door said that Lady Steele was
out; her ladyship had gone to Dumfries and Miss Douglas with
her. There was no saying when they would be back.

This was a blow. Somehow James had never thought that
Holly might be out. He was disappointed, for he had been looking forward to a chat with Holly.

"Would you come in and wait?" asked the maid. She asked
somewhat reluctantly, for if the gentleman came in it would be
necessary to give him tea, which would be a nuisance.

"What about Miss Eleanor?" James enquired.

"Miss Eleanor's having tea in the nursery as usual."

"I'll go up," said James.

It was rather amusing to watch the maid's reactions to this

announcement. At first she was astonished, and then astonishment gave way to satisfaction, for it would save a good deal of trouble if the gentleman shared Miss Eleanor's tea.

James ran up the stairs, two steps at a time. He had omitted to ask where the nursery was, but he felt sure it was at the top of the house and when he saw a wooden gate on the top landing he knew he was right. He opened two doors and looked in—the rooms were shrouded in dust sheets—but when he opened the third door he realised that he had arrived at his destination. It was a large, bright room with battered furniture and a carpet from which every vestige of colour had faded; he saw a rocking-horse and an ancient and dilapidated doll's-house. There was a large sofa by the window and in this Eleanor was curled up, reading and having her tea.

"James!" exclaimed Eleanor in amazement.

He noticed she did not rise and rush to him as she had done before and he understood the reason (they had parted on doubtful terms) but she was very pleased to see him all the same, and even more pleased when he enquired whether he might stay and have tea with her.

"Of course!" she cried. "How lovely! The only thing is . . ."

The only thing was Eleanor had no cup to offer her guest and she was reluctant to ask for a cup to be brought from the pantry.

"It's so far, you see," she explained. "I mean they don't like coming up all those stairs, it makes them very cross when I ask for things. I've used my cup or I'd give you that, but if you don't mind a mug . . ."

James did not mind in the least.

A mug was unearthed, an enamel mug commemorating the

coronation of King George the Fifth and Queen Mary. It had
languished in the nursery cupboard for years and was full of dust
and cobwebs, but Eleanor washed it thoroughly in the nursery
bathroom. By this time the slight embarrassment had completely
vanished and they sat down together upon the sofa to have tea.

"I've never had anyone to tea before," said Eleanor. "Not a
guest of my very own, like this. It's lovely. I suppose Mother and
Holly are out. I hope you aren't awfully disappointed."

James assured her that he was not, and it was true. He felt
happy and comfortable with his young hostess.

"Holly won a lot of money at that party," said Eleanor. "She
won thirteen pounds and she's awfully pleased about it. I wish
I could have been there—it was a *very* good party, wasn't it?"

"Yes," said James in doubtful tones.

"Didn't you enjoy it?"

"Not very much. I don't like parties, I'm afraid. As a matter
of fact I would rather have tea in the nursery with Miss Steele."

She smiled at him. "It's nice of you, but I don't believe it."

"Cross my heart," declared James.

Eleanor offered him more tea and pressed him to eat the only
piece of cake, and after some argument they divided it in half
and ate it bite for bite with a good deal of laughter over their
foolishness.

"James," said Eleanor, with sudden gravity. "I wanted to ask
you something, and please will you tell me *honestly*. Did you get
into trouble about me? I mean that night when I got lost. I got
home in plenty of time for breakfast and nobody said a word, so
I thought it was all right. Then when Mrs Johnstone came over
to see Mother I was rather afraid—afraid that somebody—"

"It was perfectly all right," declared James.

"Good," said Eleanor with a sigh of relief. "I've been wondering, you see."

James saw. He felt an absolute brute. He had been inconsiderate and unkind. He had been so absorbed in his own affairs that he had never realised Eleanor might be worrying.

"You mustn't worry about me," he told her.

"No, it was just that I didn't want you to get into trouble." She paused and then added, "I'm going to school."

"Really?"

"Yes. Are you pleased, James? You said I ought to go to school, didn't you? Holly says I shall like it."

"Of course you will."

"I don't know," said Eleanor doubtfully. "Holly gave me a book called *Veronica's First Term* and I've been reading it this afternoon. Veronica wasn't happy at school. One of the girls stole a pair of gloves from another girl and one of the mistresses found them in Veronica's drawer, right at the back and all covered up with linen, so of course everybody thought—"

"That's nonsense!" declared James stoutly. "School isn't like that at all. My sisters both went to school and they had a jolly good time."

"Holly says her school-days were the happiest days of her life," admitted Eleanor with reluctance.

James had heard this curious satement before. "Yes," he said. "Well, as a matter of fact I enjoyed the holidays best. It was so lovely coming home and everybody being pleased and making a fuss about you."

This was a new point of view to Eleanor; she tried to imagine her family being pleased to see her and making a fuss about her, but failed. It was impossible to imagine such an eventuality.

"School is the best thing—honestly," said James, who had begun to wonder whether it really was.

"Tell me about school," said Eleanor leaning against him confidingly.

James complied with her request. His two sisters had been at school—as he had said—so he thought himself quite an expert upon the subject, but the school described by James bore little resemblance to a modern establishment for the education of budding gentlewomen; it was a sort of cross between his own preparatory school and a convent, with a dash of Young Ladies' Seminary (as depicted by nineteenth-century novelists) thrown in for good measure.

Eleanor listened with interest. She believed James, of course, but it sounded different from what Holly had told her.

"You'll have lots of friends," said James.

"Yes," agreed Eleanor more cheerfully. "It will be nice to have lots of friends, and if I have a very special friend I shall tell her about you."

"No! Goodness, no!" exclaimed James in horrified tones. "Girls never talk about men. It isn't the right thing. It isn't done. Girls talk about—about hockey and—and things like that."

"I don't think you're right," said Eleanor, but she said it doubtfully for it seemed impossible that James should be wrong. "At Holly's school they talked a lot about their boy-friends. Holly had one, of course."

"Oh!" said James, somewhat taken aback.

"Holly has always had lots of friends. She's so pretty, isn't she?"

"Yes, she is."

"She still has lots of friends, but she likes Peter best. Some-

times she comes up to the nursery and talks to me about him and
she showed me his photograph. They love each other *very* much
but they can't be married because he's terribly poor. He hasn't a
bean," said Eleanor sadly.

"Oh!" said James again. He realised that the slang expression was a quotation, for Eleanor (who fed upon classical authors)
never used slang.

"She'll have to marry somebody else," said Eleanor. "It's just
like a story, isn't it?"

"Yes, I suppose so," said James. He felt annoyed with Holly,
which was odd, for James had no right to feel annoyed.

"It's like the girl in 'Auld Robin Gray.' I expect you know
the song, don't you? She thought her sweetheart had been drowned
at sea and all sorts of dreadful things happened and she had no
money to buy food for her father and mother, so she married
Robin Gray. Then Jamie came back, but it was too late! Poor
girl," said Eleanor sorrowfully. "Poor Jeanie, she cried and
cried."

James thought it was hard luck on Robin Gray, and said so.

"You aren't meant to think of his side of it," Eleanor pointed
out.

"But I do! I think Robin had a raw deal. He did what he
could for the wretched girl and all he got was a bag of misery."

Eleanor was surprised at James's vehemence, but she was
tired of the subject so she returned to a subject nearer her heart.
"When Holly was at school she was actually engaged—only se-
cretly, of course. The girls knew about it, but not the mistresses.
She had a ring and wore it on a ribbon round her neck."

"Oh!" said James.

"James," said Eleanor. "I don't suppose—I mean you don't

think you could—could give me a ring, do you? Just a curtain ring would do."

"No," said James firmly. He hesitated and then said, "No," again more firmly than before. The truth was he was suddenly beset with the most frightful temptation to accept this adoration which was being offered to him so sweetly and let it comfort his heart. He was so unfortunate in his love affairs! Rhoda was out of reach and Holly did not love him. If he married Holly it would be second best for both of them. Here was first and best. Here was somebody who would lay down her life for him and ask no greater boon. You could wait three years, said the tempter in James's ear. There must be no engagement, of course (that *would* be wrong). You need only say two words: "Perhaps, someday." That would be enough. You're lonely, and so is she, said the tempter. Why not let her go to school while you go to school yourself? Then, when you've learnt how to farm and she's learnt the ways of the world, you could marry her. You could take her home and love her and look after her. You could make certain that she's never lonely and frightened and unhappy again . . . and you would have Love beside you, real Love, not some other man's leavings. It would be easy, said the tempter persuasively. (The Steeles wouldn't mind, they don't care about Eleanor and your prospects are rosy.) Just one word will do, just say, "Perhaps." What's wrong with that?

But it *was* wrong. It would be positively wicked to bind this fairy creature, this Lady of Shalott, who had no idea of the world and had never seen a man except himself.

The grey eyes were gazing at James, they were very clear-sighted grey eyes. "We could wait, couldn't we?" said Eleanor softly. "We could wait and see. Perhaps when I'm grown-up you

will love me properly. Let's wait, James. I don't really want a ring
—it would be silly—and I promise not to tell anybody at all. We
could wait and see. Meantime I shall learn all sorts of useful things.
I shall learn how to cook, so that if we—"

"No, darling," said James. "No, *honestly*. It wouldn't be right.
You're my little sister and I shall always think of you like that.
Someday you'll marry somebody else—somebody nearer your own
age—and I shall come to the wedding, see? And, meantime if
there's anything you want, or if some snooping mistress finds a
pair of stolen gloves in your drawer, you must let me know and
I'll straighten out everything for you."

"I can write to you."

"No," said James. "No, you mustn't write. You won't be allowed to write to me from school. If anything goes wrong you
must write to Mamie—to Mrs Johnstone—and she'll tell me."

He put his arm round Eleanor and smiled down at her. Eleanor smiled back, but rather sadly.

"You'll understand someday," said James. "Someday, when
you're older."

Eleanor sighed. It was dreadful to be young.

Tea was finished and James had just risen to go when the
door opened and Holly appeared.

"James!" she exclaimed breathlessly. "They told me you were
here. Why didn't you let me know you were coming?"

"I never thought—" began James who was somewhat embarrassed at Holly's unexpected appearance and at her effusive
greeting.

"You never thought?"

"I mean I thought you would be here."

"Here, waiting for you, I suppose!" laughed Holly. "Really, James! Weeks pass and you never come near me and then you pop over and expect to find me waiting for you!"

"No, of course not. I mean I happened to have a free after-noon so I just took a chance."

"Well, never mind. I'm here now. What did you think of the Heddle's party? I told you it would be a slap-up show, didn't I?"

"You did—and it was," agreed James. "Much too slap-up for a country bumpkin like me."

"Nonsense!" cried Holly. "It was fun. I won oodles of money and enjoyed every moment of it. That dear little ball did exactly what I wanted every time. I only wish we had been playing for pounds as Mr Heddle suggested. Come on, James," she added taking his arm. "Come down to the drawing-room and have a glass of sherry and a nice chat."

They went out onto the landing and Eleanor followed.

"I'm afraid I can't stay," said James.

"You can't stay?"

"I'm afraid not, Holly. I've got to be back at six because the vet is coming to see a sick cow and I want to hear what he says about it."

"Nonsense! Of course you must stay. I want to talk to you." She smiled at him as she spoke in a very friendly way and for a moment James was tempted to abandon the sick cow and do as she suggested . . . but the temptation was only momentary.

"No—honestly," said James. "You see I want to learn all I can and this is such a good opportunity. I'll come another day instead."

Holly's face changed. She was really angry. Perhaps she had a right to be angry, thought James. He felt guilty and miserable

about Holly, for, although he had never been more than friendly
with her in word or deed, he had shilly-shallied about her in his
own mind. At the dance in the barn, for instance, he had been
on the point of asking her to marry him and of course Holly had
known—Holly was no fool—and that day by the river she had
given him every encouragement but again he had failed to seize
his opportunity.

"I'll come another day," repeated James uncomfortably.

"Perhaps I shan't be here another day," said Holly with a
brittle laugh. There were two spots of bright colour in her cheeks
and her eyes were sparkling.

All this time Eleanor had said nothing. She had listened intently to every word and, although she did not understand the
hidden undercurrent of the conversation, she felt the tension and
resented it. "Oh Holly!" cried Eleanor. "You mustn't be cross
with James—it isn't fair! He's been working terribly hard."

"I really have been busy," said James. "We've been draining
a meadow and I find I get awfully sleepy after working in the
open air. The days pass and . . ." he paused. It was all perfectly
true, but somehow or other it sounded like an excuse and a feeble
one at that.

"Goodness!" cried Holly. "What a fuss about nothing! Don't
bother to explain. I couldn't care less whether you come or not."

By this time all three of them were walking down the stairs
so it was easier for James to pretend that Holly was joking.

"Well, I care," said James, laughing. "I like seeing you. I
shall ring up next time I get a free afternoon and if you aren't
here, waiting for me, there'll be trouble."

"Cave-man stuff!" exclaimed Holly in mock alarm—but James
could tell from her tone that he was forgiven.

28

*J*OCK SUDDENLY made up his mind to go to Edinburgh
for the weekend. It was not often that he left Mureth, and he always left it regretfully and returned to it with joy, for he never
felt himself unless his foot was upon his own soil and he hated
the noise and bustle of town and the discomfort of town clothes.
But there was business to be done in Edinburgh; Jock wanted to
speak to his family solicitor about altering his will in James's
favour, and to find out the correct procedure to enable James to
assume the name of Johnstone in addition to his own. James had
decided to take the name at once, there seemed no sense in waiting (James Dering Johnstone sounded well, thought its prospective owner, and his aunt and uncle thought it sounded very well
indeed) but none of them had the faintest idea how the change
was to be effected.

"Mr MacGregor will know," said Jock, who had absolute confidence in the sagacity of his man-of-law. "I'll just put the whole
thing before him. And James had better come with me; it'll be
as well for Mr MacGregor to see James, and there's sure to be
papers to sign. You'll come too, Mamie. You'll enjoy it. We'll stay
at yon quiet hotel near the Braids and get our sleep."

Mamie refused the offer. She would not have let Jock go
alone but he would have his nephew as a companion, so there was
no need for her to go as well. Both Jock and James did all they
could to persuade her to accompany them; they tried to lure her

with the promise of a theatre on Friday night; she could go to a concert on Saturday afternoon; she could look at the shops. What woman could resist such a programme? Mamie resisted it. She did not want to go.

"What will you do, all by yourself?" asked Jock in amazement.

"I'll have a nice, quiet time," said Mamie, smiling. "Lizzie and I will do some cleaning, and we'll get Mrs Couper in to help. We'll have a good opportunity to get down to it properly with no meals to prepare."

"No meals!" exclaimed Jock. "You'll surely need meals!"

"Just eggs or something. An omelet and a cup of coffee doesn't take long to prepare."

Jock and James went off on Friday morning; they would return on Tuesday afternoon. It was a long weekend—much too long to suit Jock—but Mr MacGregor wanted to see them on Friday and again on Tuesday when the papers would be ready to sign, so there was no help for it, the ordeal must be endured. Willy Dunne drove them over to Drumburly and saw them into the train; he received implicit orders to meet the afternoon train on Tuesday and assured Mr Johnstone that he would be there.

The house felt very quiet after their departure, which was curious, really, for Jock and James were always out in the daytime so the house was no more quiet than on any other day. But the fact remained that it *felt* extremely quiet and although Mamie had been looking forward to a nice, quiet time she did not like it much. Even when Mrs Couper arrived the house felt quiet . . . but perhaps *quiet* was not the right word, thought Mamie, as she and Lizzie and Mrs Couper got down to the job of cleaning and polishing. Not quiet, thought Mamie (as the sound of chatter and clatter assailed her ears), not empty either; there must be some other word to describe the horrid vacuum which the departure of her men-folk had created in Mureth House.

Lizzie was a silent sort of person, but Mrs Couper liked to chatter as she worked and today she was labouring under a sense of grievance and was anxious for Lizzie's sympathy. Mamie did not want to hear the conversation, but she could not help overhearing bits of it. Mrs Dunne's name cropped up frequently, *"That Mrs Dunne!"* exlaimed Mrs Couper in tones of scornful derision. Apparently James had been giving old Mr Couper an occasional rabbit, because old Mr Couper's teeth were in such a parlous condition that he could not eat meat, and Mrs Dunne, becoming aware of the gifts, was consumed with jealousy.

It was just the sort of thing that started feuds in the cottages, thought Mamie rather miserably. James was not to blame. It was nice of James. He could not be expected to know that his kind action to old Mr Couper would create a storm. The storm was blowing up and very soon Mrs Dunne would pursue Mamie and say in honeyed accents, "Mistress Johnstone, could I speak to you for a moment?" and Mamie would have to listen whether she liked it or not.

They worked all morning and at lunch-time they knocked off and partook of boiled eggs and tea, for this was even more easy to prepare than an omelet and a cup of coffee. Mamie had hers upon a tray in the dining-room and she found it extremely dull. She began to wish she had gone to Edinburgh with the others . . . where were they and what were they eating, Mamie wondered.

In the afternoon the three of them got busy in the drawing-room and so well did they work that by tea-time it was finished and everything was back in its appointed place. The room looked beautiful; the furniture was shining brightly and there was a delightful smell of bee's-wax and turpentine in the air.

"It's nice, isn't it?" said Lizzie, looking round. "I like cleaning. You can see your work when you've done a bit of cleaning. You've done enough, Mrs Johnstone; you'll just sit down and take your tea in peace."

"We could do the pantry—"

"Not you," said Lizzie firmly. "Mrs Couper and me will have a go at the pantry. There's no need for you to bother."

Mamie agreed. She washed and changed and sat down to have her tea in peace . . . and immediately began wondering where Jock and James were at this moment and whether they were having a good tea.

Mamie was in the middle of her solitary meal when the door opened and Greta walked in. She had Topsy in her arms.

"Hullo," said Mamie cheerfully.

"Hullo," replied Greta.

Since the birth of her black child Greta had lost her fear of Mrs Johnstone and had become quite friendly. She had never expressed her thanks to Mrs Johnstone nor shown the slightest sign of gratitude, but as Mamie had not expected gratitude she was not disappointed. All Mamie had wanted was that Greta should not fly from her as if she were a leper with a bell, and this modest desire had been fulfilled.

"How is Topsy?" Mamie enquired.

Greta held out one grimy little hand and opening it displayed a black boot-button.

"Oh dear, it's Topsy's eye! Just give me my work basket, Greta."

Greta stood and watched while the eye was sewn firmly into place. "It's an operation," said Greta. "She'll need a bandage. Maybe she ought to stay in bed."

They discussed the matter seriously.

As Mamie sewed and chatted she began to wonder if there was anything she could do for Duggie. Duggie still fled at her approach. Perhaps Jock would be able to think of something to win Duggie's heart.

Mamie had just finished the operation and had returned Topsy to her mother's arms when the front door bell rang. Lizzie and Mrs Couper were still thumping about in the pantry—and were in no fit condition to appear—so Mamie would have to answer it herself.

Perhaps it was Holly, thought Mamie, as she crossed the hall. She hoped sincerely it was not Holly, for although she disliked being alone she would rather be alone than entertain Holly. She had the greatest difficulty in finding anything to say to Holly; they had nothing in common.

There was a girl standing upon the steps—not Holly but a stranger. At the bottom of the steps stood a motor-bicycle, a magnificent machine which glittered and gleamed in the afternoon sunshine. Mamie looked from the girl to the machine and then at the girl again. She had never seen a girl riding a motor-bicycle but obviously this girl did; obviously this girl had arrived at the door of Mureth House upon the motor-bicycle. The girl was tall and slender, she was wearing a lemon-coloured pullover and grey slacks and a duffel jacket open in front.

"Oh!" exclaimed the girl. "Is Mrs Johnstone—are you Mrs Johnstone?"

"Yes," replied Mamie. She said it a trifle vaguely for she was

thinking how very pretty the girl was . . . how more than pretty!
She looked intensely alive. Her blue eyes sparkled, and her hair
. . . Mamie had never seen such glorious hair before.

"I came over from Catterick," explained the girl. "It isn't terribly far and I had a splendid run. Blink went like smoke—that's
Blink," said the girl, smiling and pointing to her steed.

"Oh, good," said Mamie.

"What lovely country!"

"Yes," agreed Mamie. "Yes, it is."

"It was you who wrote to me, wasn't it?"

"I wrote to you!"

"Yes, I'm Rhoda Ware."

"Oh!" exclaimed Mamie in blank amazement.

Rhoda Ware nodded. "I only got your letter yesterday. It was
forwarded to me from home. Dad is awful about letters; he simply
won't forward them properly. He waits until there's a whole batch
of them and then puts them into a big envelope and sends them."

"I thought—" began Mamie.

"You thought I wasn't going to answer, but I only got it yesterday, you see."

"Yes, I see."

"It's awful of me to come like this without letting you know.
I should have written to you, of course. I tried to write—honestly
—but I didn't know what to say. I didn't know—what—to say,"
repeated Rhoda helplessly.

"Much better just to come," said Mamie, recovering herself.
"I hate writing letters, myself. It's so difficult to say exactly what
you mean, isn't it? And spelling is difficult, too—at least it is to
me. I expect my letter was full of mistakes, I wrote it in such a
hurry."

"It looked as if you were in a *tearing* hurry," said Rhoda with a sudden smile.

"If I hadn't written it in a hurry I wouldn't have written it at all."

"That would have been a pity."

Mamie nodded. She had regretted her letter several times since she had sent Duggie off to the post with it, but now she regretted it no longer. "Come in," she said. "I don't know why I'm keeping you standing on the doorstep. You'd like some tea, of course. Perhaps you'd like—"

Rhoda hesitated. "Is he in?" she asked anxiously. "Perhaps I won't come in if he's there—it might be—I mean I don't know whether—"

"He's gone to Edinburgh for the weekend," Mamie told her. "Of course he had no idea you were coming or he wouldn't have gone. Oh dear, isn't it a pity! But he'll be back on Tuesday. You'll see him on Tuesday. You can stay till he comes back, can't you?"

They were in the drawing-room by now. Mamie offered her unexpected guest a chair and began to pour out tea.

"You must think I'm mad," said Rhoda subsiding into the chair with awkward grace. "You must think I'm completely bats. Perhaps I am, really. I can't explain it, but the fact is when I got your letter it gave me such an awful shock . . ." She hesitated and then added, "I suppose you know the whole thing. You *must* know or you wouldn't have written."

"James told me quite a lot."

"You only know his side of it," said Rhoda quickly. "You probably think I'm a perfect beast. James wouldn't have *told* you that, but you probably think so all the same, and I don't blame you."

"I wrote to you," Mamie reminded her.

"Of course! What a fool I am! You wouldn't have written if . . ." She hesitated and looked thoughtful.

Mamie offered her a scone and some butter, rich creamy farm butter, and asked if she would like honey as well. It would be very interesting indeed to hear Rhoda's side of it but there was no sense in hurrying her.

"James and I knew one another when we were children," said Rhoda, buttering her scone and beginning to eat it in an absent-minded way. "We did things together, you know . . . all sorts of things. I was terribly fond of James but fond of him more as a brother than anything else. He was just like a brother, really. Then, when he came back from Malaya, he was just exactly the same only quite, quite different—if you see what I mean?" She paused and looked at her hostess doubtfully.

Mamie nodded. "Of course," she said.

Thus encouraged Rhoda continued, "We had both grown up but we seemed to have grown up to exactly the same height. We still understood each other."

"That's the important thing," said Mamie softly.

"Yes. Well, then he asked me to marry him. He asked me—beautifully. It was so perfect that I almost said yes. But—but I didn't say yes. There's my painting, you see. I do so love painting. I can't imagine life without it. I get absolutely lost in it. When I'm painting there's nothing else in the world. I expect it sounds silly, but—"

"No, it doesn't."

"You mean you understand?" asked Rhoda incredulously.

"I like music, you see," explained Mamie.

Rhoda was aware that this must be an understatement of

fact. She sighed with relief. "Oh," she said. "That makes things a *lot* easier. You'll realise that it wasn't because I didn't love James, but because I'm mad on painting. I had worked terribly hard and was beginning to be really worth while. It may sound stuck-up to say so, but it isn't any good telling you *anything* unless I tell you the truth. I'm good, and if I go on I shall be very good. I wanted that."

"Of course, but couldn't you—"

"No," said Rhoda firmly. "No, I couldn't. It must be one or the other—painting or James. If I married I could go on painting as a hobby but not as a career. It's different for a man. A man can do the things he's good at and be married too. A woman can't. I explained that to James and he understood. He's very under-standing. You see, if I married James he would want *all of me*— it would be no good if he didn't—and I couldn't give him all of me. We might have babies; it wouldn't be right to marry James and not have babies, and as a matter of fact I shouldn't *like* it. When I do a thing I like to do it thoroughly," declared Rhoda.

Mamie nodded again. She had realised that Rhoda was not the girl for half measures.

"I chose painting," continued Rhoda. "It wasn't entirely self-ish. It seemed to me a sort of duty. I'd been given this talent and I had no right to wrap it up in a napkin and bury it. That was how I saw it. So I said no to James. I went ahead with my paint-ing and I put James out of my head . . . or at least I tried to."

"You couldn't?" asked Mamie with interest.

"He kept coming into my head at odd moments; not when I was painting, but at other times . . . at night, mostly . . . some-times in a bus . . . sometimes if I happened to see the back of a man's head that looked like James's head. I thought it would

pass but it seemed to get worse instead of better. Then one day
in the studio I found I had stopped painting and was thinking
about James. That gave me a jolt," declared Rhoda. "It gave me
a terrific jolt. I decided I had better have a holiday so I went to
Catterick to stay with a friend . . . and then I got your letter."

Mamie refilled her guest's cup and put a large slab of fruit
cake upon her guest's plate. Her guest made no comment upon
these attentions.

"Your letter!" exclaimed Rhoda. "Goodness, it upset everything! It made a sort of earthquake inside me. I found I just
couldn't bear anyone else to have James."

"Of course not," said Mamie.

"It sounds awfully dog-in-the-mangerish, doesn't it?"

"No," said Mamie. "No, I don't think it was that. I think you
meant to marry James all the time."

Rhoda considered this. She found the idea extremely interesting and her opinion of the intelligence of her hostess rose to new
heights. "I wonder if you're right," said Rhoda slowly. "It would
explain a lot of things. You mean the idea that someday I would
marry James was latent in my subconscious mind."

Mamie would not have put it in those words, but it was exactly what she meant. "I'm sure it was," she said.

Rhoda took a large bite of cake and chewed it thoughtfully.

After a little silence they began to talk of other matters.
Rhoda knew Caroline, of course, for her home was at Ashbridge
not far from Vittoria Cottage; she had seen Caroline quite recently
and reported her as very happy indeed.

"Mr Shepperton is a dear," said Rhoda. "He really *is*. I'm
sure you'll like him. He's very quiet at first, but when you get
to know him you realise what a lot there is behind his reserve.

Leda hates him like poison, but you know what Leda is! I never could bear the sight of Leda," added Rhoda frankly.

Mamie made no comment upon this statement. She was not particularly fond of her niece, but she was sorry for her and thought she had been badly treated . . . and as it was Rhoda's brother who had treated her badly (breaking his engagement to Leda in an extremely high-handed manner and marrying the daughter of the Toothpaste King instead), Mamie felt it might be as well to change the subject to a safer one.

"I'm glad Caroline is so happy," she said.

"She deserves happiness," nodded Rhoda. "She's a perfect pet. I've always adored Mrs. Dering (I mean Mrs Shepperton, of course) and admired her too. Someday I'm going to paint her. You're like her, you know," said Rhoda, regarding her hostess with an impartial stare (exactly as if I were an orange on a plate or something, thought Mamie). "You have the same structure of skull and your colouring is the same, but of course you're much younger."

"Six years, that's all," said Mamie.

"Is that all!" exclaimed Rhoda in surprise. Mrs Shepperton had always seemed to Rhoda a thoroughly "grown-up person" and therefore of a different generation from herself, but there was something very young and innocent about Mrs Johnstone.

"Well, thank you awfully," said Rhoda, rising as she spoke. "Not only for the lovely tea, but even more for listening and understanding everything so marvellously."

"But you're not going!" exclaimed Mamie in surprise.

"I think I'd better. It may be difficult to find a room. Your nearest town is Drumburly, isn't it?"

"You can't go and stay at Drumburly!" cried Mamie in alarm.

"Isn't there a decent hotel?"

Mamie hesitated. Of course there was. No hotel could be more comfortable than the Steele Arms, and Mrs Simpson would welcome Rhoda with enthusiasm and treat her like a queen, but all the same Mamie knew that she could not let this girl—this lovely golden-haired creature—go to the Steele Arms. It just wasn't possible. The news of her arrival would sweep through Drumburly like a devouring fire and in half an hour everybody would be talking about her; wondering who she was, wondering why she had come. If she happened to walk along the High Street everybody would see her (out of the backs of their heads in some extraordinary manner, for they were much too polite to stare), and one Drumburlian would say to another, "My, she's bonny! She's a friend o' the Johnstones, ye ken. It's queer the Johnstones not having her at Mureth."

"Listen," said Mamie earnestly. "Why not just stay here with me?"

"It's awfully sweet of you, Mrs Johnstone, but I would rather—"

"And then you'll be here when James comes home."

"But that's just it!" cried Rhoda. "Don't you see I can't stay here, because James would feel—would feel he had to—to—"

"You can't go to the Steele Arms. People would think it odd, and it *would* be odd," declared Mamie.

"Odd! How could it be odd? It would be much more odd to arrive here out of the blue and stay here. I never thought of such a thing for a moment. It simply isn't done."

"It is, here," said Mamie firmly. "What isn't done, here, is letting your friends go and stay at a hotel."

Rhoda began to laugh.

"You *will* stay, won't you?" pleaded Mamie. "I'm all by myself and it's so dull for me. Please stay, Miss Ware."

"I shan't stay if you call me Miss Ware," declared Rhoda laughing helplessly.

"Rhoda," said Mamie smiling. "Please, Rhoda."

They went out together and found Blink still waiting patiently for his mistress. Rhoda unstrapped her suitcase and her painting outfit (she never went anywhere without paints and canvases and other paraphernalia connected with her art), Lizzie and Mrs Couper were summoned and the spare room was prepared.

29

*W*HEN MRS COUPER had helped Lizzie to make up the bed in the spare room and fill it with hot-water bottles she went home to prepare supper for her family. She was not surprised to find Mrs Bell and Daisy on the look-out for her, nor did the arrival of Mrs Dunne "to borrow a pickle of tea" astonish her in the least. She had barely reached her doorstep when Willy Bell appeared from the byre and Willy Dunne from the stable; and the group was further augmented by her husband and her father-in-law and by Wilson who had come down for Charlie's milk. Mrs Couper glanced round to see if they were all there before she began her tale and, as nobody was missing except Daniel Reid (who was raking his sheep upon the hill and therefore had missed all the excitement), she began her tale forthwith. Luckily Mrs Couper was unlike Lizzie and scorned to beat about the bush.

"It's a Miss Rhoda Ware," said Mrs Couper. "She's come over from Catterick on her motor-bike, unexpected-like, but she's having the best sheets with initials in the corner and pillow-cases to match."

The audience nodded gravely. Obviously Miss Rhoda Ware was an honoured guest.

"She's about medium height and nice and slim, and she's got the bonniest hair you ever saw. It put me in mind of yon king-cups in the marsh—gold as gold—all wavy and shining. Her eyes are blue like wild hyacinths and sort of twinkly. She's got nice features and a lovely skin. Her mouth is a bit painted up, but not her nails. She was wearing a yellow jersey and grey trousers—mind you, she looked awful nice in them."

"Trousers!" exclaimed Mrs Dunne.

"You wouldn't expect a lady to be wearing a kilt, riding a motor-bike," said Daisy sweetly.

"I wouldn't expect a lady to be riding a motor-bike," retorted Mrs Dunne."

Mrs Couper went on hastily for she was not going to have her story ruined by an argument between these two old antagonists.

"I went with her to the garage," continued Mrs Couper. "I offered to put the bike away myself, but she'd not have that at any price. She said she'd saved up to buy Blink—that's what she calls it—so it was 'terribly precious.' She talks very English, but not stuck-up like some, and she talks a lot—friendly and jokey as you please." Mrs Couper paused and looked round to make sure everybody was listening with all the ears they had. She lowered her voice and added, "Lizzie says her photy was standing upon Mr James's bedside-table."

There was a stir amongst the audience but nobody spoke.

"M'h'm," nodded Mrs Couper. "It was a wee snap, but Lizzie's sure it was her."

"Did you not go and look at it yourself?" enquired Mrs Bell and Daisy in one breath.

"It's not there, now."

"Not there!"

"He must have put it away," explained Mrs Couper. "He had it there when he first came—Lizzie saw it when she was dusting —and then, about two, three weeks ago, she saw it was gone."

"That was just about the time he started in with Miss Douglas!" exclaimed Daisy.

"Maybe she's come a bit late," commented Mrs Dunne with her usual amiable smile.

"Och, women!" said Willy Bell in disgust. "The photy might have got broken, mightn't it?"

The group began to melt, for it was a busy time of day; it melted all the more rapidly when Mrs Couper pointed to a slim figure coming up the path towards the steading and said, "That's her!" And thus it was that when Rhoda reached the little row of cottages there was not a creature to be seen.

Rhoda had come out for a walk before supper, she had come to look at Mureth Farm, at the barns and byres and cottages. James had told her a great deal about Mureth, but descriptions, however glowing, rarely do justice to their subject and Rhoda found Mureth more beautiful than she had dreamed. Those old stone barns—what a gorgeous colour they were! And the whitewashed cottages with their shining windows and neat little front gardens full of bright flowers! The view down the valley was wide and free: the winding river, the rounded, rolling hills. The air sparkled so that it was a positive joy to breathe . . . and over the whole place there was a stillness, a peaceful sort of feeling, it was like the feeling one has when the words of a benediction have been uttered and have died away.

Rhoda wandered about. She had been given complete freedom by her hostess. ("Go wherever you like," Mamie had said. "Come back when you feel inclined. We can have supper any time, so don't hurry.") She had been given the freedom of Mureth and she made the most of it. She took out her notebook and made a few sketches—lightning sketches of this and that.

Presently Rhoda noticed a woman come out of one of the cottages and look round, but the woman took no interest in Rhoda, none whatever. How queer, thought Rhoda. In a little place like this, so isolated and cut off from the outside world, one would imagine a stranger might cause some interest to the inhabitants! Rhoda had expected some of the farm-workers to speak to her, perhaps to ask who she was and what she wanted, but obviously Mureth was not interested in strange young women.

There were few evenings when a fire was not welcome at Mureth House. Mureth stood high and even in summer the nights were cool. On this particular evening a particularly fine fire of logs burnt in the drawing-room grate. Mamie had seen to it herself, for she had a rooted conviction that English people are tender plants and she was determined that her guest should be as comfortable as possible and should find Mureth perfect in every respect.

The window was uncurtained but the light was fading, so an electric lamp stood beside the piano. Mamie was playing. When she raised her eyes and looked towards the fire she could see the back of Jock's big chair and one long, slender leg, clad in a silk stocking, stretched out sideways. The only other evidence of her guest's presence in the room was a thin, blue spiral of smoke, rising in the still air.

Mamie loved music as Rhoda loved painting, she could play for hours, losing herself completely in the melody which flowed from beneath her fingers. When she played for Jock she played tunes that she knew he liked, but tonight she was playing for herself and had chosen the composer whose music spoke to her heart and satisfied her best. It was Edvard Grieg. Perhaps the reason for her love of Grieg was the fact that his music had been written amongst the hills, because it seemed to express the moods of nature. It was wild like the storms of winter and brilliant like the clear spring sunshine, it ran sweetly like the burns and its elfin merriment was like the laughter of kelpies.

The music was in full flood when suddenly Mamie remembered her guest . . . perhaps she was boring her guest! Her fingers faltered and there was silence in the room.

"Go on," said a sleepy voice. "I'm not musical, worse luck, but that seems to me a very pleasant noise."

"You're not musical?"

"Not really. Unless I like it very much I prefer silence."

"Perhaps that means you *are* musical," said Mamie doubtfully.

"I don't think so, I don't always like the things I ought to like, you see. I liked *that* because it made pictures for me . . . which isn't the right reason for liking it."

"It's quite a good reason—"

"But not the best."

Mamie considered the point. "What sort of pictures?" she asked.

"Hills and clouds," said Rhoda dreamily. "Rivers and waterfalls and little gnomes dancing in the moonlight . . ."

"That's what it means," Mamie told her. "Grieg's music is all pictures. He was a Norwegian but descended from Scots ancestors and I like to think he owes something to his Scots descent. It's just my own idea of course but somehow his music seems to fit Mureth as if he knew this part of the world and loved it."

There was a little silence and then Rhoda said, "There are no great Scotch composers, are there?"

"Some of the songs are beautiful."

"Sing," said Rhoda. "I'm sure you sing—you've got a lovely speaking voice—but don't sing 'Annie Laurie.' It's a heavenly song but it ought to be sung by a man. It always sounds so ridiculous to hear a woman declaring that for bonnie Annie Laurie she would lay her down and dee. You know, Mamie," continued Rhoda (who already had asked and received permission to address her hostess in this familiar way), "you know I think there's only one thing that sounds sillier than a woman singing a man's song."

"A man singing a woman's song! Oh dear!" exclaimed Mamie, beginning to laugh. "Oh Rhoda! Oh goodness?"

"Out with it!" demanded Rhoda. "Tell me all and tell it quickly."

"It was a terrible thing, really," said Mamie, trying to control herself. "We had a young minister at Drumburly while Mr Sim was away for his holiday and Jock said we must have him to dinner. He was dreadfully shy, and neither Jock nor I are good at polite conversation, so after dinner we suggested music. He had a really beautiful voice, a light tenor and very well trained, but when he stood up and sang 'My Mother Bids Me Bind My Hair' . . ."

"He didn't!" cried Rhoda.

"I—disgraced—myself," said Mamie dissolving into helpless mirth.

Rhoda chuckled delightedly. "It's almost too good to be true."

"I know," agreed Mamie, wiping her eyes. "The sad part is it's such a lovely song and I used to sing it often—Jock likes it —but now I can't sing it at all."

When they had finished laughing Mamie came over to the

fire and heaped on more logs. "This fire burns better with a little coal," said Mamie. "But unfortunately we can't get coal now, because, since it was nationalised, all the coal has turned into black stones. The cellar is full of them. Jock says he's going to make a rockery when he can find the time."

"I think I shall like Jock," said Rhoda thoughtfully.

Mamie smiled. She felt pretty certain that Jock would like Rhoda; nobody could say Rhoda wore a disguise. "But I hope I'm not talking about him too much," said Mamie in sudden alarm.

"Why shouldn't you talk about Jock? I expect I shall talk about James if . . ." she paused.

"If what?"

"If he gives me the right to talk about him," said Rhoda uncertainly.

There was a little silence.

"Supposing he's changed his mind," said Rhoda. "I mean you said in your letter . . . I mean there's Holly. It's a silly name, isn't it? I've been wondering ever since I got your letter what Holly is like."

"She's *very* pretty," replied Mamie truthfully. "She's tall and slim, with dark hair—"

"Are they just friends or—or—?"

"I expect he's kissed her," said Mamie in an absent-minded sort of tone, as if it did not matter much one way or the other. "Yes, I'm pretty sure . . . at the dance, you know. I saw them go out together. It was such a lovely night and the moon was shining. Holly is the sort of girl men kiss."

"Oh, she is, is she?" said Rhoda, struggling to be calm.

"You know what I mean," said Mamie.

Rhoda knew exactly what Mamie meant. "She's got oomph,

has she?" said Rhoda a trifle bitterly. "She's got what it takes. James has kissed her—in the moonlight, I suppose—and probably more than once."

"You can't blame him," Mamie pointed out in tones of cold reason. "He's quite free, isn't he?"

"Quite free," agreed Rhoda. "Oh, goodness, what a fool I've been!"

"But it will be all right now," said Mamie comfortingly; for, having got Rhoda into this condition and made certain that she really and truly wanted to marry James, Mamie felt that a little comfort was indicated. "It will be all right now you're here. If you're quite certain you want James."

"Do you think I would do?"

"Do?"

"For James," explained Rhoda. "*You* know what it entails being a farmer's wife and I should hate to take on anything I couldn't manage. James intends to be a farmer and when he's finished learning about it he'll want a farm of his own."

(So she didn't know, thought Mamie, looking at her.)

"That's what he wants, isn't it?" asked Rhoda.

"He has decided quite definitely to be a farmer," said Mamie, choosing her words with care.

"Could I learn to be a farmer's wife?"

"I think you could do anything you really want to."

"You mean anybody could?"

"No, I mean you could."

Rhoda had a feeling this was true. "You'd help me, wouldn't you?" she said.

"Of course I would!" cried Mamie. "I'd do *anything*. Jock will help James and I'll help you—not that you'll need much help.

There's nothing in it at all. I mean if it was difficult I couldn't do it, and I seem to manage all right, so you see there's nothing whatever to worry about. No, I'm not worrying about that."

"You *are* worrying about something?" asked Rhoda.

"Will your father mind?" enquired Mamie. "Will he be disappointed if you give up your painting?"

"Mind! He'll be delighted. Dad thinks my painting is just a hobby. He's very old-fashioned; he thinks marriage is the proper career for a woman and he's terribly fond of James. James's mother will be pleased too. Everybody will be pleased," declared Rhoda unenthusiastically. "Everybody will think it 'most suitable.' That will be one of the hardest things to bear."

These sentiments were so unexpected and so different from Mamie's own that she could scarcely believe her ears. She thought of her own struggles to marry Jock and how she had wept and prayed in secret before she had been able to marry him in the teeth of her parents' opposition and open displeasure.

"Don't you understand?" asked Rhoda in surprise, for Mamie had understood everything else quite easily. "Don't you understand, Mamie? If James hadn't a brass farthing and everybody was dead against him I should go ahead like a steam engine—nothing on earth would keep me from marrying James."

"But as it is?"

"Oh well, you can't have everything absolutely perfect," said Rhoda, smiling at Mamie's troubled face. "Not in this world, you know. So, if James will give me a second chance, I'll marry him in spite of everybody's approval."

30

THE FOLLOWING morning was Saturday, of course. Mamie had some shopping to do in Drumburly and she was delighted when her guest asked permission to accompany her. She did the honours with pride, pointing out Drumburly Tower and retailing its history, pointing out the old Town Hall with its statue of Robert the Bruce.

Rhoda was suitably impressed with the beauty of the country and of the little grey town; she did not say much but what she said was exactly right and her hostess was increasingly pleased with her.

"I'm afraid I'll be some time," said Mamie, as they parked the car. "You won't be bored, will you?"

"I'm never bored," replied Rhoda smiling. "Or at least never bored by myself. Sometimes people bore me, but not often. I'll stray about and do a few sketches, so don't hurry."

Rhoda strayed about Drumburly and found a good deal to interest and amuse her. The place looked foreign to Rhoda's eyes and this surprised her for she had not crossed the sea. The people looked foreign too, and, from chance remarks which fell upon her ears as she wandered up the High Street, they seemed to be talking a foreign language.

The bridge was lovely. She transferred its graceful arches to her notebook in a few firm strokes and indicated a couple of old men who were leaning upon the parapet gazing down into the

flowing water. While she was thus engaged she was accosted by
a third old man, who was anxious to give her a great deal of information about the subject of her sketch. Rhoda was quite ready
to listen; she listened intently but she could not understand a word
he said. He tried again, several times, but it was no use. When it
became evident that their efforts to communicate with one another were hopeless they smiled and parted: he with the sorrow-
ful conviction that the bonny young lady was "wanting," she with
a strong feeling that if she was going to be domiciled in this part
of the world something must be done. I suppose I could learn it,
thought Rhoda. Mamie said I could do anything if I really wanted
to . . . and so musing she walked back to the Steele Arms where
she was due to meet Mamie for a mid-morning cup of coffee.

Curiously enough Mamie had seen nobody she knew in Drumburly so she was unable to talk about her guest and broadcast the
news of her arrival, but of course there was Mrs Simpson at the
Steele Arms. No sooner had Mamie and Rhoda sat down at a
small table in the lounge and ordered coffee than Mrs Simpson
appeared in person, with beaming smiles, and whisked them away
to her private parlour to have their "elevenses" with her. They
chatted of various matters. Rhoda was informed that it was here,
in this very room, that Mamie had received an offer of marriage
from Jock and accepted it. This made the parlour even more interesting which was saying a good deal, for it was interesting in
itself, being of an unusual shape and full of fine old furniture.

Mrs Simpson invited Rhoda to look out of the window, so
Rhoda knelt upon the broad window-seat and leant over. The river
ran below, washing the thick stone walls of the ancient house; beyond the river was rolling country and trees and hills. There were
always hills, thought Rhoda; whether you were looking at a barn

or a bridge or a piece of undulating land your eyes came to rest upon a lovely sweep of hills against the blue wash of the sky. If she left here and never came back—which was a possibility she was bound to face—she would always remember Drumburly and Mureth set in this casket of hills.

It was now time to go home, so they said good-bye to Mrs Simpson and went to get the car. Mamie was even more delighted with Rhoda than before; she had been quite perfect with Mrs Simpson, neither too reserved nor too familiar, but just her natural self. It was obvious that Rhoda did not suffer from the foolish shyness which was the bane of Mamie's existence; she could "talk to people" like Jock.

After lunch Rhoda went out by herself; she wanted to see the river of which she had heard so much. James loved everything about Mureth but he loved the river best and Rhoda was prepared to love it too.

It was pleasant to feel free. Sometimes when you stayed with people they insisted upon entertaining you, filling every moment of your day so that you felt "cribbed, cabined and confined," so that you felt bound to reciprocate and be more appreciative of everything than was natural. At Mureth you could do as you liked. You could go out or stay in, you could talk or be silent without constraint. Mamie was a companion after Rhoda's own heart. She's exactly my age, thought Rhoda, as she wandered down the river-bank, pausing to sketch a tree or to catch, with a few firm strokes of her pencil, the curve of clear water round a jagged piece of rock.

Mamie and Rhoda had intended to have more music that evening but they found too much to say. It was amazing how much they had to say to one another for their lives had been so different

—Mamie's life had been quiet and sheltered, Rhoda's had been gay—but the fact was they were interested in one another and they were both completely sincere. Rhoda chattered freely about the Art School and about the strange people she had met, but she did not monopolise the conversation by any means; she was ready to listen as well as talk and she encouraged her hostess to describe the local people. She heard all about the extraordinary party at Tassieknowe and about James's adventures upon the hill chasing the "sheep-lifters."

"Did you have a nice walk this afternoon?" Mamie wanted to know.

"Lovely," nodded Rhoda. "What are those stones for, Mamie? There's a big half-circle of stones in a meadow near the river. They look important, somehow, but I can't see any reason for them being there."

"That's the Stone Circle. It was made by Sun-worshippers."

"Sun-worshippers!" exclaimed Rhoda. "But how marvellous— a sort of Stonehenge on your own doorstep! Tell me about it."

"Jock could tell you much better than I can," said Mamie, who felt unable to explain the peculiarities of the circle herself.

"Are people here interested in it?" Rhoda asked.

"Some of them are. They call it the Stanes. Old Mrs Couper's mother used to talk about going to kirk as 'going to the Stanes' and Jock says it was because that was the old name for a place of worship and it was handed down from parent to child from the days of the Stone Circles."

"How amazing!" said Rhoda in a low voice. She slid on to the floor as she spoke and producing her notebook laid it upon Mamie's knee. "There's one of the Stanes," she added looking up and smiling.

It was a very rough sketch—a few firmly delineated strokes and some shading—but in spite of that it was quite recognisable.

"Rhoda!" exclaimed Mamie in astonishment.

"You like it?"

"It's wonderful! I don't know how you do it."

Rhoda laughed. "Knack and hard work is the answer. As a matter of fact it's a very attractive subject. You see the idea, don't you? Here's the big stone in the foreground and the old gnarled thorn-tree, and in the distance that lovely sweep of hills. I should like to paint it tomorrow afternoon unless you want me for something else."

Mamie was pleased that her guest should have found something to interest her and it was arranged that they would go to Drumburly Kirk in the morning and Rhoda would paint in the afternoon. If the picture were not finished it could be finished on Monday afternoon (not on Monday morning as Mamie suggested because the shadows would be different).

Having settled this to their mutual satisfaction Mamie turned over a page of the notebook and uttered an exclamation of surprise.

"Oh, that's just a man," said Rhoda. "He came along the river while I was sketching so I bagged his back view. It seemed a very distinctive sort of back. I never saw his front."

"It's Willy Bell!" There was no doubt about it—none at all—although the sketch consisted of a few lines.

"Willy Bell," said Rhoda nodding. "It's a nice name. I should have liked to talk to Willy Bell but he took no interest in me. Cows are what interest Willy Bell, not strange females. It's funny how none of the people here take the slightest interest in me. You'd think in a quiet place like this—"

"But they do, they're madly interested."

"No, darling, I'm sorry but you're quite, quite wrong. Yesterday afternoon when I went up to the farm there was nobody about at all, and then a woman came out of one of the cottages . . . that's her," said Rhoda flicking over the pages of her notebook and pointing to a rotund back bending to pick up something from the ground.

"Mrs Dunne," murmured Mamie with awe.

"All right, if you say so. It was Mrs Dunne. She looks well-fed, anyhow. She stood for a moment outside the cottage door and looked round and her eyes passed over me as if—as if I were the pump," said Rhoda seriously.

Mamie began to laugh.

"Don't laugh," said Rhoda trying to assume a wounded expression. "Don't laugh, Mamie. It was rather galling. I mean I've always imagined I was quite a pleasant sight, or at least an interesting sight, but no, not to Mrs Dunne. Having viewed the prospect, including the pump, with a slight air of boredom she turned her back and stooped down—as you see."

"She could see you out of her back," declared Mamie, laughing immoderately. "Everybody in Mureth is talking about you—talking about nothing else."

31

RHODA HAD never been to a Presbyterian Kirk before. It was surprisingly different from an English church. Everything was different: the building, the service, the singing and the people. Even the atmosphere was different. She was impressed by the simplicity of the service—it was moving—and she was further impressed by the fierce sincerity of the minister and by his extraordinarily well-reasoned sermon. Rhoda had quite a good brain (and knew it) but even she found the sermon "a bit stiff," for Mr Sim's theme was the ethical interpretations of history and the varying interactions of the temporal and spiritual powers . . . and as Rhoda looked round at her fellow-worshippers she could not help wondering whether they were taking it all in or whether their rapt expressions were due to preoccupation with domestic affairs.

Lizzie had come with them in the car. She sat at the end of the Mureth pew dressed very neatly in a brown tweed coat and skirt. She looked quite different from her usual self—even her face looked different—and Rhoda decided if she had met Lizzie in the street attired in her Sabbath garments she would not have known her. Lizzie was sitting like a statue, anyone would think she was absorbing every word, but if that were the case she was a great deal more intelligent than Rhoda had thought.

The building was full of interesting faces, faces of character, rugged and individualistic. Rhoda's fingers itched for a pencil . . . and then she remembered where she was and collected her wandering thoughts and fixed her eyes firmly upon the black-clad figure in the high pulpit.

As usual, after the service, the congregation met and talked in the kirk-yard, so at last Mamie had the pleasure of introducing her beautiful guest to her friends. Various people enquired for Jock and were informed that he and James had gone to Edinburgh on business but were coming home on Tuesday. Lady Steele was there with Eleanor, and Mamie was delighted to find that her ladyship was as friendly as ever and obviously bore her no grudge for her outspoken remarks.

"Eleanor is going to school next term," said Lady Steele. "We went over to see the school and it is quite delightful. The girls seemed very pleasant, they chatted to Eleanor in a friendly way."

"They said they were glad I was coming," declared Eleanor with a surprised inflexion in her voice. "Wasn't it nice of them, Mrs Johnstone?"

Mamie agreed that it was and added that she was sure Eleanor would enjoy herself at school—but she did not feel quite as confident about this as she would have liked.

"Where's Holly?" said Lady Steele, looking round. "Oh, there she is, talking to Dr Forrester! Wait a moment, Mamie, I must get her and introduce her to Miss Ware. Holly knows Miss Ware's brother."

Mamie was not particularly anxious for the introduction to take place but there was no possibility of escape. She waited while Lady Steele fetched her niece and introduced her to Rhoda.

"How lovely to meet you!" exclaimed Holly with a dazzling smile. "Of course I know Derek—and I've heard about you, too. James mentioned you one day when we were having coffee together at the Steele Arms. You live quite near his home, don't you?"

"Quite near," replied Rhoda gaily. "James and I have known one another all our lives."

"I expect James has told you about me."

"No, I don't think so—"

"How funny!" laughed Holly. "I thought perhaps he might have told you he was teaching me to fish. I'm afraid I'm not a very intelligent pupil but he's extraordinarily patient with me."

"I think we ought to go," put in Mamie, but nobody took any notice of the interruption.

"Where is James?" asked Holly. "I was so surprised when I didn't see him in church."

"Oh, didn't you know he'd gone to Edinburgh?" exclaimed Rhoda raising her eyebrows in astonishment.

"How silly of me!" Holly declared. "Of course I knew he was going, but I didn't realise it was *this* weekend. The cow must be better, I suppose."

Rhoda gazed at her.

"Yes," said Holly, nodding. "He was terribly worried about the cow. He came over to see me on Wednesday, but I was out when he arrived and he couldn't stay long because of the cow. I was frightfully disappointed, of course."

"Of course," agreed Rhoda, sympathetically.

"It was really very naughty of James not to let me know he was coming—contrary to all rules and regulations," declared Holly laughing a trifle ruefully.

"Perhaps it was a sudden impulse," suggested Rhoda.

"Oh, yes," nodded Holly. "He was so funny about it. He said

he never thought for a moment that I wouldn't be there, waiting for him."

There was a moment's silence.

"But how odd," continued Holly, with a puzzled frown. "How *very* odd of James to dash off to Edinburgh just before you arrived!"

Rhoda laughed gaily. "Oh, but you see I was naughty, too," declared Rhoda. "I never told James I was coming. It was quite unexpected."

"A sudden impulse, perhaps," suggested Holly sweetly.

The conversation took place in a circle of friends. It seemed a very amiable conversation. Both young women were gay and smiling and it must be admitted that, standing there together with the golden sunshine upon them, they were a most attractive sight. Rhoda's fairness was set off by the dark beauty of Holly so that each gained rather than lost by comparison with the other; but all the same Mamie was uneasy—she was even a little scared —so she cut in with an abruptness quite foreign to her gentle, self-effacing nature.

"We really *must* go," declared Mamie. "It's nearly lunch-time."

"Come and have tea tomorrow," suggested Lady Steele. "The girls could have a nice chat, couldn't they?"

"No," said Mamie. "Not tomorrow, I'm afraid."

"What about Wednesday?"

"No," said Mamie, struggling to find some excuse. "Thank you awfully, but I'm afraid—I mean we're going to be very busy all this week . . ." and with that she swept Rhoda into the car and drove off without more ado.

There was no opportunity to talk on the way home for Lizzie was with them, sitting in the back seat, and with Lizzie there it was impossible to discuss any important matters. But Lizzie was no bar to thought and Mamie was full of uncomfortable thoughts. Mamie had been rude to Lady Steele. Other people could refuse invitations gracefully, could think up a white lie on the spur of the moment, but Mamie was incapable of this social accomplishment . . . and she had been scared and flustered which had made her even more gauche than usual. But the regrettable fact that she had been rude to Lady Steele was not the only uncomfortable thought which was bothering Mamie. She glanced at Rhoda from time to time and wondered what she was thinking of her new aquaintance. Rhoda's face was turned away, she was looking out of the side window, but Mamie was aware that her guest was not her usual cheerful, carefree self.

Having said nothing about Miss Douglas during the drive home it was a little difficult to broach the subject, and it was not until they were halfway through lunch—for which Rhoda seemed to have little appetite—that any reference was made to the meeting in the kirk-yard.

"I'm frightened," said Rhoda suddenly. "Mamie, I'm simply terrified. I think I'll go back to Yorkshire tomorrow."

"Oh, Rhoda!"

"Don't you see? James may have changed his mind. You can't be certain he hasn't changed his mind. You aren't certain, Mamie."

Mamie hesitated.

"You see! You can't say you're certain, can you? And if he comes back and finds me here, waiting for him! Oh hell!" exclaimed Rhoda, getting up and walking over to the window. "Why did I come—pursuing him like this? Why didn't I write or something?"

"But Rhoda, why suddenly—"

"Because of that girl. You were wrong about her, Mamie. She isn't the sort of girl men kiss, she's the type men fall for in a big way. She's a traffic-stopper, that's what she is . . . and you heard what she said, didn't you? It was naughty of James not to tell her he was coming to see her . . . and he expected to find her waiting for him . . . and James is teaching her to fish . . . and she isn't an intelligent pupil but he's extraordinarily patient with her!"

"They did go fishing together," said Mamie doubtfully. She would have liked to comfort Rhoda (as she had done before) to tell her not to worry and to assure her that everything would be all right; but she, too, had been alarmed at the possessive manner in which Holly had spoken of James.

"I shall go tomorrow," declared Rhoda. "It would put James in an impossible position if I were here waiting for him. You see that, don't you, Mamie? I simply must go. You can tell him I've been here—no, you mustn't tell him. You mustn't mention my name."

"Rhoda, listen—"

"No, darling, I couldn't bear to listen. I know what you're going to say. I'll go back to Catterick tomorrow and I'll write. I'll write him a friendly letter and then he can do as he likes, can't he? He won't feel bound to—to—"

"Don't go tomorrow," said Mamie. "You can wait until Tuesday morning."

Rhoda was silent.

"Please, Rhoda," urged Mamie, rising and going over to join

Rhoda at the window. "Do *please* stay till Tuesday morning. They won't be home till tea-time and it's so lovely for me to have you . . . and there's the picture, remember; you said you couldn't finish it in one afternoon."

Rhoda put her arm round Mamie's waist and they stood there together, looking out. "All right," said Rhoda huskily. "I'll stay and finish the picture and give it to you, only you must promise not to show it to James. Oh, Mamie, haven't I made a hash of everything."

Rhoda spent Sunday afternoon at the Stanes, painting industriously, and returned in a more cheerful frame of mind. This was because the picture was coming along even better than she had hoped. In all Arts there are occasions when the human tool is made an instrument of some Higher Power; such visitations are infrequent, alas, but when they take place they are glorious indeed. Rhoda experienced such a visitation this afternoon—her veins became full of ichor so that she could do nothing wrong. Somebody guided her brush and she surrendered herself to guidance, freely and gladly.

Rhoda painted until the shadows began to alter and then packed up and walked back to Mureth on air.

"Look," said Rhoda, putting her unfinished canvas upon the drawing-room mantelpiece and standing back to view it from a distance. "Look, Mamie, I've got the masses blocked in."

Mamie was disappointed. She was aware that the picture was not finished, of course, but she could see no sense in it at all. To her untutored eyes it was a mess—a mess of bright colours which bore little or no resemblance to the subject it was intended to represent. Mamie had liked the sketch much better, she had seen promise in the sketch. She tried to hide her opinion of the picture but without success for Mamie was not versed in the art of subterfuge.

"You wait," said Rhoda cheerfully. "I shouldn't have let you see it until it was finished. It was idiotic of me, but I forgot you knew nothing about painting." And so saying she removed her canvas and carried it away.

That evening was passed very pleasantly with music from *Peer Gynt* (which is picture-music *par excellence* and therefore eminently suitable for the entertainment of a painter) and soon after ten o'clock they went upstairs to bed. Mamie made certain that her guest was comfortable and supplied with a book and biscuits and a hot-water bottle, and having said good night she went along the passage to her own room.

This was when Mamie missed Jock most, for this was the time they always chatted and discussed the events of the day. She wondered if Jock were missing her. She wondered what sort of room they had given Jock—a quiet room she hoped. She wondered if the bed was comfortable.

Mamie sighed and began to brush her hair. Jock often brushed her hair; he liked doing it and did it well, with smooth firm strokes. It was because Jock liked brushing it that Mamie had never had her hair cut short like other women.

At this moment the telephone-bell rang and Mamie (picking up the receiver of the extension which stood beside her bed) heard Jock's voice.

"Mamie!" said Jock's voice. "I just thought I'd give you a ring and have a wee chat. It's not too late, is it?"

"Oh, Jock—no, not a bit too late!"

"The fact is I've been showing James the town and we've just got back. Are you in bed?"

"I'm in the middle of brushing my hair."

"Give it a hundred strokes, mind."

"I'm missing you frightfully," Mamie told him.

"Good," laughed Jock. "It wouldn't be fair if I was doing all the missing."

"So you're glad I'm unhappy!"

"You're not really unhappy, are you?"

"No, of course not."

"Not lonely?" asked Jock anxiously.

"Not a bit lonely. I've got a visitor, she's—"

"You've got what?"

"I'll tell you on Tuesday," Mamie said. She had just remembered that Rhoda did not want her presence to be made known to James, and, for all Mamie knew, James might be standing beside Jock at the telephone. "I'll tell you all about everything on Tuesday. I suppose you've got things fixed with Mr MacGregor?"

"On the way to being fixed. Apparently it'll take a while to put through, but Mr MacGregor will come down to Mureth for a weekend and finish the business. You'll see Willy Dunne remembers to fetch us?"

"Of course!"

"How's Mrs Dunne?" asked Jock, and Mamie could tell by his voice he was smiling.

"It's all very well for you to grin like that," she declared. "You think it doesn't matter when they fight. Mrs Dunne ran after me this morning and—"

"And wanted to speak to you for a moment?"

"Yes, but, Jock—".

"Why do you let her worry you! Tell her you're busy."

"I can't. She sort of hypnotises me. It's about the rabbits."

"Rabbits?"

"She's cross because James sometimes gives old Mr Couper a rabbit. He's only got six teeth, you know, and—"

Jock was laughing now. "De'il tak' the auld besom!" he exclaimed. "Tell her when she's ninety and has six teeth in her head she'll get rabbits, too."

This conversation comforted Mamie. She had been worrying about the Dunne v. Couper feud over James's rabbits, but now she saw how silly it was. She could not tell Mrs Dunne exactly what Jock had said, but she could mention Mr Couper's teeth—or lack of teeth—and pour oil upon the troubled waters. Jock was wise; he was well balanced; you could lean upon him as if he were a rock.

She lay in bed and thought about Jock. It was wonderful to have Jock. She wanted everybody to have the same sort of happiness which had been granted to her and Jock; she wanted James and Rhoda to have it. What a pity Rhoda had made up her mind to go! Mamie understood her reason perfectly, but it was a pity all the same. Rhoda had said she would write, but a letter was a poor medium of expression. A letter was unsatisfactory—cold—capable of misinterpretation. If only Rhoda would stay and meet James and talk to him Mamie felt certain that all would be well. All *must* be well, thought Mamie. There was no comparison between the two girls, they were as different as night from day. Night and day, thought Mamie, that's what they are! Rhoda is like sunshine. Oh God, please let it be Rhoda!

With Rhoda, James would be safe. They would live at

Boscath, across the river; she and Jock could keep an eye on them and see that everything went smoothly. They could meet and help one another—four people in harmony! Later there might be more than four people! There might be a baby with golden hair and blue eyes—a little son—so that Mureth, and all it stood for, would be safe for another generation.

But if James married Holly it would be very different. Lady Steele had said Holly never stuck to anything for long and Mamie was aware that, unless you happened to enjoy a quiet life for its own sake, sticking power was an essential ingredient in the wife of a farmer. Holly would soon tire of the country, she would become discontented and miserable. And Mamie knew that Holly disliked her—and despised her—so it would be difficult to help Holly. She could never drop in at Boscath if Holly were mistress there . . . and last, but by no means least, Jock did not like Holly.

Oh dear, thought Mamie, turning over restlessly. If only one could arrange people's lives! If only I could persuade Rhoda to stay! If only she and James could meet—unexpectedly—suddenly—without thinking about it beforehand!

She knew it was hopeless, of course. Rhoda was determined to go and Rhoda was a girl with a mind of her own. Nothing Mamie could do or say would alter Rhoda's decision.

32

O n MONDAY morning Mamie suggested that Rhoda might like to go round the cottages and be properly introduced to the inhabitants of Mureth, but Rhoda refused politely. She explained that as she did not want James to be told of her visit to Mureth it was better that she should not be seen. She did not believe Mamie's assertion that everybody in the place knew all about her already—she simply did not believe it. Mrs Couper had seen her—and Lizzie, of course—but neither of them was interested in her; and nobody else had looked at her nor shown the slightest sign of being aware of her existence.

Mamie left it at that. Perhaps it was just as well. She, herself, had promised faithfully not to tell James of Rhoda's visit but she could not prevent other people from mentioning it to him, could she? If James heard that Rhoda had been at Mureth in his absence . . . yes, thought Mamie. I wonder what he will do.

Monday afternoon was beautifully sunny and warm and, as this was to be Rhoda's last day at Mureth, Mamie packed a picnic tea and went down with her to the Stanes. She was anxious not to miss a moment of Rhoda's company and it would be interesting and instructive to see Rhoda at work upon the picture. She would not bother Rhoda. She would take a book with her and read while Rhoda painted.

Rhoda painted and Mamie sat and read with her back against a warm mossy stone. There were cows in the meadow but they remained near the river. Some of them were standing in the water, swishing their tails to keep off flies. It was very peaceful.

Every now and then Mamie raised her eyes and looked at Rhoda, who had erected her portable easel and stood before it with her palette and her brush, painting easily and surely. There was no hesitancy in her movements and she looked completely happy and absorbed. If Mamie had ever doubted Rhoda's assertion that she was a good painter, and was on the way to being very good indeed, she would have doubted it no longer. You had only to look at her, thought Mamie.

And what a pleasure it was to look at her! How perfectly beautiful she was! She had donned a butcher-blue overall for her work and the colour suited her admirably, showing off her lovely fair skin and the glory of her hair. The overall was smeared with paint of various hues and colours but oddly enough this seemed to add rather than to detract from the good effect.

Mamie rarely spent a thoroughly lazy afternoon, for there was always something to do, something that needed doing, so today was a very special sort of day—a holiday. I shall never forget this, thought Mamie. Even if she goes away and I never see her again . . .

They had tea early—Rhoda did not waste much time over tea—but before she resumed work she invited Mamie to look.

"You've been *very* quiet," said Rhoda, in tones of praise. "I'd almost forgotten you were there. You may think that's a bit rude, but it isn't really. Come and look at it, Mamie."

Mamie came and looked.

"You see the idea now, don't you?"

"Yes, of course," said Mamie without much enthusiasm.

"You're too near. Stand back a little. Isn't that yellow lichen on the stone a perfectly gorgeous colour—and I've got it exactly."

"Yes," agreed Mamie. "Yes, it's very nice, Rhoda. I think it's very clever of you—"

"You'll like it when it's finished. It's going to be good," said its creator joyfully. "You wait, Mamie. It's going to be very good indeed." There was no false pride about Rhoda.

When she had admired the picture sufficiently Mamie walked home for, although this was a holiday, there were one or two things that she wanted to see to before tomorrow, when Jock and James would be arriving. She took the picnic-basket with her, but she forgot her book and did not remember it until she was on the doorstep of Mureth House.

What a bother, thought Mamie, hesitating. She had left the book lying on the ground. Should she go back and get it or would Rhoda see it and bring it with her? It was a very special book, a really lovely book about Mozart which had been given to her by Jock for her birthday. Mamie decided that it would come to no harm. If Rhoda did not bring it she could send Duggie to fetch it . . . yes, that was the best plan.

She went into the house and through the hall to the pantry and began to wash up the picnic cups and saucers. As she washed and dried them and put them away all clean and shining in the cupboard she thought how lovely this afternoon had been . . . like peaceful music, thought Mamie. If you let the music play in your heart it made you happy. That was Mureth's secret. It was not really magic at all. You opened your heart and the peaceful music played.

Mamie was thinking of this—she had almost finished her task—when suddenly she heard a familiar sound. It was Jock's voice raised in his usual cheerful bellow.

Jock's voice! But it couldn't be Jock! Not until tomorrow!

"Mamie! *Mamie!*" It certainly was Jock.

"Jock!" cried Mamie, dashing into the hall.

"Here we are!" shouted Jock, whisking her off her feet in a bear-like embrace. "Here we are, my girl! Surprised, aren't you? Gosh, it's good to be home! We thought we'd come today instead of tomorrow. Couldn't stand it a day longer! How are you? Are you all right?"

"Quite all right," gasped Mamie.

"Sure?" he enquired anxiously.

"Perfectly all right."

"I was a bit worried about you."

"Nonsense, Jock."

"Yes, really," declared Jock. "It sounded as if you were feeling a bit down in the mouth."

"Och, away!" exclaimed Mamie laughing. "That wasn't why you came home a day sooner than you intended."

Jock laughed too. "Partly," he said. "And partly because I was just about fed up with town."

"We both were," declared James, appearing in the doorway with a suitcase in each hand.

"We both were," nodded Jock. "Town is noisier and dirtier than ever. D'you know this: I put on a clean collar when I got up and by lunch-time it was grubby-looking. Well, to cut the story short James said, *why not 'phone Mr MacGregor and tell him to send the papers to sign*—to send them here, d'you see— and that was what we did."

"It's lovely, Jock!" cried Mamie. "I'll run and tell Lizzie. You'll be wanting tea, of course."

"We haven't had a decent cup of tea since Friday."

"Oh, Jock, what nonsense!"

"You ask James—he'll tell you . . ."

All was bustle and confusion. The taxi which had brought them from Drumburly was paid and despatched; tea was prepared; suitcases were carried upstairs to the bedrooms. Mamie was so busy and so excited at the unexpected pleasure of their arrival that she forgot all about her guest who, presumably, was still painting in the meadow. It was not until they were actually sitting down to tea that Mamie suddenly remembered Rhoda . . . and then she remembered her only because, of course, Mamie had already had tea.

"Oh!" exclaimed Mamie in consternation.

"What's the matter?" asked Jock.

"Oh!" said Mamie, her brain working furiously. "Oh dear, I'll have to go down to the Stanes—"

"You'll have to go down to the Stanes!"

"Yes," said Mamie rising. "I was down there this afternoon and—and I left my book." It was an inspiration to have thought of such a marvellous excuse to tell Rhoda what had happened and find out what she wanted to do, and of course it was perfectly true. Mamie had left her book at the Stanes.

"You left your book?" asked James.

"I was reading," explained Mamie. "It was such a lovely afternoon, so warm and sunny. I sat and read for quite a long time and then, when I came away, I forgot about the book and left it lying there. The meadow is full of cows so I think I had better go down and—"

"I'll get it!" said James. "I'll go, Mamie."

Mamie was about to say she would rather go herself, but suddenly she saw that this was exactly what she had prayed for. It was a direct answer to her prayer.

"Oh, James," said Mamie. "But you're tired, aren't you?"

"Not a bit tired."

"You want your tea."

"Of course he wants his tea!" exclaimed Jock in amazement. "There's no need for James to go *now*, surely? He can have his tea and walk down later. What book was it, anyhow?"

"My Mozart book," said Mamie plaintively.

"It won't take me ten minutes," said James, smiling at her and rising and making for the door.

"Take your tea first, lad!" cried Jock, who was astonished beyond measure at Mamie's thoughtlessness.

But already James was off. He was running down the path, pleased and happy at the opportunity of doing something for Mamie (even this small service was something, thought James. Better than nothing, anyhow). For James had just been made heir to two large, well-stocked farms and to a small fortune besides —in fact to everything belonging to the Johnstones with the exception of a few small bequests. Jock had known exactly what he and Mamie wanted, and had instructed his solicitor accordingly, and James had sat there and listened, getting hotter and more embarrassed every moment. Mureth was not to be divided, said Jock Johnstone firmly. It was not to be pared down in any way. It was all to go together (every stick and stone of it and the capital to run it as it should be run) and it was all to go to James. If James had been their only son the arrangements made for him by the Johnstones would have been generous. Mr MacGregor said so, and James fervently agreed.

So it was only natural that when Mamie expressed some anxiety over a valued book, left out in a meadow full of cows, James was off to get it at once—or sooner. Tea! He didn't want tea. Goodness, no! The only thing he did regret was the fact that he had not thought of changing his shoes. Town shoes are not designed for running over stony paths and through long grass, and it might have been quicker if he had changed them.

James approached the Stanes not by the winding river but across the fields. He knew the way well, of course, for it was here that he and Couper had laid their drains. He noticed as he passed that already the drains were doing their stuff and the sedgy meadow was drying nicely. Marginal land! Soon this waste piece of ground would be fit for grazing. It would grow food instead of reeds . . . another fertile meadow to add to Mureth property. Worth while, thought James. A man's job, farming!

He skirted a little wood and so came to the green meadow by the river where the sun-worshippers had placed their stones. There was a barbed-wire fence between him and his objective. James had forgotten about the fence; indeed he would not have thought twice about the obstacle if he had not been wearing his best suit. But he *was* wearing his best suit, the only decent suit he possessed. Better find a gate, thought James.

He looked up and down the fence and, as he did so, his eye rested upon the Stanes; he caught a glimpse of blue amongst them. A girl moved out from behind the biggest stone and stood there with her back towards him. She was wearing a blue over-all. Her hair was gold. James felt a queer movement inside him —as if his heart had missed a beat. Gold hair! Only Rhoda had hair like that. He rubbed his eyes and looked again . . . and now he was sure. It was Rhoda. She was here—here at Mureth!

"Rhoda!" he shouted, leaping over the fence and running across the meadow as fast as his legs would take him. "Rhoda! Rhoda . . ."